NIGHT OF THE WHITE BUFFALO

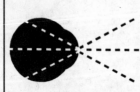

This Large Print Book carries the
Seal of Approval of N.A.V.H.

NIGHT OF THE WHITE BUFFALO

MARGARET COEL

THORNDIKE PRESS
A part of Gale, Cengage Learning

GALE
CENGAGE Learning·

Farmington Hills, Mich • San Francisco • New York • Waterville, Maine
Meriden, Conn • Mason, Ohio • Chicago

GALE
CENGAGE Learning®

LIBRARY OF CONGRESS CATALOGING-IN-PUBLICATION DATA

Coel, Margaret, 1937–
    Night of the white buffalo / by Margaret Coel. — Large print edition.
      pages ; cm. — (Thorndike Press large print core) (A Wind River mystery)
    ISBN 978-1-4104-7619-7 (hardcover) — ISBN 1-4104-7619-7 (hardcover)
    1. O'Malley, John (Fictitious character)—Fiction. 2. Holden, Vicky (Fictitious
character)—Fiction. 3. Murder—Investigation—Fiction. 4. Arapaho
Indians—Fiction. 5. Indian mythology—Fiction. 6. Wind River Indian
Reservation (Wyo.)—Fiction. 7. Large type books. I. Title.
PS3553.O347N54 2015
813'.54—dc23
                                         2014040144

Published in 2015 by arrangement with The Berkley Publishing Group,
a member of Penguin Group (USA) LLC, a Penguin Random House
Company

Printed in the United States of America
1 2 3 4 5 6 7 19 18 17 16 15

ACKNOWLEDGMENTS

I am especially grateful to Robert B. Pickering, Ph.D., for his engaging and informative book *Seeing the White Buffalo,* which sparked the idea for this novel, and to Dan O'Brien for his lovely book *Buffalo for the Broken Heart.*

And a thousand thank-yous to my friends Laura and Ron Mamet on the Wind River Reservation for providing several close-up experiences with a buffalo herd from a flatbed bouncing over the pasture while Ron forked off bales of hay at feeding time.

Several people, including the Mamets, took the time to answer my questions with patience and generosity, thus keeping me from wandering too far afield of reality. Others pored over the unfinished manuscript and made helpful suggestions so that the story might ring true. My sincere thanks to: Michael Bennett, Fremont County and prosecuting attorney; Ed McAuslan, Fremont County coroner; Virginia and Jim Sutter, members of the Arapaho Tribe, all in Wyoming; John Dix, in Virginia, my nephew and go-to guy for anything related to baseball; and in Boulder, John Tracy, professor emeritus of the University of Colorado; Sheila Carrigan, attorney and former judge; Karen Gilleland; Beverly Carrigan; Carl Schneider; and my husband, George.

Not to be overlooked are my editor, Tom Colgan, and my agent, Rich Henshaw, who gave me excellent advice and suggestions for this story.

For some very special people in my life: Eleanor, Violet, Aileen, Sam, Liam, and Lilly.

"I shall see you again," White Buffalo Woman told the people, promising to return in times of need.
— *Seeing the White Buffalo,*
Robert B. Pickering, Ph.D.

1

Late June, the Moon When the Hot Weather Begins

The confessional was warm and stuffy. The round light in the ceiling shone on the pages of the novel he was reading and radiated heat around the small area. He could hear the wind picking up outside, the June beginnings of the hot, dry winds that would scour the Wind River Reservation all summer. A cottonwood branch scratched at the corner of the church like an animal nibbling at the stucco.

Father John Aloysius O'Malley flexed his legs in the cramped space and checked his watch. Ten minutes before five. Confessions ran from three to five every Saturday afternoon, and the last penitent had left twenty minutes ago. He had heard the church door open and close, had felt the swish of fresh air wafting into the confessional through the slats on either side. Usually the same

9

handful of parishioners came with a litany of the same sins. Got drunk. Yelled at the kids. Had impure thoughts about the next-door neighbor. Forgive me, Father.

He hadn't heard anyone else enter the church, known as the new chapel the Arapahos had built at St. Francis Mission almost a hundred years ago, after the old chapel had burned down. He closed the Craig Johnson novel he was reading — Wyoming setting, people and places that seemed true and real — and switched off the light. Immediately the confessional felt cooler, or at the least not as warm. He had heard confessions at St. Francis Mission on the Wind River Reservation for more than ten years, longer than he had imagined he would be here. Six years was the usual assignment for a Jesuit, then on to a new place, new people, before a priest could become too attached, too set in his ways, too much at home.

He was at home with the Arapahos, a Plains Indian tribe he had once thought of as a footnote in a history book. Strange that he should be in this place. God worked in mysterious ways. Years of struggling with the thirst, in and out of rehab, stumbling through life teaching, or pretending to teach, in a Jesuit prep school in Boston. Then the assignment to an Indian reserva-

10

tion in the middle of Wyoming. He'd had to look up the place on the map. He had no idea where he was going. To the middle of nowhere, to the ends of the earth.

Father John got to his feet and was about to head out when the door to the penitent's side on his left opened. He sat back down. In the dim light he watched the large, muscular figure folding himself downward on the other side of the screen. The kneeler creaked and groaned; a little tremor ran through the wooden confessional. The man wore a dark cowboy hat pulled low over his eyes. He propped his elbows on the ledge and dipped his face into his hands. He looked like an immense, dark shadow. Sharp smells of tobacco, whiskey, and perspiration trailed across the screen.

"You there, Father?" He had the roughened voice of a man who spent his days in the wind.

"I'm here."

"Can't remember what I'm supposed to do. It's been a long time."

"Start with what's bothering you. What brought you here?"

The man didn't say anything for several seconds. His breath came in quick, shallow spurts, as if he were trying not to cry. Finally he said, "I come for forgiveness."

11

"What are your sins?"

"I committed murder."

Father John felt as if he had taken a punch in the gut. On the other side of the screen, inches away, knelt a killer who wanted forgiveness. He thought he had heard almost everything in the confessional or in his office during counseling sessions. Adultery, robbery, theft, all kinds of violence against fellow human beings, even rape. He had heard it all. But no one had ever confessed to murder. "How did it happen?"

"I know what you're doing. You're looking for some way to forgive me. Defend myself? Defend somebody else? It wasn't like that. I did it on purpose, what they call premeditated murder."

"Why did you do it?"

"I didn't have no choice."

"We always have choices." Father John tried to recall any recent unsolved murders on the rez. There weren't any.

"Maybe in your world. I come from nothing." The man was quiet for a moment, as if he had sunk into another time. "Lucky to get a bologna sandwich when I was a kid. Lived out of a truck. Dad always on the move trying to stay ahead of the law, until he took off. Left me and Mom and the truck, so Mom picked up waitress jobs, which wasn't so bad. Least we got some food. Took off when I was fourteen, been on my own ever since. What I got I worked hard for. I been trying to hold on, and everything was gonna go away."

"Did the man you killed steal from you?"

"It wasn't nothing like that. Why did I think you'd understand?"

"I'm trying."

"It was premeditated, okay? Get that in your head."

"What do you expect from me?"

"I told you. Forgiveness."

"Are you sorry for what you've done?"

"Sorry? Like I said, I had no choice. Why should I be sorry for something I had to do? Only one thing . . ." The man drew in a long breath and plunged his face deeper into his hands until only the crease of his cowboy hat was visible. "It's like there's no more sleep for me. I close my eyes and I see his face, the way he goes all pale when I lift the rifle, the way he tries to turn around, like he's gonna run away from a rifle. I know the thoughts going through his head, like I'm thinking them myself. We could've been the same man, killer and victim."

Father John waited a moment before he said, "There's nothing I can say that you haven't already figured out. You know what

13

you have to do."

The man was rocking back and forth, shaking his whole body. "No police."

"You know it is the only way to help yourself."

"Help myself to prison."

"Acknowledge what you've done. And accept your just punishment. Ask God for forgiveness."

"That's what you're supposed to do. Tell me God forgives me. Go in peace. Go sleep. Say a Rosary or something. Isn't that what confession's all about?"

"Pray very hard for the courage and the strength to accept responsibility."

"I don't know why I come here." The kneeler groaned as the man shuffled his weight back and forth. "It's not like when Mom dragged me to some two-bit church in a flea-bitten town in Arizona or Nevada or someplace. She used her spit to wipe up my face and smooth my hair. 'Tell the priest your sins and you're gonna be forgiven and everything's gonna be okay for us,' she said, ' 'cause God knows we're sorry for whatever we've done, like getting mixed up with that sonofabitch you think was your father and following that no-good all over creation. I'll say I'm sorry for doing that, and you can say you're sorry for back talking me all the time and being so lazy when I need you to help me out.' So I'd go into the confessional and tell the truth. How I beat up a kid in the school yard, stole money out of Mom's purse, smoked a joint. The priest said, 'Don't do that again. Make an act of contrition. Say three Hail Marys. Your sins are forgiven.' "

"Do you know about atonement?"

"What?"

"It's not enough just to say we regret our sins."

"I don't regret what I had to do."

"But you know what you did, taking a human life, was a terrible thing. Deep inside yourself you know that, and that's why you can't sleep. You are going to have to come to terms with what you did. You have to begin to regret it and acknowledge it."

"How's that gonna atone for anything? How's that gonna make up? The guy's still dead."

"Until you acknowledge your guilt, you won't know. But God will give you the grace and the strength to know what might be done."

"God, what a bunch of crap. I never should've come. I'm outta here." The dark figure on the other side of the screen started to rise, and the wood creaked and shivered.

He swung around, as if he might burst through the closed door, splinter the wood, send it flying across the vestibule.

"Hold on." Father John got to his feet and flung open his own door, but the tall, dark figure in blue jeans and dark shirt was already across the entry. Lifting his right arm, as if to block a tackle, he pushed the door open and plunged outside. The door slammed shut, rocking on its hinges.

Father John took the entry in a couple of steps and ran outdoors. He stopped on the concrete stoop, unsure of which way to go. The quiet of a Saturday afternoon suffused the mission. No vehicles about. Only smears of boot tracks in the hard-packed ground below the concrete stairs. The yellow stucco administration building on the other side of the narrow dirt drive, the old stone museum at the bend of Circle Drive, the redbrick residence on the far side of the field of wild grass, all looked like a still life painting. The wind scythed the grasses and whistled in the branches of the cottonwoods scattered about the grounds.

He took the steps two at a time and crossed to the corner of the church. The dirt drive that ran past Eagle Hall was empty. At the far end stood the thicket of cottonwoods, sage, and willows that bordered the Little Wind River at the edge of the mission. Clouds of dust and tumbleweeds rolled down the drive.

No sign of the big man in the dark cowboy hat. A killer. Blown away on the wind like a ghost.

2

*August, the Moon of Geese Shedding Their
Feathers*

The sun had dropped behind the Wind
River range two hours ago, but the day's
heat locked onto the blue shadows and the
starlit darkness that spread over the reservation. Parallel flares of yellow headlights
stretched ahead on Blue Sky Highway. Vicky
Holden rolled the passenger window down
a couple of inches. The moving air felt warm
on her face. Adam had turned the air
conditioner on high, but she preferred the
fresh air with the familiar smells of sage and
the gritty dryness of the blowing dust.

"You did a great job." Adam turned his
head in her direction, a quick, perfunctory
movement, then went back to staring out
the windshield.

Vicky wasn't sure about that, but this
handsome man, this Lakota lawyer behind
the wheel of a new BMW, didn't give out

18

compliments freely, not even to her. Had she stumbled in her talk to the women students at the tribal college about careers in law for Native people, especially women, Adam would have been the first to tell her. She appreciated his honesty; it helped to ground her, keep her on track.

She had been late leaving the office in Lander this afternoon. An unexpected client had walked in the door, and she was unable — as Adam always told her — to turn away Arapahos from the reservation who happened to find their way to her office and venture inside, nervous, hands shaking, blanched looks on dark faces. Never been to see a lawyer before. Not sure of what to say or do. Only certain they had been caught up in the vast, impersonal, and rigid world of the white man's law and knowing they needed help.

She had said, "Come in. Sit down. Tell me your name."

The woman was Arapaho, in her twenties, close to the age of Vicky's own kids, Susan and Lucas. She set an infant's car seat on the floor and made her way into Vicky's private office, cuddling a small infant in a blanket that looped around one shoulder into a big knot at her waist. A city Indian, as Susan and Lucas had become. Vicky had grasped that fact immediately. Married to a warrior from the reservation, learning the old ways, trying to connect somehow with an inscrutable past that was hers and not hers.

"Mary. Mary Red Fox. He's cheating on me, my husband, Donald." She had a low, breathless voice. "I need to get out. He says I can go anytime I want. Pack up, take what I came with, which was nothing except the clothes on my back, leave everything else. Leave my baby. He says that's the way it was with the people. Kids go with the father, and he can have as many women as he wants."

Vicky sat down at her desk across from the woman. The part about polygamy had some truth to it in the Old Time, usually for the chiefs and headmen who could afford more than one wife and needed several wives to handle social obligations: feasting the leaders of other tribes, feasting the white men invading the plains in never-ending streams of wagons. Donald Red Fox was wrong about the rest of it.

"In the Old Time," Vicky said, pulling the memories out of the long ago — sitting around the kitchen table in her grandparents' little house, listening to stories of how it used to be — "children belonged to their mothers and their mothers' families. In any case, this is now, and no judge is going to separate you from your baby unless . . ." She left the rest of it unsaid. Mary Red Fox didn't need to be told that if there were any evidence she was an unfit mother, the court would award custody to the father. The girl was upset enough. Forehead wrinkled, little beads of perspiration popping in the creases. She had left the reservation and driven to a small brick bungalow on a corner in Lander with a sign in front that said VICKY HOLDEN, ATTORNEY-AT-LAW. It had taken courage.

Through the beveled-glass doors that separated her office from the reception area, Vicky saw the outside door open and close. Adam Lone Eagle paced back and forth, casting impatient, distorted glances through the glass. His boots made a swishing noise on the carpet.

"I wish . . ." Mary bit at her lower lip and bent her shoulders around the infant, who was making little mewling sounds. "I wish I didn't still love him. It wouldn't hurt so much, leaving him."

"Any chance of working on your marriage?" Divorce was final, like a death that came after a long illness. What was left was guilt and wondering and second-guessing.

The scars from her own divorce from Ben Holden felt like ridges of inflamed tissue deep inside her. "Have you tried counseling? Would your husband agree to go?" Probably not, she was thinking. An Arapaho warrior with a stranger, most likely a white man, telling him what to do?

"I don't know."

"Father John O'Malley at St. Francis Mission is very understanding and sympathetic. Practical," Vicky added. There were cases when Father John had advised her own clients to get a divorce, for the sake of their lives, for the sake of their children.

"I can ask him."

Adam was still pacing, still shooting glances through the beveled glass. It had taken another ten minutes for Vicky to explain that if counseling didn't work, the woman should come back. They could start divorce proceedings. "Do you have family?"

"In Denver."

"You might want to think about going to them before your husband is served with the divorce papers."

Mary Red Fox had nodded, pushed herself to her feet with the precious bundle tied to her chest, and asked how much she owed.

"We'll see how things go."

■ ■ ■ ■

Now Adam said, "Looks like somebody's in trouble."

Vicky stared beyond the headlights flashing over the asphalt at the dark hulk of a truck pulled off to the side of the highway. "Probably drunk," Adam said, a musing, perfunctory tone in his voice. She realized that another truck — large and black — stood in the shadows beyond the parked truck.

Headlights burst into the darkness as the black truck swerved into a U-turn and shot toward them, weaving into their lane. Adam stomped on the brake pedal, sending the BMW skittering toward the borrow ditch as the truck sped past. Vicky watched the taillights flare like red firecrackers in the side mirror.

"Jesus. What the hell was that?" Adam drove slowly, tentatively, as if he expected the dark phantom of yet another vehicle to rear up in front of them.

Vicky rolled down her window and leaned outside. Something wrong about the skewed way the parked truck sat alongside the ditch, rear tires sloping downward, as if the driver had stopped suddenly and unintentionally. As they drove past, she caught a glimpse, like a reflection in a mirror, of a man slumped over the steering wheel, off balance as if a strong wind might push him backward onto the seat.

"He needs help, Adam."

"We don't know what just went down here. Could've been a drug deal."

"Stop, Adam. Please. We have to see if he's okay."

"Vicky . . ." Adam shook his head, braking lightly, finally bringing the car to a stop. He shifted into reverse and, turning to look past the driver's window, steered backward, then veered to the right and pulled in where the other truck had stood. "What do you think you saw?" He was looking into the rearview mirror, studying the truck behind them.

"The driver looks sick or hurt. He's alone."

Adam leaned past her, opened the glove compartment, and withdrew a small black pistol that gleamed in the dashboard lights.

"What are you doing?"

"Stay here." He opened the door and got out.

Vicky yanked at her handle, pushed the door open, and jumped onto the slope of the borrow ditch, holding on to the door to steady herself. Adam had already closed the narrow space between the rear of the BMW and the front of the truck, the pistol tucked into the back of his blue jeans, the grip riding above his belt.

"Go back." The words came like a hiss of steam over his shoulder.

Vicky was beside him, staying in rhythm with his footsteps toward the driver's door, her gaze fastened on the head propped sideways against the steering wheel. They were still a few feet away when she saw the hole in the man's forehead, the wide eyes fixed and blank, staring out the opened window.

"He's been shot." Adam stepped in front of her, as if to shield her from the sight. She felt the pressure of his arm on hers. "Let's get out of here."

"We have to get help."

"The man's dead, Vicky." She looked back as Adam turned her around and began pulling her along the asphalt. He was right. Death had its own stillness.

She yanked herself free, hurried ahead to the BMW, grabbed her bag off the floor, and began rummaging for her cell phone. Tapping in 911, she started back to the truck. Adam blocked the way, like a cottonwood that had materialized on the highway.

An intermittent sharp bleeping noise sounded in her ear.

"Get into the car." A little shock ran through her as Adam grasped her arm and started wheeling her backward. "We have to get out of here."

"What is your emergency?" A disembodied phone voice.

Vicky twisted herself free. "A man's been shot on Blue Sky Highway." Vicky could hear the frantic pitch of her voice. "South of Trosper Road. He's in a . . ."

"Ford," Adam said.

"Dark Ford truck pulled over in the southbound lane."

"I'm sending the police and an ambulance. What is your name?"

"Vicky Holden. I'm with Adam Lone Eagle. We are attorneys in Lander."

"The police will want to speak with you."

"We will give our statements tomorrow," Adam said, as if he were part of the conversation, an arm around her shoulders now, urging her back to the car.

Vicky pressed the off button. "We have to stay with the body."

"For godssakes, Vicky. We don't know what happened. There's been a number of random shootings on highways on the rez. The shooter likes firing at pickups and trucks for kicks. Now he's finally killed somebody. You want to wait around for an hour in the darkness until a patrol car arrives? How do we know the shooter wasn't in the other truck? Ran this guy off the road, walked back, and shot him. What if the shooter decides to come back, make sure the guy is really dead? We'd be like sitting ducks out here in the middle of the rez. Christ. You want us to be the next victims? Let's get out of here."

He was right, she was thinking. Realistic, looking ahead, the pistol tucked into his belt. And yet, it was wrong. She swung around and faced him. "I'm staying with the body."

"It's crazy and dangerous." Adam tossed his head about, taking in the darkness that stretched away from the highway. They might have been in no-man's-land, somewhere on the moon, a killer watching them, waiting. Or making a U-turn on the highway, on the way back. "You can't help him. He's dead. No one can help him."

"Have you no respect?" Someone always stayed with a body until the body was buried. The dead were never left alone. Wasn't that true of the Lakota, as well? Where had Adam lost the way?

"Cops will prowl around the area, look

for casings, bullets, footprints. They don't need us messing up things."

"Go on, if you want."

"What are you talking about? Leave you here alone?" He did a half turn, and for an instant Vicky thought he might walk away. Leave her in the darkness with the body.

He turned back. "It doesn't make sense, Vicky. It's foolish and risky." He was still glancing around at the darkness. "We could be here the rest of the night answering questions, giving statements. Is that what you want?"

"I told you, you can go on."

Adam was shaking his head, a slow, tense motion of resignation and bewilderment. "We'll wait together."

3

The sound of a ringing phone came from far away. Father John fought his way to the surface of consciousness and propped himself up on one elbow. A bluish light pulsated in the cell phone on the nightstand, the ringing sharp and persistent. Yellow numbers glowed across the top: 12:46. He picked up the phone and slid the tip of his finger along the button. "Father John," he said.

"Art Banner here." The voice had the snap of a whip. Father John felt the muscles in his stomach tighten. The chief of Wind River Law Enforcement would not call St. Francis Mission in the middle of the night unless something terrible had happened.

"What's going on?"

"White man that raises buffalo off Trout Creek Road was shot on Blue Sky Highway this evening. Clean shot in the middle of the forehead. Killed instantly, the coroner

29

says. Thought you might know him. Dennis Carey."

Father John drew up a picture in his mind of the tall, big-shouldered cowboy with the bolo dropping from the collar of his buttoned-up shirt, serving buffalo burgers at every powwow, every celebration on the rez. His wife, small and attractive with reddish fire in her hair and a white, grease-smeared apron draped in front of her, flipped the burgers on a charcoal grill in the back of the booth. They weren't parishioners, but a couple of times this summer Dennis had stopped by the mission with packages of buffalo meat. Something on the man's mind, Father John had thought, but when he'd invited Dennis to have a cup of coffee and chat awhile, the man had made excuses. Had to get back to the ranch, mend the fences, haul hay out to feed the buffalo herd. Both times he had bolted away, leaving Father John with the unsettled feeling there was something painful and sad and hard to talk about.

"I've chatted with Dennis and his wife a few times," he said. "Ordered buffalo burgers at the powwows. Dennis brought buffalo meat to the mission." He was barely acquainted with the man, he thought. Two white men from outside the rez, from a different culture, from different places, planted on a reservation. White men among Arapahos and Shoshones. Probably the reason that Banner, an Arapaho himself, assumed he would know the man.

"We'll be here for a while yet, then I'll head over to the ranch to notify Carey's wife."

"I'm on my way."

Coolness sliced through the night air, the day's heat having receded ahead of the wind blowing off the high peaks of the Wind River mountains. It was the first Monday in August, the Moon of Geese Shedding Their Feathers, as the Arapahos kept time. He flipped on the CD player on the seat next to him as he drove around Circle Drive, past the old mission buildings, quiet sentinels from another time bathed in shadows. The white steeple of the church rose overhead, gleaming in the moonlight. The music of *La Traviata* filled the cab, drowning out the shush of the wind over the half-opened windows. He had been back with Verdi lately, the arias beautiful and familiar. Like reconnecting with an old friend.

He drove through the tunnel of cotton-woods with thick, heavy branches arching the road and turned left onto Seventeen-

Mile Road. Another death, he was thinking; another murder. There had been so many senseless deaths in the decade he had been at St. Francis. An important part of his pastoral mission, tending to the dead and to those left behind. It never got easier. Never routine.

The reservation seemed suspended in time, as if life had stopped for the night. The flat, open plains ran into the darkness, small houses popped up here and there alongside the road, an occasional light flared in a window, and shadowy objects — pickups sloped sideways with missing wheels, swing sets and abandoned refrigerators and cartons — lay scattered about the dirt yards. Only a few other vehicles on the road. Taillights flickered ahead, and an occasional pickup passed in the opposite direction.

An uneasy feeling, almost as if he were being watched by invisible eyes, had settled over him. The rancher had been shot in the forehead, Banner said, killed instantly. There had been several random shootings on the highways in the past year, but Carey's death looked like a premeditated killing. He could still hear the cool, certain voice of the man in the confessional almost two months ago now, the words acid-burned into his mind.

It was premeditated, okay? Get that in your head.

The man had killed someone, and yet no murders had been reported on the rez in several months before the man had come into the confessional. If he was telling the truth, the body of his victim might be anywhere. In one of the dry arroyos, in a mountain cave or rock pile. In the Old Time, Arapahos had buried people in the rock piles on the mountain slopes, covered the corpses with boulders to protect them from wild animals. Is that what the killer had done?

Or he could have committed the murder somewhere else. Miles away from the reservation, a different county, a different state. Anywhere. Then why had he found his way to a mission on the reservation?

The man was still out there someplace. He could still be on the rez, driving the roads, mingling with the people. Now someone on the rez had been killed.

What if the man in the confessional had shot another victim? He hadn't asked the man if he planned any more murders. He should have asked, and that regret had kept him awake night after night. The seal of the confessional was inviolate; he could never betray the penitent. Yet he could have talked to him, tried to convince him to go to the police. He would have offered to go with him. He had gone after the man. Walked down the dirt drive between the church and the administration building, desperate to catch a glimpse of him somewhere. But the man had disappeared into the thick stand of trees along the Little Wind River; there was no other explanation. In the middle of sleepless nights, he had imagined the killer watching him walk back and forth from behind a cottonwood, Father John searching and calling out: "Where are you? Come back. Let me help you."

Laughing at him, perhaps, except that Father John didn't think so. Something about the man — the tension of an internal struggle, a deep-seated regret he couldn't acknowledge, and a need for forgiveness so profound it had driven him to the confessional — made any kind of joy or laughter seem ludicrous.

Father John found himself heading south on Blue Sky Highway, the old Toyota pickup shivering on the pavement. He wondered how he had gotten here; he had been lost in thought. The voice of Cheryl Studer filled the cab: *E strano! E strano!*

In the darkness beyond the headlights he could see the faint glow of emergency lights, the dark hulks of vehicles parked along the highway. He pulled in behind the nearest vehicle, the gray coroner's van. The rear doors stood open. He got out and walked past the van and a Wind River patrol car toward the uniformed officers and coroner's assistants huddled in the middle of the highway. Red, blue, and yellow roof lights splashed their faces. A gurney had been placed alongside the truck, which sloped into the borrow ditch, and on the gurney was the lumpy plastic bag that, he knew, held the body of Dennis Carey. Faint sounds of *La Traviata* drifted through the night.

Chief Banner stepped back from the others. "Couple of officers knew him, and he's got ID on him. You want to bless the body?" He nodded toward the man standing at the head of the gurney, who began unzipping the bag. The plastic made a crinkling noise. "It's not a pretty sight."

They never were, Father John thought. He stepped closer. A surprised look in the face, the wide-open eyes staring into nothingness, as if Dennis Carey hadn't believed he was about to die in the middle of life. A round black hole had been drilled into the middle of his forehead.

Father John made the sign of the cross over the body. "Be at peace." He could see

35

Dennis Carey getting out of a pickup, lifting the lid on the cooler in the bed, handing Father John packages of buffalo meat. "Coffee?" Father John had asked, but the man wouldn't stay. Some part of him, Father John was sure, had wanted to stay. "Go with God. May He forgive you any sins you may have committed. May He take you to Himself."

He stepped back as the coroner's assistant re-zipped the bag, then started wheeling it toward the rear of the van. Another officer began stretching yellow police tape around the truck and out several feet in a U across the pavement.

"Who found him?"

"Vicky called it in. She and Adam passed the truck on their way back to Lander." Banner threw a glance at the policemen milling about. "They hung around for awhile, said they saw a large black truck pull out onto the highway just as they drove up. Didn't get the license or make in the darkness. You just missed them."

Father John looked around, as if Vicky might reappear. It didn't surprise him that she had stayed in the darkness with the body. Arapahos always stayed with the dead until the burial. He wondered if Adam had thought it a good idea. If the killer had been

36

in the second truck, he could have returned. He could have decided to eliminate the people who had driven up and possibly gotten his license plate number. Who knew where the killer was? He could be out there in the darkness now, watching. None of it would have mattered to Vicky, he knew. She was stubborn; she clung to so many of the old ways.

He realized Banner was talking about how murder on the rez was in the FBI's jurisdiction. "We've handled the preliminary forensics," he said. "Made casts of boot prints around the truck and tire tracks on the side of the road. Some are going to belong to Adam and Vicky. My guess is Carey knew his killer. Looks like whoever did it drove around him and pulled over. Carey pulled in behind, rolled down his window, and waited. He wouldn't have done that if a stranger had tried to pull him off the road. He would have found a way to drive on. But he pulled over and waited. The killer walked up and shot him."

Father John felt a chill run through him, as if he had stepped into a surreal world: the matter-of-fact voice of the chief, the faintest notes of the opera in the background, the gurney disappearing into the van, the glow of the interior lights, the roof lights pulsing, and the darkness beyond. A world where an acquaintance or friend could walk up, pull a trigger, and extinguish a man's life.

"I'll follow you to the ranch."

Banner swung about and walked to the car wedged between the truck and the coroner's van, which was starting to nose out onto the highway. Father John waited until the van had skirted around the officers and the yellow tape and headed south for Lander. The morgue was in the basement of the old Fremont County courthouse. He got into the pickup and followed Banner south through a bend before turning right. *O mio rimorso!* was playing on the CD.

4

Father John stayed a couple of car lengths behind the police car that shimmered silver in the moonlight. A slow left turn onto Trout Creek Road, then another left onto a narrow dirt road. The old Toyota pickup bounced and skittered. Dust rolled backward and sprayed the pickup's windshield. He dropped another car length behind. He and the police chief were driving farther and farther away from the houses, the debris-strewn dirt yards, the paved roads.

The chief's brake lights came on, and Father John followed them onto a two-track. The pickup was gyrating so hard he had to grip the wheel to keep from being tossed against the side window. The CD skipped and stuttered as the two-track undulated over the plains toward what looked like a log ranch house, the windows lit up like Christmas.

Banner was knocking on the front door as

Father John pulled in next to the police car and hurried up the stone steps. The wooden slats of the sofa and chairs on the porch rattled in the wind. From inside came the clack of footsteps that stopped on the other side of the door. Father John had the sense of a presence on the other side, of a hesitation.

The door inched open the width of a brass chain, and Banner stuck his wallet badge into the opening. In an instant the door closed, then swung open, the metal chain clanking against the wood. Peering up at them with narrowed eyes and a fixed expression of dread was a small, attractive woman with reddish hair plastered against her head and fastened in the back. In her red plaid shirt and blue jeans washed gray, she looked capable of riding onto the pasture and roping a buffalo calf. She barely came to Father John's shoulder.

"Sheila Carey?" Banner tilted his head toward Father John. "Father O'Malley from the mission. May we come in?"

"What are you doing here?" A deep well of suspicion rose in the woman's voice.

"I'm afraid we have bad news."

She stepped back and motioned them inside, then walked around a small table and perched on the edge of a sofa. "What-

40

ever it is, let's have it."

Banner dropped into the upholstered chair on the other side of the table, and Father John nudged a wooden chair out of a corner and sat down a few feet from the chief. He wondered how they must appear to the small woman staring wide-eyed at them, two big men bearing down on her with terrible news. The chief cleared his throat. It was never easy, Father John thought. "Your husband, Dennis, was shot this evening on Blue Sky Highway."

The woman pitched herself to her feet. There was a sharp thwack as her leg hit the edge of the coffee table. "That's ridiculous." Now she was looking down at them. "Dennis is at a meeting in Riverton. Monthly meeting of local ranchers. Afterward they go to a bar, sit around, drink beer, and gossip like a bunch of old biddies. He'll be pulling up any minute."

"I'm so sorry." Father John stood up and reached across the table for the woman's hand. She yanked herself away.

"How dare you show up in the middle of the night and tell me Dennis is dead. He cannot be dead. He's on the way home. See . . ." She darted for the front window and peered past the edge of the drapes. "I can hear the rumbling of his truck. He's

41

out on the dirt road now. I'll see his head-lights coming up our road soon." She pivoted about and stared at Father John a moment, then at Banner. "How dare you tell such lies!"

She was swaying on her feet, and Father John walked over and took her arm to steady her. "You had better sit down. Your husband didn't survive."

She shrugged away again, and wrinkles of understanding began to crease her face. "Didn't survive? How can that be? He was fine. He went to a meeting. How can he be dead?"

Father John took her hand and tried to lead her back to the sofa, but she was like dead weight, stuck in the middle of the floor. A door opened and shut in the back of the house, and a cowboy, black hat pushed back on his head and bunched fists hanging at his sides, materialized out of the darkness in the kitchen. He looked His-panic, dark-skinned with flashing black eyes, and a short, stocky build. He stopped a couple of feet into the living room. "You need help, Mrs. C? I seen the police car and old truck out front."

Behind him, like a shadow, was another cowboy, lean and young and tense looking, acne popping on his forehead.

"Chief Banner." Banner got to his feet and faced the two men. "Who might you be?"

"Hired hands," Sheila Carey said. "Carlos Mondregan, the foreman, and Lane Preston."

Banner nodded. "Father O'Malley and I have brought Mrs. Carey some very bad news. Her husband was shot this evening."

"What?" Mondregan's mouth opened into a wide O. "Shot? Where?" The other cowboy stepped backward, as if he had been pushed.

"On Blue Sky Highway. He was probably on his way home."

"I should've gone to the meeting with him. I should've gone. Nobody would've gotten close to him if I'd been there. God, Mrs. C." Mondregan swung toward the woman who was rocking back and forth, eyes darting about the room. "What do you want me to do?"

"I have to go to him."

"I'll take you," Mondregan said.

Banner told them the coroner had removed the body to the morgue. "We'll arrange for you to see him and make a positive identification."

"Positive identification? You mean, there could be a mistake?"

"I'm afraid there is no mistake."

Sheila Carey ran her tongue over her lips.

"Oh my God. It's true then, isn't it?"

"Is there anyone I can call for you?" Father John said.

She dropped onto the sofa and dipped her face into her hands. "There's nobody else." Her voice was shaky and muffled. She peered through the Vs of her fingers. "Carlos and Lane have been helping out on the ranch. But it's just me and Dennis in our own little world here, like it's been ever since we met eight years ago. Both of us looking for something, and we found each other. Dennis is a real cowboy." She dropped her hands, closed her eyes, and sat rocking back and forth, as if she had escaped into another time, another place. "A real cowboy. Wandered around the West for years, working other people's ranches, drinking too much, hooking up with no-account women. Same for me, except for the cowboying and women. I hooked up with loser guys. It was like I had a beacon on me to attract losers. Wandering all over, like Dennis, with a lot of lousy, miserable jobs and rat-infested apartments. Things are gonna change, be different, he told me that first night. We're gonna get us our own spread, and we're gonna raise buffalo. He had a thing about buffalo, Dennis did. Buffalo are wild, can't ever be tamed. He

44

felt a kindred spirit with them. So he got a good job on a ranch outside Grand Junction, and I hired on at a restaurant. No more drinking and carousing. We saved every penny. Two years ago, we put a down payment on this spread. Mortgage to knock out your eyeballs, but it was Dennis's dream. Our dream." She was crying now, as if the present loomed in front of her.

Father John went over and sat down beside the woman. He waited a moment before he said, "Are you sure there isn't someone we can call? A friend on the rez?" Had Dennis and Sheila Carey been Arapaho, the moccasin telegraph would have spread the news by now. The house would be filling up with relatives and friends. Women working in the kitchen, fresh coffee brewing, casseroles and cakes appearing as if by some conjuring trick. People would be pressing around Sheila Carey, patting her shoulder, holding her hand. Sipping coffee, eating, crying.

"Now he's dead. I know he's dead." This seemed to take all the woman had left, because she fell sideways onto the armrest. Banner and Carlos both jumped forward as Father John put an arm around her shoulder and lifted her into a sitting position. Her head lolled against the back cushion. She

45

blinked at the ceiling, then made an effort to pull herself upright. "There is something you can do."

He waited, and after a long moment, she went on: "Bless the grave. Dennis would want to be on the ranch." She ran her tongue over her lips. They looked cracked and sore. "You can do that, can't you?"

"Yes, of course," he said. He glanced up at Carlos. "She could use some water."

The cowboy swung about and disappeared into the dimness at the back of the house. The sounds of running water and glass clanking on metal drifted out of the kitchen.

"I can get an ambulance," Banner said.

"No! No ambulance!" A surprising amount of energy pumped through the exclamation. "No hospital. No drugs to help me cope. I had enough of that in that other life. You gotta arrest that bastard."

"Who are you talking about?" Banner asked. "Do you have an idea of who might have shot your husband?"

"Oh, I got ideas all right." She grasped the glass that Carlos held out and gulped at the water. "I got more than ideas. That cowboy Dennis had to let go in June. Threatened he'd come back and settle things."

"If he's still in the area, we can pick him

46

up. What can you tell me about him? Name? Local connections? Where did he go?"

"He was no good. I told Dennis not to hire him the minute I laid eyes on him, and believe me, I know a loser when I see one. But Dennis said he needed help. Long stretch of fence to repair, dams about to calve. So he hired him. Rick somebody. Thomas. Thompson. Tomlin, maybe. He didn't work out, just like I knew would happen. Drunk half the time. How would I know where he went? He wasn't from around here. After Tomlin and another hand took off, we were lucky to hire Carlos and Lane."

Banner started to his feet. "I know this is hard, Mrs. Carey, but if there's anything about Rick Tomlin you happen to remember, give me a call." He pulled a card from his shirt pocket and set it on the table. "Agent Gianelli will also want to talk with you."

"The fed?" Mondregan's eyebrows shot up.

"I don't want cops and feds all over the place," Sheila said.

"Mrs. Carey, your husband was murdered."

"We were supposed to be blessed."

Both cowboys leaned in close. "You sure

you want to talk about this now?" Carlos said.

"Talk about what?" Banner sat back down.

"Can't stay a secret, not on the rez with people coming around. Word'll get out."

She drained the glass of water, then set it on the coffee table. "We had a great blessing. Ironic, isn't it? Dennis gets killed just when we've had a blessing." She was staring at Banner. "It's a blessing when the white buffalo calf gets born, isn't it? In the Arapaho Way?"

Banner made a sucking noise, as if he were trying to catch his breath. "When did this happen?"

"About a week ago," Carlos said.

"When were you planning to notify us?" Banner leaned forward, not taking his eyes from the woman, and Father John tried to remember what he had heard about the white buffalo. A being so rare, a white buffalo calf was considered by all the tribes to be sacred, a special blessing from the Creator, a reminder that the Creator was with the people. People from all over would descend on the ranch to see the white buffalo calf.

"Not until we finish repairing the north fence," Carlos said. "We gotta control the crowds."

"I'm asking Mrs. Carey."

"We didn't expect . . ." She broke off and sobbed quietly into the palm of her hand. Finally she lifted her head. "Nobody expects a white buffalo calf to be born. It just happened. Dennis spotted it in the pasture. He couldn't believe his eyes. Pure white buffalo calf with black nose and black eyes. Not an albino. I didn't know what that meant until he told me. Our calf is the real thing, as rare as a gold nugget the size of my fist. We were blessed. That's what he said. We were blessed. Some blessing!"

Banner had extracted a white handkerchief and was patting at his forehead. He stood up and, looking down at the woman slumped on the sofa, said, "When do you plan to make the birth public?"

"It was Dennis that was gonna handle it."

"We need a couple days before we can get the fence fixed," Carlos said. "Maybe longer. We can't have people trampling the pastures. We gotta fix a pathway they can use to go see the calf."

Banner stuffed the handkerchief into the back pocket of his uniform trousers. "We're going to need time to plan for crowd control." He was looking sideways into the middle of the room. "Roads will be jammed." He switched his gaze between the

49

woman and the cowboys hovering nearby, then he tapped the card he had laid on the table. "I would appreciate a heads-up before you make the announcement. Like I said, if you remember anything that might help us locate your husband's killer, call me immediately."

"Oh God," Sheila said. "Why did this have to happen?"

Father John got to his feet, leaned over, and patted the woman's shoulder. "I'm at the mission if you want someone to talk to."

He followed the chief across the living room and out the door. The night was getting cooler, and the wind had picked up. The chief hurried to his car and slid inside, shoulders rounded with determination. The engine had barely coughed into life when Banner pulled a U-turn and headed out onto the two-track. Father John got into the pickup and started after the red glow of taillights that jumped and bounced ahead. The woman was right, he was thinking. A white buffalo calf born on the rez, and a few days later, her husband shot to death. How could the calf be a blessing? And yet Indian people everywhere believed the calf was a blessing, a symbol of the Creator's presence. Hundreds, probably thousands of visitors would descend on the rez to see the white buffalo calf. And Sheila Carey, left to cope alone with only the help of hired hands. Dear Lord. He turned off the two-track and onto the dirt road, a few scattered stars shining through a sky black with clouds, the red taillights plunging into the darkness ahead.

5

Father John tossed the Frisbee into the tall grass surrounded by Circle Drive and watched Walks-On lope after it. The early-morning sun burned at his neck, but a hint of the night's coolness lingered in the air. He had slept fitfully, a few hours of tossing and turning, images of the surprised look in Dennis Carey's face stamped in his mind. But something else had nagged at him: the uneasy feeling that the man in the confessional had killed again and, somehow, Father John should have stopped him. The feeling had kept him awake most of the night and followed him this morning like a shadow he couldn't identify or ignore.

The dog disappeared into the stalks of grass and reappeared with the red Frisbee clenched in his jaw. He ran back, a shaky, unbalanced sprint filled with confidence and enthusiasm, as if the fact that he was missing a hind leg was of little importance.

Walks-On had been tiny, not much larger than a brown paper bag tossed out of a car, when Father John had found him in the ditch on Seventeen-Mile Road. He had been at St. Francis a couple of years then, still wobbly with the effort to stay sober, grateful to have a place to work, to be a priest.

Even now it made him flinch to think he might have driven past if the puppy hadn't moved his head. Father John had pulled over, gathered the broken body in his arms, laid the dog on the front seat, and driven for the vet's office in Riverton. A week later he had gone back and claimed him, when no one else had. A puppy with an amputated hind leg who had grown into a muscular golden dog, full of life, seemingly unconcerned about his loss. A lesson in that, Father John thought.

He threw the Frisbee again, this time angling it toward the residence. The slope in Walks-On's shoulders meant that he understood: the game was over. Father John made his way across the field on the dirt path worn by countless past Jesuits. Like so many aspects of St. Francis Mission — the black-and-white photos that lined the administration corridor, the theology and philosophy books in the library, the files in the archives — the dirt path was a reminder that he followed in the footsteps of other men, better men. He never wanted to let them down.

A white pickup turned off Seventeen-Mile Road and flashed through the tunnel of cottonwoods as Father John hurried up the church steps and let himself inside. Mass was supposed to start in ten minutes. He had played catch with Walks-On longer than he should have. Now he walked down the aisle, genuflected before the altar and the tabernacle Arapaho women had made from tanned deerskin to resemble a tipi, and made his way into the sacristy. He could hear the front door opening and closing with the arriving parishioners as he put on the chasuble and walked out to the altar. The red, blue, and yellow geometric patterns in the stained glass windows glowed in the morning sun: lines symbolizing the roads of life, triangles for the village, circles for the buffalo. At least a dozen Arapahos knelt in the pews, most elderly and set in their ways, used to starting the day with the quiet solemnity of Mass.

"Let us offer our prayers," he said, "for the soul of the rancher, Dennis Carey, who lived among us and died among us last night on Blue Sky Highway, where he was shot to death." From the nodding heads and blinking eyes, Father John knew the news had spread. The moccasin telegraph never shut down, not even in the middle of the night. But he sensed something in the hands fidgeting with prayer books and rosaries, the worried looks shadowing the brown faces. Somewhere on the reservation was a shooter who had been taking random shots at pickups moving in the night down empty highways. Now a man was dead.

He gave a short sermon on a part of Luke's Gospel he had always liked: how Jesus had encouraged his disciples to place their trust in God and to live without anxiety. At the consecration, he lifted the bread and the grape juice that alcoholic priests could substitute for wine and repeated the words of Jesus: "This is my body; this is my blood." Silently he prayed for the grace to trust in God for whatever the future might hold.

After Mass, he stood outside and shook hands with the elders and grandmothers, another ritual that started the day, he thought, for them as well as for himself. Walks-On had wandered over, and the old people took turns patting his head, which, he suspected, was the way the dog liked to start his day.

Miriam Many Horses waited until the others had set out for the pickups parked on Circle Drive before she stepped over. Usually she brought her father, Clifford, to Mass. This morning she was alone. She was in her fifties, but she looked older, with a tanned, weathered face and a red-and-blue scarf tied around sloped shoulders. "Dad wasn't up to coming to Mass this morning."

Clifford Many Horses put up with a lot of afflictions, Father John knew. Diabetes, arthritis, and lungs that collapsed regularly into pneumonia, but the old man seldom missed daily Mass. Father John could think of only a few mornings when Clifford and his daughter hadn't sat in the last pew. Clifford's pew, he thought of it. "Is he okay?"

"Ninety years old and getting worn out." She smiled. "Otherwise he's a tough old bird."

Father John nodded. Tough and determined, he thought. Nothing had kept Clifford from doing what he set his mind to. Ran away from the rez to join the army at age fifteen. Slogged through Africa and Italy and finally Germany. On his way to fight in the Far East when the United States dropped atomic bombs on Hiroshima and Nagasaki and the war ended. Back home on the rez with a purple heart for a bullet he had taken in his hip, he'd bought a couple of cows and a steer and started building a herd. Then he'd built a family. Miriam was the youngest of six children, the one who'd stayed close to the old man after her mother, Dorothy, died, took him to church, saw that he had a good meal every day.

"My father would like to talk to you. How about lunch at noon?"

"I'll be there."

Father John could hear Miriam's pickup rumbling around Circle Drive and out through the cottonwoods as he went back into the church and made his way down the aisle, checking the pews for anything left behind. Odd the things he sometimes found. Cigarette packs, notepads, pencils, keys, eyeglasses. Small enough objects to have slipped silently out of pockets. The pews were empty this morning. He genuflected again at the altar, taking an extra minute to say another prayer for the dead man on the highway and the widow whose life had changed in a moment.

Outside, Walks-On raced ahead across the grass and up the steps to the residence. Father John let him in the front door and followed him down the hall to the kitchen, where the dog stared at his empty bowl, then stared up at him.

"How are you, my boy?" Bishop Harry sat at the round table hunched over the *Gazette* spread in front of him, working at a cup of coffee. A fringe of whitish gray hair wrapped around the old man's pink scalp. His eyes were pale blue and lively, fired by the sunlight that filtered past the flimsy white curtain at the window. From the basement came the hum of the washing machine. "You must have had quite a night. I heard about the poor man who was shot."

Father John lifted the bag of dog food out of the cabinet and shook it into the bowl. Then he filled the dog's water bowl and set it down. "Elena?" The moccasin telegraph usually reached the housekeeper before it reached the mission.

"You are to help yourself to oatmeal."

From the basement came a lurching, halting noise before the washing machine settled into a normal rhythm. Something else at St. Francis that was old, outdated, and in need of replacement. Like the stove and refrigerator that he half expected to give out at any moment, the roofs on the old buildings that leaked in every rainstorm, the gutters that needed patching, the creaking doors, and the worn carpets. There was

58

never enough money to keep the mission buildings running smoothly.

"I went with Banner to notify the widow." Father John spooned oatmeal into a bowl, poured in milk, and sat down across from the bishop.

"Ah, yes. The hardest part of our job." For a few seconds, it seemed, the bishop wasn't an old man sent to St. Francis Mission to recover from two heart bypass surgeries; he was the bishop of Patna, India, overseeing thousands of Catholics, visiting the families of the sick and dying, consoling those who'd lost their loved ones, watching hope disappear in their eyes. Their brothers, sisters, cousins, fathers were with God now, at peace, he'd probably told them. It wouldn't have made the task any easier.

"I don't have to ask how she took it."

"Her life changed last night. Nothing will ever be the same. Her name is Sheila Carey. Her husband was Dennis. They ran the Broken Buffalo Ranch off Trout Creek Road."

The bishop was nodding. "I trust she has family and friends."

"She seems alone, except for a couple of hands who work there. She asked me to bless her husband's body. She wants him buried on the ranch."

"They're Catholic?"

"I don't think so." He took a bite of the hot, creamy oatmeal, surprised at how good it tasted, morning after morning.

"Whatever comfort you can bring in this time will be welcome, I'm sure."

Father John could hear the slow, halting shush of footsteps on the basement stairs, a sense of determination and purpose in each step. He knew the effort it took for Elena to climb stairs now. The door opened into the kitchen, and she walked over and set a hand on his shoulder. "You okay?"

He had to smile. So much solicitation about how he was feeling after last night! For an instant he was transported back to the kitchen in the little apartment on Commonwealth Avenue in Boston, Mom standing over him, worried about the boys he'd had to fight his way through on the way home from baseball practice and the black eye she kept trying to cover with an ice pack.

"I'm fine, thanks," he told the old woman. In her seventies at least, although she might have crossed into her eighties. Her age was her business, as she had reminded him on numerous occasions. She had kept house and cooked for a parade of Jesuits down the decades. She could remember every single one, all the odd habits. Father Jerome, the

60

vegetarian; Father Lawrence with his leg brace; Father Michael, who'd talked to himself in Latin; Father Bruce, who'd lost himself in philosophy treatises and forgotten to come to dinner. Elena had related all the stories, and he suspected that when he was gone she would tell stories about him to the next priest.

"Gives me the creeps," she said, walking over to the sink and turning on the faucet. "Somebody out in the darkness shooting at cars like they was in a shooting gallery."

"Chief Banner thinks Carey knew his shooter. He had pulled over."

She seemed to take this in as she slid a stack of plates past the soapsuds into the sink. "Well, that don't make sense. Who's dumb enough to pull over and wait for somebody to shoot him? I'd say the same crazy shooter took a shot at him, and that's why he pulled over."

Father John exchanged a glance with the bishop. He didn't say anything. He had learned long ago not to argue with Elena. She had her own way of looking at the world, and it had amazed him, at times, how clearly she saw it.

"Might be Arapaho," she said.

Father John finished the oatmeal, got up, and poured himself a cup of coffee. He carried the coffeepot to the table and refilled the bishop's cup. The crazy shooter might be someone from the rez, either an Arapaho or a Shoshone. He leaned against the counter, sipped at his coffee, and waited to see if she had anything else, but she was caught up in washing, rinsing, and stacking dishes. "What makes you think so?" he said finally.

"Raps don't like that buffalo ranch." She added a plate to the stack and, patting the suds on her hands with her apron, turned toward him. "Those white people never hired Indians. Only cowboys ever worked there are white. Outsiders. They come from all over, from what I hear. Only thing is, they don't come from the rez."

The cowboy Carlos Mondregan was most likely Hispanic, Father John was thinking. The other cowboy with the pimply face was white. Neither was Arapaho or Shoshone. He wondered why a rancher in the middle of the reservation wouldn't hire local Indians, who knew more about handling buffalo and horses than anybody else. He waited for Elena to continue, provide an explanation, but she turned back to the sink, plunged a hand into the soapy water, and dislodged the stopper. The water swished downward.

"You know," he said after enough seconds had passed to change the subject, "I'm pretty sure I could manage the laundry."

Elena gave a shout of laughter. She found another plate at the bottom of the sink, rinsed it under the faucet, and set it in the drainer before turning toward him. "And mess with my washing machine and dryer? They need special care. They don't work for just anybody."

"You could teach me." He pushed himself away from the counter and took another sip of coffee.

"Ha! How long would that take? I could get ten loads of laundry done."

She would never relinquish the task, he was thinking. Laundry was part of taking care of the house, which she considered her house even though she lived a mile away with her daughter's family. Her place, her work. Judging by the grin on the bishop's face, the old man also knew that they were here at Elena's forbearance.

6

"A minute of your time, Counselor." Tom Glasgow, Fremont County prosecuting attorney, stood in the doorway on the other side of the high-ceilinged corridor. The courthouse was empty, the double doors to the court itself closed. From the bottom of the stairs, Vicky could hear the outside door opening and shutting and the quiet tread of footsteps on the vinyl floor.

She stepped back from the courtroom doors and considered the prosecutor's request. Another plea offer, no doubt, and she had already turned down one offer. Glasgow would offer her client, Arnie Walksfast, a plea of aggravated assault with the stipulation that Arnie would get two years in prison. She hadn't said anything, just walked out of the prosecutor's office. She had no intention of pleading Arnie guilty to a felony. Now she could see the mixture of eagerness and stress in the prosecutor's face. He was tapping his knuckles against the door frame. Maybe Glasgow didn't have the case he thought he had. Brimming with confidence the last time they had met, certain she would accept the plea bargain. *We have Walksfast cold. Up to you how much time he gets.*

"Okay."

She crossed the corridor. Glasgow had already backed into the conference room. Two men seated at the long, shiny table stumbled to their feet. "You remember my assistants, George Reiner and Martin Lewis."

The men nodded in her direction as she took the chair Glasgow held for her. He dropped onto the chair at the top of the table and opened a file folder. "As you know, we have witnesses who were present when Mr. Walksfast assaulted Richard Tomlin in the parking lot at the O.K. Bar. They will testify to the brutal beating the defendant delivered to an innocent man."

"We are also prepared to call eyewitnesses." Vicky placed both hands on the table. The two assistants shifted in their chairs. "Our witnesses will testify that Tomlin insulted, taunted, and finally assaulted my client because he is Arapaho, then followed him into the parking lot and assaulted

65

him again. They will testify that my client was defending himself."

Vicky took hold of the armrests and started to lift herself out of the chair. Another waste of time. She was eager to get inside the court and have a few minutes alone with Arnie before the judge started the trial. Floating like a gnat in the air was the possibility of Arnie opening his mouth, saying something he shouldn't say, and sending himself down to Rawlins without any help from the prosecuting attorney. She meant to caution him again to remain calm and answer only the direct questions.

"Hold on," Glasgow said. "We have an offer in the best interests of your client." The heads of the two assistant prosecutors bobbed up and down.

"Since when do you care about the best interests of my client?"

"Look, Counselor. Your client pleads guilty . . ."

"It will not happen." Vicky was halfway to her feet.

"Misdemeanor charge of reckless endangerment." He rapped his fist against the table and hurried on. "One year in jail. Beats a felony conviction and ten years in Rawlins. You interested?"

"Why would you do that?" She wasn't

sure Arnie would agree to plead guilty to anything. He insisted he was not guilty, that Rick Tomlin had thrown the first punch inside the bar, that he had the right to defend himself.

"Interested or not?"

"You haven't answered my question." Vicky glanced between the other two men, and in the way their eyes slid away from hers, she could sense the answer. "Let me guess. You've lost a witness. An important one, I'd say. Who is it? The so-called victim?"

"It looks as if Rick Tomlin has left the area. My office has been trying to get ahold of him for two weeks. His boss out at the Broken Buffalo said he packed up his saddle and knapsack six weeks ago and drove off. Tomlin was so adamant about testifying against Walksfast, I was sure he'd be here today. No such luck."

Vicky was on her feet, heading toward the door. "I'm moving for a dismissal as soon as the jury is seated." She turned back. "Once jeopardy attaches, you won't be able to bring my client to trial on this charge again."

"Dismissal? I doubt the judge will go along," Glasgow said. "You forget we have other witnesses willing to swear your client assaulted a man, knocked him down, beat his head against the asphalt, and might have killed him if they hadn't jumped in. Your client is still looking at ten years."

"It's a risk, Glasgow. Like trying a homicide case without a body. I have a stronger chance of getting the charges dismissed."

"Arnie Walksfast faced an assault charge last year and skated away. Won't happen this time."

"He had asked for a lawyer, but the police continued to question him. Not smart to ignore a man's rights."

"Say you get a dismissal with jeopardy attached, which is unlikely, but maybe the judge enjoyed his coffee and cinnamon roll this morning and is in a real good mood. The chances are slim. Say it happens, your client will be back here before we've filed the case away. You interested?"

Vicky walked back and sat down. Arnie Walksfast was an alkie. He needed treatment. She had already gotten a substance abuse recommendation, hoping to persuade the judge to put Arnie into rehab if he was found guilty. "Reckless endangerment," she said, "and time in rehab. No jail time and no fines."

Glasgow tapped out a rhythm on the file folder and sent the folder skidding across the table. One of the assistants bent forward and coughed into his fist. The other kept his eyes fixed on the folder. After a moment, Glasgow tipped his head back and stared at the ceiling. "I can go for one year in jail, suspended except for thirty days in rehab and completion of other terms of probation, such as staying out of trouble."

"Deal," Vicky said.

District Judge Gregory Hayword slumped behind the bench and peered through thick eyeglasses at the papers strung in front of him. He cleared his throat and readjusted the layout of the papers, as if he were unaware of anyone else in the courtroom. Vicky could hear the hush behind her, the handful of spectators holding their collective breath.

The judge cleared his throat again, looked up over the top of his glasses and called out the case number. "Arnold C. Walksfast," he said.

Vicky stood and told the judge she was representing the defendant.

Glasgow was also on his feet. "We have agreed to a disposition subject to the court's approval," he said. Then he laid out a guilty plea to reckless endangerment with any jail time suspended on condition that Arnie complete terms of probation and thirty days in rehab.

"Is this your understanding?" The judge was peering at Vicky.

She nodded Arnie to his feet. It had taken a while to persuade him to agree to a guilty plea. Part of the reason, she suspected, was his aversion to entering rehab. If he didn't take the plea, she had emphasized, he could face ten years in the state prison. He had been up on assault charges before, she had reminded him. Assault and public drunkenness and disorderliness, and had gotten off on a technicality. Did he really want to try the judge's patience with another assault charge less than a year later? And there was Glasgow, willing to cut what was a very good deal. Charges reduced from a felony to a misdemeanor. She had half expected him to postpone the trial until Tomlin could be found. It was obvious Glasgow believed that Tomlin had left the area for good.

"What is the factual basis for this change in plea?" Now the judge had turned to Glasgow.

"We were unable to locate the main witness. It seems he has left."

"Left Fremont County?"

"That is correct, your honor. When we were unable to locate Mr. Tomlin, we spoke to Dennis Carey, his former employer at the Broke⋆ Buffalo Ranch. I'm sure you are aware that Mr. Carey was shot and killed last night on Blue Sky Highway. He told us Mr. Tomlin had driven off without leaving any forwarding address. He left about two weeks after the assault occurred. It's possible he was reluctant to testify against Mr. Walksfast because of the defendant's violent tendencies."

"Your honor." Vicky could feel her fists clenching.

The judge held up one hand, eyes still on Glasgow. "Let's not jump to conclusions. The fact is the man Mr. Walksfast is charged with assaulting is not here to testify. He could be in Montana, or Utah, or Colorado by now. Six weeks ago, you said? He could be in the Yukon. I'll go along with the plea."

Now the judge fastened his gaze on her client. "Well? I'm waiting. How do you plea?"

"Guilty." Vicky could sense the reluctance in the man beside her.

"Substance abuse recommendations, counselor?"

"Yes, your honor. Level three-point-five is recommended for my client. A residential program. As for a bed date, my client could check into the clinic in Riverton today."

The judge was staring down at the papers scattered before him. "Mr. Walksfast," he said, looking up slowly, "I am going to sentence you to one year in the Fremont County Jail. On the recommendation of the prosecutor, I am going to allow you to serve your sentence on probation. But I am imposing a condition. You must successfully complete thirty days in alcohol and drug rehabilitation at the White Buffalo Calf clinic in Riverton. If you mess up, your probation will be revoked and you will serve the rest of your sentence in jail. This is an opportunity for you to straighten out your life. Do you understand?"

"Yes." The word sounded garbled, as if Arnie had suppressed a cough. "Your honor," he added.

"A deputy will take you directly to the clinic." The judge banged his gavel, then peered over his eyeglasses at the clerk. "Call the next case," he said.

"I'm out of here," Arnie said, starting to move past her.

"Hold on." Vicky set a hand on the man's arm. She felt a sense of relief. Arnie was the kind of drunk who could sober up for months, then lose himself in days of raging drunkenness. His luck — their luck, she thought — had held again.

72

"It's all over. I'm in the clear. I told you I didn't do nothing wrong."

Vicky nodded to the deputy who had walked over and stood waiting. "I need a few minutes with my client," she said. "We have to check in at the probation office." Then she motioned Arnie ahead, past the prosecuting attorney, who pulled his eyes away, as if he were looking away from an accident. The handful of spectators, Arnie's relatives, made their way into the aisle. Someone had opened the double doors to the corridor. She stayed close behind Arnie, willing him to keep moving toward the doors.

An elderly woman with short, gray hair and a pinched, smiling face reached for Arnie's arm as he passed and pulled herself in alongside him. Smiling! Betty Walksfast had heard what she had wanted to hear, Vicky thought. She had missed the rest of it: If Arnie messed up, he was going to jail.

A young woman, all white and blond with startled blue eyes, held back a moment, then darted after them, her nervousness as palpable as a ticking clock. Lucy Murphy, Arnie's current girlfriend. In the two years Vicky had represented Arnie Walksfast, he'd always had a girlfriend. Indian, Hispanic, white. Vicky moved to the side to make room in the aisle. She was aware of the scuff of footsteps falling in behind them.

They reached the corridor, and Vicky steered Arnie past the door marked Probation. Fifteen minutes later, Arnie had been assigned a probation officer. She led him back into the corridor through the relatives milling about. They kept going past a heavy glass door. Across the entry, down the sidewalk, and out into the parking lot, the deputy walking beside them. The young woman was on the other side, close to Arnie, his mother and the other relatives, all drawing the same conclusion. Arnie had done it again! Never should have been charged. Someone always out to get him; always blaming him.

Vicky stepped ahead and motioned Arnie toward her, away from the crowd. The deputy stayed a few feet back and held out his arm like a roadblock to keep the others away. "Give them a moment," he shouted.

"I have to know, Arnie," she said, keeping her voice low, her eyes on the brown, skittering eyes of her client. "Did you have anything to do with Tomlin's disappearance?"

"What? You're supposed to be my lawyer. You're supposed to trust me."

"If he isn't in court, he can't testify against you."

"How do I know where he went? I seen him one time at the O.K. Bar. Drinking a beer, minding my own business, and that sonofabitch started calling me names, pushing me around. 'Go back to the rez, redskin,' " Arnie was tossing his head about like a pony fighting a halter. "I don't have to take that crap."

"Look at me." Vicky moved in closer. The tobacco and coffee-infused stench of the man's breath floated around her. "If you are lying to me, I will withdraw from your case. Do you understand?"

Arnie stared at her for a long moment, eyes narrowed, mouth hanging open, as if he were trying to grasp the implications. A front tooth was broken, sliced off at an angle, which made him look younger, a kid settling into his grown-up face. "I'm telling the truth."

Betty dodged past the deputy, walked over, and grabbed her son's arm. "The judge cut you some slack," she said. "Only thing that prosecutor wanted was to put you in prison."

"We had our own witnesses. No way was I going to be found guilty."

"We have two witnesses." Vicky glanced at

Lucy Murphy, inching her way like a shadow next to Arnie. "The prosecutor wouldn't have had any trouble proving one of them, your buddy Ernest Whitebull, was too drunk to be credible. You have to go to rehab immediately." This for Betty, whose face was now frozen in comprehension.

Arnie shuffled from one foot to the other. "I need time to get my things together. Why do I have to go right away? Tell the deputy he can pick me up later."

"Now, Arnie. The deputy doesn't take orders from me. I'd like to report to your probation officer how seriously you are taking this, how eager you are to recover, how sorry you are for the fight at the O.K. Bar."

Arnie seemed to be turning this over in his head. Vicky could almost see the gears slip into action. But it was his mother, Betty, who said, "Vicky's right. We got to listen to your lawyer."

Still hovering close to Arnie, the young blond woman had a sad, defeated look about her, as if she hadn't yet been abandoned but understood it was about to happen. "I can bring your things to you," she offered in a small, tentative voice.

"Jesus." Arnie exhaled a breath. "I don't see the rush."

"Come on." His mother took his arm and

tried to steer him toward the deputy, who had walked over. "The sooner you get rehab over with, the better."

"Jesus," Arnie said again.

A few cars, pickups, and campers lumbered along the streets of Lander. Clumps of sagebrush, dried and brown in the August sun, sprouted from the dried yards. Vicky kept the windows rolled down partway. The wind whistled around and fanned at her hair. She drove with one elbow propped on the top of the door, her hand holding her hair out of her eyes.

You're my lawyer. You have to trust me. Vicky laughed at the thought of trusting Arnie Walksfast. Maybe when he was sober, but you could never trust him to stay sober. It was Betty who had called after Arnie was arrested. "They're out to get him, Vicky." Vicky hadn't asked who *they* were. They could be anybody. Police, feds in the big and sometimes frightening — yes, frightening — white world with its laws and regulations.

She had agreed to take Arnie's case. To quiet the panic in Betty's voice at the thought of losing her son to the prison system. Her own son, Lucas, a few years older than Arnie, was moving up the corporate ladder in a high-tech firm in Denver, living like a white man in a condo by the South Platte River within walking distance of Confluence Park where an Arapaho village had once stood. The thought of someone taunting Lucas, insulting him, assaulting him, left a hard knot in her stomach. She had visited Arnie at the Fremont County jail, gotten him out on bond, prepared a defense. Whether or not Arnie was innocent, he deserved a defense.

Vicky swung around the wide curve, stopped for a red light, then turned into a parking lot and drove toward the redbrick building of the local FBI offices. She spotted Adam standing on the sidewalk, his hands in the pockets of his khakis, eyes trained on the highway on one side of the lot. Not until she had parked next to his BMW did he seem to realize she had arrived. He walked over and opened her door. She could still feel the coolness that had settled between them last night when she had insisted upon staying with the body of Dennis Carey. A white man she had never met. Adam, nervous beside her, glancing around as if he expected the killer to rise up out of the borrow ditch and point a gun at them. She had thought of Grandmother Nitti and Grandfather Joseph, her parents and aunties and uncles, the lady who'd served lunch in the cafeteria at St. Francis School when she was a kid, the grandmother who'd made fry bread at the rodeos, all the dead she had known. Someone had always stayed with the body until one of the holy old men could bless it, paint it with the sacred red paint that would identify the spirit to the ancestors.

She lifted herself out of the Ford, conscious of the protective and — was it her imagination? — apologetic pressure of Adam's hand on her arm as he guided her across the sidewalk and through the front door of the redbrick building.

7

Federal agent Ted Gianelli, twenty years ago a linebacker for the Patriots, stood in the corridor, the pebbled glass door open behind him. "Saw you drive up. Come on in." He had a booming voice that rolled around the walls and the vinyl flooring.

Vicky felt the pressure of Adam's hand on the middle of her back as they followed the fed into a warren of offices with fluorescent lights humming overhead. Right, down a short hallway past a cubicle with a dark-haired woman behind the desk, head bent into the phone at her ear. Left, down another hallway and into a small, tidy office with a bank of windows that overlooked the parking lot. Opera music played softly from the iPod jammed among the massive gray legal books that lined the side wall. A flood of memories washed over her. In John O'Malley's old pickup, opera floating out of the CD player between them on the front seat; in his office at St. Francis, opera wafting from the CD player on the bookshelf. Opera was something they had in common, John O'Malley and the fed. She had grown accustomed to the music, even recognized a few arias. "Celeste Aida" was playing now.

Gianelli motioned them to the pair of chairs. Vicky sank down and Adam dropped beside her. The fed settled himself behind the desk and leaned back, tapping a ballpoint against the palm of his hand in rhythm with the aria. "I've read the Wind River police reports." He nodded toward the computer on the table in front of the bookcase. "Sometimes it takes a while for the details to emerge. Let's start at the beginning. What time did you come upon the victim?"

Adam cleared his throat, as if he were the only lawyer in the courtroom and the judge were addressing him. "Must have been close to eleven. The meeting at the tribal college in Ethete adjourned at ten, and Vicky . . ." She was aware of the nod in her direction; she kept her eyes on the fed, ready to read his reactions. What was he looking for? Something new, something they had neglected to tell Banner? A detail they hadn't realized could be crucial? "After she spoke, Vicky stayed to talk to students. We drove out of the parking lot about ten thirty and headed south."

Is that what they had told Banner? Left at ten thirty, reached the victim's pickup about eleven? It was possible. Vicky felt a shiver run through her. Parts of last night were a blur, a mixture of anger and frustration, fear and shock, with a white man collapsed over a steering wheel, a black hole in his forehead and trickles of blood on his cheeks.

"I spoke to the monthly meeting of women students about careers in law," Vicky heard herself explaining. She wondered what on earth difference it made. She and Adam could have been munching on hamburgers at the convenience store in Ethete. Except that one clear, inane memory might trigger another, and that might make the difference. "It was a small group, about twenty students."

"Traffic was light." Adam looked relaxed, leaning back, hands on the armrests. "Folks are staying home at night with that crazy shooter loose. No one knows when he might show up and send a bullet into your windshield."

"It has been a few weeks since we've heard from him." Gianelli shook his head.

"What about last night?"

"Maybe, but we don't think so. Still early

in the investigation, but no bullet holes in the truck. So traffic was light. How many vehicles on the highway near the shooting scene would you say?"

Adam was shaking his head. "The highway was empty. That's why I was surprised to see two vehicles pulled over on the side of the road, headlights on. We were still a good hundred yards away when the first vehicle pulled out and made a U-turn. Had to be going seventy when it passed us."

"Did you get the make? Any part of the license?"

"License?" Adam snorted. "It was pitch-black out there except for the headlights. Big, dark-colored truck, like a Chevy."

"I was watching," Vicky said, the memory spurting in her mind. She was in the passenger seat, watching the headlights coming toward them. The dark hulk rushing past. "The driver wore a cowboy hat." The memory was getting clearer, like a pebble in a creek starting to reflect the sunlight. "I'm sure it was a man."

Gianelli scribbled in the notepad he had produced from a desk drawer. "What made you stop?"

Adam drew in a ragged breath. She waited for what he would say: she could almost hear the words moving through his head. *I didn't want to stop.* "I expected the second vehicle to pull out. A pickup with its head-lights on. I figured the engine was running. I was concentrating on driving past, in case the driver was drunk and decided to pull in front of me."

"I caught a glimpse of the driver slumped over the steering wheel," Vicky said. Another memory as clear as glass. "He looked sick or passed out. I asked Adam to stop. He slowed down and pulled in ahead of the pickup. When we walked over, we saw the man had been shot."

No one said anything for a moment. A matter of respect. *Aida* played softly. "We called 911 and waited for the BIA cops." Adam's voice was crisp and businesslike. As if that were all of it, the facts. "They showed up twenty minutes later."

"Did you recognize the victim?"

Adam shook his head. "Not until one of the officers ID'd him. Dennis Carey, white rancher on the rez. We've seen him cooking buffalo burgers at powwows. He came to the farmers' market this summer to sell buffalo meat."

"Anything else?"

"We stayed with the body out of respect," Vicky said.

Gianelli made some more notes, then

looked up at her and nodded. He had worked among Arapahos and Shoshones on the rez long enough to glimpse their ways. "If you think of anything else, give me a call."

Vicky got to her feet and started past the desk toward the hallway, conscious of Adam close behind, the large presence of him. Then she turned back and, looking past Adam, said, "What about his wife? How is she doing?"

Gianelli drew in a long breath. The answer was obvious, Vicky knew. How did she expect the woman would be doing after her husband had been murdered? Still she had asked, a matter of politeness. She had to find the time to stop at the ranch, tell Dennis Carey's wife that she and Adam had stayed with her husband. He hadn't been alone.

"Well as can be expected," Gianelli said. "Eager for us to find the killer. She's been very cooperative."

The heat reflected off the asphalt, the sun blinked on the hood of the Ford. Adam opened her door, and Vicky slid behind a steering wheel that was like a hot iron burning her fingers. Gusts of dry air banked and swirled around the interior. "We have to talk about this, you know." He was leaning around the door.

This. The word looped through her mind. Last night, all of it. She had told him she wanted to go to her own apartment. Alone. He hadn't protested, even though they had both expected her to spend the night at his house. Spaghetti dinner at the little restaurant on Main Street in Lander, the meeting at the tribal college in Ethete, the drive home under a field of stars. They had both assumed . . .

Adam had walked her into the glass entry of her apartment building and pressed the elevator button. They had stood silently next to each other, the elevator gears and chains rattling. She had stepped into the elevator alone. Through the narrowing space of the closing doors, she watched Adam spin about and dive past the glass door into the darkness. *Woman Alone,* she had thought, as she made her way down the corridor and into her own apartment. The name the grandmothers had given her after she returned to the rez, divorced from Ben Holden, opening a one-woman law practice, clinging to the belief that she could make a difference, that she could help her people. A woman who had stepped ahead of the warriors and made herself a chief, as if such a thing were possible. Destined to be alone. In the glow of the kitchen light inside her apartment, she had made herself a cup of tea, then carried the cup over to the window bench. She had sipped at the tea and watched the streetlights flickering, the lone car crawling down the street, glad to be alone.

Now she was aware of Adam leaning into her window. She tried to focus on what he was saying. Dinner tonight? "We can go to Hudson and have a good steak."

Vicky didn't say anything. She stared straight ahead at the red-brick building. The distance between them had been opening for some time. She had known and not known, she realized, not wanting to bring it into her consciousness, where it would demand attention. Since last night, the distance had expanded around them like a black cloud coming across the plains.

"Okay." She heard her own voice, disembodied in the heat. It demanded attention. She was still staring at the building.

"I'll pick you up at seven." Adam closed the door. She started the engine, rolled down the other windows, and backed into the lot, trying to ignore the black-haired man watching her in the rearview mirror, waiting until she had driven off.

■ ■ ■ ■

Out on Blue Sky Highway, Vicky called the office as she headed north. "I'll be in after lunch," she told Annie Bosey, her secretary. She had seen herself in Annie the morning the slim young woman with shoulder-length black hair had stepped into her office. "Hear you're looking for a secretary, and I'm a good one," Annie had said. "I got two kids to feed." Vicky had hired her on the spot.

"I had cleared your day for the trial. I hear you reached a plea bargain."

My God. The moccasin telegraph was a thing to behold. It had worked in the Old Time on the plains, when the criers walked through the villages, shouting out the news of the day. "If anyone calls . . ."

"Got it. You'll be in after lunch."

Vicky pressed the end button. The plains flashed past the windows, sagebrush and wild grass swirling in the wind, little clouds of dust blowing across the highway. Everything looked brown under a sky crystalline blue with a snowy bank of clouds floating past. She had a sense of coming home. This was her place, all the brown emptiness and the blue sky and the sun glowing red and orange on the foothills.

She made a left onto Trout Creek Road, trusting to memory. The RJ Ranch, it had been called when she was growing up. A white man had purchased the land a hundred years ago, when the government had allowed Indians to sell reservation land, and white men had owned it ever since. The law had changed as reservations began to diminish, and tribes were always trying to buy back land owned by outsiders, but white people had hung on to the RJ. About twenty years ago, the owners had decided to raise buffalo and had changed the name to the Broken Buffalo Ranch. She'd heard that new owners had bought the ranch almost two years ago.

She took a left onto a dirt road that ran ahead into a two-track. A tight-looking barbed-wire fence came into view, tall enough to keep buffalo from jumping over. They could jump like deer, she remembered Grandfather saying. Wild animals, tough and hardy. They could never be domesticated; they were always themselves.

Ironic, she thought. Dennis Carey and his wife, a white couple, raising buffalo in Indian country.

The ranch house seemed to grow out of the plains ahead, lifting itself upward like a crop of corn. The two-track led through a gate with *BB* carved into the overhead post and down a narrow dirt road toward a log house with a porch that stretched across the front. Beyond the house, she could see sides of the barn and outbuildings and an assortment of ranch vehicles: a tractor and flatbed, several pickups and trucks and a yellow forklift parked next to the stack of hay bales. A barbed-wire fence with a gate in the middle ran between the buildings and the pasture. Out in the pasture was the buffalo herd, great brown hulks as placid as cows. Until you got close to them, she thought. *Intelligent animals.* Grandfather's voice in her head again. *They gave themselves as food and sustenance for their Indian brothers and sisters. Don't want to be ranched, corralled inside pastures. The plains are home. They used to roam for miles and miles. If you corral them, be very careful. They could kill you.*

Vicky stopped close to the house and waited. If Sheila Carey didn't come to the door, she would write a note of condolence, leave her number in case Sheila wanted to talk about last night, secure the note on the porch, out of the wind, and drive back to Lander.

She was digging in her bag for a notepad when the front door opened. A small, at-

90

tractive woman with reddish hair stepped onto the porch, came down the steps, and walked over, a mixture of surprise and curiosity in her eyes. "I'm so sorry to bother you," Vicky said across the top of the window rolled halfway down. "I'm Vicky Holden. Adam Lone Eagle and I found your husband. I just wanted to . . ."

"You'd better come in."

8

Sheila Carey was the picture of a grieving widow. Face drawn and blanched, red hair haphazardly knotted in back with strands poking into the air. Her gray western shirt and blue jeans looked worn and crumpled, as if she had slept in them. She didn't say anything until they had crossed the entry into the living room, where she nodded at an upholstered chair as worn-looking as her clothes. "You want coffee or something?" She might have been talking to herself the way her eyes flitted about the room.

"Nothing, thank you. I'm sorry to intrude." Vicky sat on the edge of the cushion. "I thought you might like to know how we found your husband." A pounding noise outside sounded muted and far away.

"I need some coffee." Sheila started toward the kitchen in back. "You want to change your mind?" The question was tossed over one shoulder.

"All right. Thank you." In the Old Time, Vicky was thinking, it was unthinkable to turn down any offer of sustenance, and no one who came to the village left hungry. You never knew when you might eat and drink again. She glanced about the living room. Typical of a ranch house, familiar even. Overstuffed sofa in a wood frame, wood armrests nicked and stained. Gray carpeting with pathways worn silver and, in the middle, the kind of rag rug that had lain on the floor of her home when she was a kid. A square pine coffee table littered with coffee-stained mugs and plates covered with crumbs. From the kitchen came the faint sounds of clinking glass and shuffling foot-steps. A cabinet door slammed.

Sheila Carey was back, carrying two mugs of coffee. She set one down on the table close to Vicky. "I didn't ask. You take any-thing?"

"This is fine." Vicky lifted the mug and took a sip. The coffee was hot and strong and smelled of cocoa. She waited as Sheila settled herself on the sofa and sipped at her own coffee. When the woman was ready, Vicky knew, she would start the conversa-tion.

"The cops told me two lawyers came across Dennis's body. You and . . ."

"Adam Lone Eagle. He's my . . ." Vicky hesitated. He was nothing to her, no relation that could be categorized. Husband, fiancé, brother, uncle, cousin. He was none of these. He was her lover. "Friend," she said. Then she told the woman about last night, how they had left the tribal college at ten thirty, saw the two trucks parked on Blue Sky Highway about eleven.

"Two trucks? You saw two trucks? The cops didn't say anything about two trucks. Neither did the fed."

Because they are investigating your husband's murder, Vicky started to say, then stopped. Investigators gather information; they don't give it. "Yes. A large, dark-colored truck was parked ahead of your husband's truck. It took off as we approached."

"You saw the truck?"

"It was very dark. We couldn't make out the model. It was like a large shadow that sped past in the oncoming lane."

"You saw the driver?"

"Only a glimpse. It looked like a man."

"The man who killed my husband."

"It could have been a passerby who didn't want to stay. I'm sure the police and the fed are trying to find the truck and get some answers."

"Please." Sheila coughed a little laugh. She leaned over and set her mug on the table. Her hand was shaking. "The cops can't even find the crazy shooter that's been terrorizing the highways. I begged Dennis not to go out. 'Don't go to that stupid meeting,' I told him. Those ranchers don't care about raising buffalo. They think we're nuts running a buffalo herd. Nothing but trouble from the . . ." She lifted one eyebrow. "Keeper of the animals, or whatever you Indians call buffalo. Takes dedication and persistence to raise buffalo. Nobody gets into this business without a strong back and a big wallet. One bull, one bull can cost eighty thousand. Who wants to take that on? Oh, the environmentalists, they think we're saints. Last year a blogger came out here and interviewed Dennis. Heaped on the praise for raising buffalo that graze lightly and don't destroy the Earth. And meat that's good for everybody's health. That's not why we got into this business. Dennis liked the fact that buffalo are wild, can't be tamed. The Broken Buffalo was Dennis's dream, and I went along like always. You know how that is?"

Vicky didn't say anything. Was that what she had done? Gone along with Ben Holden until she had summoned the courage to leave? Was that how it was with Adam? Going along?

Finally she said, "We called 911 when we saw your husband had been shot. We stayed with his body until the police came."

"What if the killer had come back?"

"We weren't thinking of that possibility." Except that Adam had been thinking of it.

"It was foolish of you. But thank you for staying with him. I don't mean to be rude."

Vicky took another drink of coffee. Had she expected Sheila Carey to thank her for watching her husband in death? She wasn't Arapaho. What were the white rituals for death? Vicky had attended the funerals of friends and colleagues in Lander. Memorial services, graveside rites. She had been the outsider, wondering about the rituals that touched these white mourners.

She said, "Do you think the random shooter killed your husband?"

"I know who killed my husband."

"You know the killer?"

"It's obvious. I told the cops. I told the fed. I told anybody who would listen. One of the two hands used to work on the ranch. Dennis had to fire them in June. Too unpredictable, out drinking and fighting in town. One got involved in an assault case. Bar fight in Riverton."

"Tomlin?"

"You know him?"

"I never met him. I represent the man accused of assaulting him. The trial was this morning, but Tomlin didn't show up."

"Sheriff's deputies came here looking for him. I told them, 'Go look in Montana or Canada.' You ask me, that cowboy couldn't get away from here fast enough. Same for the other hand we took on last fall. Worst mistake we ever made, hiring on hands. We'd tried to run the ranch ourselves, Dennis and me, but Dennis said it was too much. So a year ago last spring, Dennis hired the first cowboys that drove up. That was a mistake. Always wanting money. Advances on paychecks. Do we look like we're made of money? Dennis told them, we harvest some of the herd or sell a bull, and you'll get paid. But that wasn't good enough for Tomlin and the other hand. Accused us of trying to cheat them. Dennis paid them as much as he could, and they took off, mad as hornets. You could tell they weren't going to let it go."

"You believe they came back . . ."

"Tomlin. He drove a big, four-door Chevy truck. Blended right in with the darkness."

"You've told the fed?"

"I didn't know you saw the truck. I'll be

97

sure to tell him. That bastard Tomlin de-
serves to rot in prison. If the cops can find
him. So far the Broken Buffalo's been nothing but bad luck. Things had just started to
look up." She hesitated and dropped her
gaze to the table, as if she were considering
whether to continue. Then she seemed to
shake herself back into her line of thought.
"Enough of that. We have to go on, like
Dennis would've wanted. Carlos and Lane,
the new hands, are hard workers. Been
repairing the fences, getting the ranch
ready." She stopped again and pinched her
lips together a moment. "For the burial,"
she went on. "I plan to bury Dennis's ashes
on the ranch. It was his dream," she said
again, looking off into a space somewhere
in the middle of the room. "As soon as I
can get the fed to release his body. Why does
it have to take so long?"

How many times had she been asked that
question? Vicky was thinking. The anguished
voices, the survivors, and even that word,
survivors, was suffused with anguish. In the
Arapaho Way, the body had to be buried in
three days so the spirit could go to the
ancestors. Perhaps it was the same for
whites, wanting the body of their loved ones
to be at peace.

"I can make a call to Gianelli, if you'd like."

"Oh, would you? We're anxious to . . . you understand, we're anxious to get on with it. There's a lot of work on the ranch. Too much for a single person. I'll have to work with the hands. Taking care of the herd doesn't stop just because . . ." She halted again. "I don't mean to sound hardhearted. It's just that we have to pay the bills. We have to eat."

Vicky tried for a reassuring smile. The woman's husband hadn't even been dead for twenty-four hours, and Sheila Carey was eager to get on with it? People were different; you could never anticipate reactions. She slipped a business card out of her bag and set it on the table. "If there is anything else I can do, please call me." Then she stood up and walked to the door. Opening it, she looked back. The woman remained on the sofa, slump-shouldered, hands grasped between her knees, which rose over the top of the table.

Vicky got into the Ford and was about to back around when she saw the dark, husky-looking cowboy with a straw hat pushed back on his head walking over. He had short, bowed legs, which gave him the hip-hop walk of rodeo riders. She rolled down the front windows. The hot smell of manure and wood clippings spilled into the car.

The cowboy set his arm across the top of the door and leaned into the open window. "I hear you found Mr. Carey's body." He had large teeth, tobacco stained in various shades of brown.

"That's right." There's no way he could have known that unless he had been in the kitchen eavesdropping. She thought about the pounding outside that she had heard earlier. When had the noise stopped? "You must be one of the new hands."

"Carlos," he said. "Hired on the first of July. I been helping Dennis keep things running. Now I'm going to help that little lady in there, who needs all the help she can get."

"You mean running the ranch?"

He stared at her out of narrowed, flashing eyes. "What else? You seen the killer?"

"It was dark," Vicky said. What else indeed, she was thinking.

"All the same, you seen him?"

"I saw someone behind the steering wheel of a big truck. He wore a cowboy hat."

"Every hand in these parts wears a cowboy hat."

True, she thought. "Is there anything else?"

"Nothing," he said. "Go in peace."

9

Reg hartly slowed his pickup past the fence that enclosed the pasture. Appaloosas grazing on the stubbly grass lifted their heads, chewed, swallowed, and sent long, slow gazes his way. He parked behind a battered white pickup faded almost to yellow. There was an emptiness about the old ranch house. The steps creaked and groaned as he climbed to the porch. The morning was already hot; no telling how high the temperature might get today. The creeks were drying up. Narrow borders of sand along the banks. White, billowy clouds floating over the jagged peaks of the Rocky Mountains. Not a drop of rain in them.

Reg knocked at the screened door, which banged against the frame and jumped on its hinges. Not the kind of neglect Josh would have stood for if he were home working on the ranch. His ranch, he called it, except that old Ned, his father, wasn't ready to retire, and the spread along the Gunnison River on the Colorado Plateau outside Grand Junction belonged to Ned. Things would be done his way. Reg had tried to talk Josh out of leaving. Cowboying, moving from ranch to ranch, was no kind of life. You never could get a stake in a place of your own that you could leave to your son.

He remembered how Josh had laughed at that. Set the glass of beer down so hard that the foam had spilled onto the bar, threw his head back and laughed as if Reg had turned into a stand-up comedian, spouting truths as sharp as arrows. Well, you had to laugh or you would cry. "He's going to realize he can't run the ranch without you," Reg had said. Josh still laughing. "He's going to have to pull back. Your mother's been after him to take it easy for years. Someday he has to listen."

"You don't know my old man. He's gonna live forever. He can lift ninety-pound bales of hay. I got to get out of here." He had left six months ago. A knapsack, an extra pair of boots, and his saddle, all piled into the bed of his pickup truck. Going to Wyoming, he said. You could always cowboy in Wyoming. Besides, he wanted to work with buffalo, and there were buffalo ranches in Wyoming. Crazy animals.

Reg realized the door had opened and the old man himself was standing on the other side of the screen. "You heard from Josh?"

Reg shook his head. He opened the screen door and stepped inside. "I came to see how your wife's doing." The living room looked dusty and unkempt, empty beer bottles on the floor next to the sofa. A bachelor's place.

"Poorly. Right poorly. Ada is dying, no doubt about it, but she's taking her time, waiting for her boy to come home. He's all she's got. All we got. Never should have left. This here is our home. You want to see her? Pay your respects? She's gonna ask you about Josh. Give her some kind of story that might ease her a bit."

Reg followed the bent back and knobby spine around the sofa and down a dim hallway into a dimmer room with a lace cover over the bed, the kind his grandmother used to crochet, and the tiny figure of Ada Barker under the cover. Thin, blue-white fingers spread over a swollen belly. "Josh?" Her voice was as high and thin as a cricket's.

"It's Reg Hartly, Josh's friend." He set a hand over the old woman's. It felt like a cool sheet of parchment. "Just came by to see how you're doing. Your old man taking good care of you?"

It wasn't the right thing to say. He knew by the way she flinched, by the tremor in her hand, that it wasn't right. "He sent my boy away, and now I can't tell him good-bye."

"Now, Ada, you know that's not true." Ned cleared his throat, as if he could make the truth disappear. "Josh wanted to try things on his own, like lots of young fellas. Get his feet wet out in the big, wide world. Learn a few lessons. It'll do him good. He'll be back. This is home," he said again.

She stared for a long moment at her husband standing at the foot of the bed, then closed her eyes, as if she couldn't summon the strength for the argument. And what did it matter? Josh was gone and she was dying.

"Is there anything I can do for you? I got my chariot outside if you feel up to a drive on this beautiful day. I can carry you . . ."

The thin hand slipped away from his, and she gave a little wave, like a dead leaf, directionless, falling from a tree. "No more chariot rides for me." She managed a smile that stretched her thin lips over the stubs of teeth, as if, for a second, she had drifted into a memory. "I was a belle once," she said.

"You were the prettiest girl in Mesa

County," the old man said. "Remember the ancient surrey wagon that belonged to my grandpa? One time he let me hitch up a couple horses and take you for a ride. That was because he loved you, Ada. Wanted you to be his granddaughter. Nobody else ever got to ride in that surrey." Ned looked over at Reg. "After he died, I took a good look at the thing and hauled it to the dump. Sure didn't look like the wonder Granddad had been hanging on to all those years. I think he was hanging on to part of himself."

Moisture pooled in the old man's eyes, and he swayed slightly, as if he were trying to stand up against the wave of memories. "I been calling Josh. Sending him letters. Even got a kid down the road to text him, whatever that is. Now don't you worry, Ada." He looked back at the doll-like figure under the lace cover. "He's gonna get one of them messages and drive up here any minute now. Why, when I heard Reg's pickup coming up the road, I thought it was Josh."

"You get him back, you hear?" There was a fierceness in the old woman's voice, summoned from somewhere deep within her. For an instant she lifted her head and gestured with it toward the man at the foot of the bed, then let it drop back onto the

106

pillow. "Least you can do after you sent him off. Couldn't let go, just couldn't let go so he could be a man right here where he belongs. You bring him back so I can die in peace."

"I'm doing my best." The old man stifled a sob. "There's nothing in the world I want more than you feeling good again and Josh running the ranch. You and me can just sit on the porch and watch the horses and the sun setting behind the mountains. Won't that be great, Ada? Now you think real hard on that, and no more talk about dying. You think about Josh, 'cause he's coming back. You think about living."

She had closed her eyes, but Reg wasn't sure whether she had fallen asleep or was just closing herself away from the lies. No more lies. Ned nodded toward the door, and Reg found himself tiptoeing behind the old man, not wanting to disturb the woman any further.

"Want a beer?" Ned was already on his way across the living room and into kitchen.

Reg went after him and sat down on a hard wood chair at the table covered in red-and-white-checkered plastic. How many times he and Josh had sat at this table. Doing homework. Josh was good at math. He had made sense out of the problems Reg had struggled with. Talking about the future. A couple of cowboys, born and bred, not good for anything else. What did they need math for? You're gonna be running this place someday, Reg had told him. You're gonna need to keep the accounts. Good thing you and numbers get along. Yeah, someday, Josh had said. Soon's the old man decides to take it easy.

High school, later, a fading memory, and Reg hiring out on neighboring ranches. No place of his own, no family place. His own father had cowboyed all over Colorado, had never gotten a stake for himself. But Josh had worked for his father. Always the hired man. "I'm no better off than you," he'd said once. He had been in the dumps that day, downing three or four beers, crushing the cans and heaving them toward the trash basket. He had missed, and Reg could still hear the tinny sound of the cans clanking on the vinyl floor. He could see the loss in Josh's eyes, as if life had passed him by and he had missed everything. He'd left the next week.

The old man set a can of beer in front of Reg and dropped onto the chair across the table. He popped his can. "Don't mind saying, it hurts to see her dying with a broken heart. I keep going over and over it. I should've let him take over like he wanted. Grow our herd, put in hay in the south pasture. Oh, he had all kinds of plans. Even worked out the numbers. Sure, he'd have to borrow from the bank, but he could pay it back, or so the numbers said. But my grand-daddy and my own dad never borrowed a cent. Me neither. That's why we own this place, free and clear. Slept at night without worrying when the bankers were gonna show up and run us off our own land. That's what I wanted for Josh. Free and clear, and maybe that meant holding back on his dreams until he could pay cash."

He took a long drain of beer and smacked his lips. "Nothing turned out like I was hoping."

Reg opened his own can and took a long sip. The beer was cold and foamy, and he realized how thirsty he was. "Listen," he said. "Maybe I can help find him."

"What you gonna do? Text him? Call? Send an e-mail? He's been ignoring all that."

"I was thinking I could go to Wyoming." Why not? He had been thinking about leaving the plateau anyway and trying to hire on someplace else. Two years of drought here, and ranchers cutting back on the hired help. He hadn't had a job in almost a month. Things could be better in Wyoming, and he could get a line on Josh, wherever he was.

"Leave here? Go to Wyoming? You got rocks in your head like my boy? It's enough he's missing. You don't need to go missing with him."

"You know where he was working?"

The old man scooted his chair back, set both hands on the table, and levered himself to his feet. He headed into the living room in a lopsided gait, swaying as if he were on the dance floor. Reg could hear the squeak of a drawer opening and closing, then the old man was back, carrying a small stack of postcards and a stack of envelopes tied in blue ribbon. He flopped back down, pushed the envelopes to one side, and lined up the postcards into a neat pile in front of him.

"First we heard from Josh was in early April. He'd been gone a month, and we didn't know if he was dead or alive. Ada worried all the time. That's when she started getting sick, all that worrying, made the cancer grow. Take a look." He pushed the card across the table.

On top was a neon red-and-yellow caricature of a cowboy on a bucking bronco, hat swinging in the air. Reg turned the card over. "Getting settled in the cowboy state!

Rough drive over South Pass, big spring blizzard. Winter's still hanging around. It is what they say it is here, bad. Hope you are doing okay. Your son, Josh."

"He doesn't mention a job."

"Hadn't got on anywhere yet, my guess. A lot of ranchers don't hire 'til spring comes on. All they can do in winter is keep on the help they have. He didn't want to worry us. And my boy wasn't never gonna admit he was a failure." Ned pushed another card after the first.

An Easter picture, rabbits in cowboy boots and white hats, holding baskets of candy. April 23 was scrolled at the top on the other side. "Hope this finds you doing good. Got hired onto a ranch that raises buffalo, so finally got the chance to work with those big boys. Hope you have a good Easter and will eat a slice of coconut cake for me."

"Could be a number of buffalo ranches in Wyoming."

"Three more postcards and an envelope with a picture," Ned said, trailing the rest over the table.

Reg picked up the envelope and shook out a photograph of a two-story log cabin house. Scrawled across the bottom in Josh's handwriting: "This here is the ranch where I hired on." The postcards were more cartoonish pictures of cowboys, old pickups, and horses that looked like nags. Reg turned over the first. "Buffalo ranching is sure a hard job. Gotta take hay bales out every day, break them up and toss the hay to the herd. We show up without hay, they'd most likely turn over the flatbed and kill us. Still cold and snow on the ground. I got me a new wool muffler that covers my face. Write me at Broken Buffalo Ranch, Fort Washakie, WY."

"Did you write him?"

"Came back. Marked unknown at this address."

Reg picked up the next card. "Spring coming on. A couple cows pregnant. Owner's real glad, since he's trying to grow the herd. Scratching out a living here, you ask me. Got to get back out to the pasture before the buffalo riot. Your son, Josh."

The last postcard had what seemed to Reg a lonely note running through it. "Sure do miss the ranch and both of you. This place is pretty isolated. Indians all around. Sure would like to hear from you. Thinking about heading home sometime soon. Your loving son, Josh."

"Broken Buffalo Ranch surrounded by Indians," Reg said. "There's an Indian reservation up there, isn't there? You suppose that's where he landed?"

"I gave the kid down the road fifty cents to look it up on the internet. Yeah, my boy was on a reservation surrounded by Indians. Arapahos and Shoshones."

"He never got your letters?"

The old man tossed the blue-tied envelopes toward Reg. "See for yourself."

Reg untied the ribbon and made a fan of six or eight envelopes. Unknown stamped on the front of each one.

"You going up there and talk to that buffalo rancher?"

"That's what I'm thinking." Reg finished his beer, then took out the tiny tablet he kept in his shirt pocket. A miniature pen was hooked onto the side. He opened the tablet and wrote: Broken Buffalo Ranch, Indian reservation.

"Someone else who might help," Ned said. "If Josh was in trouble . . ."

"You think he got into some kind of trouble?"

"I'm saying if he did, he might've gone to talk to a priest. Ada poured a fierce amount of faith in that boy when he was a kid. He might've quit going to church, but he didn't get over it."

10

Father John spotted the woman in front of the blue bi-level house surrounded by pink, orange, and green bi-levels in what was known as Easter-Egg Village, the federal government's idea of a residential neighborhood. He swung the Toyota to the side of the road. The old pickup had been balking and kicking down Seventeen-Mile Road. Now the engine gasped and went silent, like a dying patient fed up with the effort of breathing. "Di Provenza il mar" faded into the shush of the wind over the half-open windows. He turned off the CD player and got out, hoping the pickup would get a second breath in a little while.

"Appreciate you coming over." Miriam Many Horses watched him come up the weed-cracked sidewalk, cigarette smoke curling from the fist next to her thigh. "Lunch is ready. Dad's waiting inside. He doesn't know I'm still smoking. That quitting thing isn't working so good." She gave a little laugh and nodded him up the concrete steps to the front door. "Don't tell him."

Father John smiled and shook his head. Addictions were hard to kick. Often quitting didn't go well. "I'm trying to think what I could tell your father that he doesn't already know," he said.

"He doesn't know what's going on on the rez."

Father John stopped and looked down at the woman at the foot of the steps. She came to his shoulders, drawing hard on the cigarette, cheeks caved in. "What's going on?"

"Moccasin telegraph's being real cagey. Bits and pieces of information all morning, but nobody's got the whole story."

"What's the half story?" The telegraph could be erratic. Sometimes St. Francis Mission was the first to hear the news. Usually bad news. Sometimes the mission was the last, which meant this could be good news. He didn't think so by the frown lines etched in the woman's forehead.

"Vacations, time off, even sick leaves canceled at the BIA police department. Getting ready for something, but not saying what. I don't remember the last time my

115

niece's husband got an order like that. Get ready, it's coming, whatever it is."

Father John looked out across the dirt yard. A tumbleweed skittered one way, then another. He could feel the woman's eyes burrowing into him. Chief Banner must have called an all-departments meeting this morning and given the directive. There would be other directives. Meetings to discuss traffic control measures, the onslaught of drunken drivers from across the country, hordes of people lined up to buy gas or hot dogs at the convenience store in Ethete. How many people — hundreds? thousands? — coming to see the white buffalo calf? He remembered reading about a white calf born on a farm in Wisconsin a few years ago. Thousands and thousands of people had come. Arapahos and Shoshones had loaded up pickups and set off for Wisconsin. The minute the word was out, people would start coming here. All he had to do, he realized, was tell Miriam Many Horses what he had learned last night at the Broken Buffalo Ranch.

"I'm sure we'll know eventually," he said.

"Yeah, eventually. While we're waiting, we might like to get prepared. Big storm? Tornado brewing? Flood?" She gave a sharp, raspy laugh; Father John laughed

116

with her. It was hard to imagine enough rain on the dry plains to worry about a flood. "See, when we don't know, we get crazy imagining stuff." Miriam stamped the cigarette butt into the dirt, then picked it up and slid it into the pocket of her blue jeans. "Go on in. Door's never locked."

The living room was narrow, running to the kitchen in back, but comfortable looking, with a worn sofa and chairs and a couple of throw rugs spread over the vinyl floor. Clifford sat at a small yellow table beneath the kitchen window. The old man made a motion toward getting to his feet when Father John walked over and set a hand on his shoulder. The bones felt sharp and fragile at the same time. "Don't get up, Grandfather." He used the term of respect for elderly men on the rez, who deserved respect for their long lives and hard-won wisdom. Just like the grandmothers.

"Sit yourself." Clifford waved a brown, long-fingered hand toward the chair at the corner.

Father John started to sit down, then asked Miriam, bustling along the counter, if there was anything he could help her with.

"Help me by eating a big lunch, make the work worthwhile." She stopped slicing sandwiches into triangles and glanced over one shoulder. "Not that there's much work in making bologna sandwiches. I didn't have to butcher the cow. Coke or coffee?"

"Coke sounds good." A cold drink and a little caffeine might keep him alert, Father John was thinking, with the warm sun slanting through the window and laying a bright path across the tabletop.

Miriam set a plate with triangular sandwiches, a handful of potato chips, and a dill pickle in front of her father. The elderly were always served first in the Arapaho Way. As if their time to partake in the joys of life were limited. An identical plate appeared before him. She set down two glasses of Coke. "Brownies for dessert," she said, sliding a plate of chocolate brownies into the middle of the table. "You promise you'll eat your sandwiches first. Dad?"

"Yeah. Yeah." The old man waved her away. "You done good, Daughter."

"Well, I'll be back soon as I get off my shift at the restaurant." She cupped the old man's shoulder. "Don't worry about supper. I'll bring you something." Then, to Father John: "You hear about what's going on, you let me know, okay?"

He smiled up at the serious-looking face. She would hear the news as soon as Sheila Carey tended to the burial of her husband.

He thanked her for lunch.

After the front door had closed, Father John waited while Clifford devoured half of his sandwich and sipped at his Coke. It was not polite to rush the conversation and inquire as to what was on the old man's mind. The time was not yet right. He worked at his own sandwich, surprised again at how good a bologna sandwich slathered in mayonnaise could taste. It took him back to his childhood, eating bologna sandwiches at a table not much larger than this yellow table, his mother bustling around the kitchen preparing dinner, with lunch not yet over. He shook away the memory, as if it didn't belong to him. So long ago. Another time, another life.

Clifford finished the sandwich and started pushing the chips around the plate with one finger. "I've been wanting to talk to you."

"What is it, Grandfather?" Father John could feel his muscles tense. The old man was ninety. The news could be anything. A bad diagnosis, bad news about his nephew in Afghanistan, worry over someone in the younger generation following the wrong road.

"Miriam don't know what's going on, but I do."

Father John didn't say anything. He waited

for the old man to collect his thoughts.

"Seen a vision a couple weeks ago. Early morning, starting to get light. I was sitting out back watching the sun rise and praying, like usual." Father John nodded. The elders prayed every day that good things would come to the people. "Then I seen a beautiful young woman with black hair and black eyes come across the prairie toward me. She wasn't walking; she was floating. That's how I knew she was a spirit. She had on a white deerskin dress decorated with beads and embroidery more beautiful than I ever seen. She spun around three times, and I saw that she was a buffalo. A beautiful white buffalo. Then she was gone, like she melted into the air. So I knew she came to tell me she was coming back as a white calf, like she promised to do whenever the people needed help. I knew a white buffalo calf was going to be born. She is a sign of the Creator among us. She is like a visitation of the Blessed Mother."

The old man stared across the table into space, as if the White Buffalo Woman might reappear. After a moment he waved a hand against any objection Father John might make. "White Buffalo Woman came to the Lakota. She gave them the sacred ceremonies and left them the sacred pipe. But she came for all the tribes. That's why we revere her. Now with the troubles, some crazy guy shooting at cars for the fun of it, man getting murdered, she's come back, just like she promised." He craned his head and stared at Father John, a pleading look in the rheumy black eyes. "It's true, isn't it?"

Father John took a couple of seconds before he said, "It's true."

"The sacred calf, here with us." The old man started nodding, something peaceful and rhythmic in the motion, and for a moment Father John thought he might drop off into sleep. Instead, he straightened his shoulders, and said, "I got the news on the moccasin telegraph that the cops are canceling vacations and leaves. I knew they're getting ready for the visitors. Won't just be Indian people. White folks, all kinds of folks will come to see the sacred calf. I figure the calf is out there on the Broken Buffalo Ranch, and I heard you and Banner went there last night after that white man got killed. The widow tell you about the calf?"

"She isn't ready to make it public."

"Can't stay secret forever. The cops know. Word's already starting to leak out."

"She wants to see that her husband is buried and at peace."

Clifford pushed the chips around the plate

and studied the design he had made. It resembled a buffalo head. "I seen something else in the vision," he said. "A cloud black as a storm. The cloud moved real slow off to the west before it turned into a black hole that looked like it had been drilled into the sky. Then it was gone. Soon's I heard about the rancher getting shot last night, I understood the vision: something sacred has come to the rez, but evil is still among us."

Father John sat very still for a long moment. There was no rational, logical way of explaining visions. Since he had been at St. Francis Mission, he had learned to accept that not everything could be explained.

He left the old man in the living room sitting in his recliner, the toes of his boots splayed in opposite directions. He could hear the faint snoring sounds as he let himself out the front door. In the pickup, with the driver's door hanging open, he checked his cell. A message from Sheila Carey. Could he stop by the ranch this afternoon? He had to jiggle the key in the ignition before the engine kicked over and the pickup shivered around him. He made a U-turn onto the dirt road, headed back to Seventeen-Mile Road, and turned west.

The staccato sounds of a hammer thumped

through the soft noises of the wind. Father John slowed the pickup over the rough mounds of dirt that passed for a road across the plains to the Broken Buffalo Ranch. He could see two cowboys working on the fence that enclosed the pasture north of the barn. Out in the pasture, several buffalo nosed among a clump of cottonwoods and willows. By the time he pulled next to the house, one of the cowboys, brown straw hat pushed forward, came walking toward him. It was Sheila Carey.

"Looks like we're going to need some extra hands," she said as he let himself out of the pickup. Beyond the house, he could see the tractor, flatbed, forklift, and trucks standing idle near the barn. "That agency in Riverton, Ranchlands Employment, is supposed to send over cowboys. Haven't seen one yet. Don't know any cowboys looking for a job, do you?"

He stopped himself from saying, "White cowboys?" The woman looked flushed from the heat and the sun; little specks of perspiration glistened on the V-shaped patch of skin that showed at the collar of her blouse. A widow, her husband not dead twenty-four hours. "I can ask around."

"You do that." She tossed her head back toward the fence where Carlos was positioning another post. "I hear word is out on the moccasin telegraph. People know something's going on."

"It won't be long before they figure out the white calf is here. When do you plan to make the announcement?"

"That's what I wanted to talk to you about. The coroner released Dennis's body today. I made arrangements to have him cremated. It was what he wanted," she added hurriedly. "I'm planning to bury his ashes here tomorrow. There's a real pretty place behind the barn, a kind of meadow. I was hoping you'd be willing to say a few prayers. Dennis wasn't what you'd call a believer, but prayers would be nice. I thought maybe you could talk one of the Arapaho elders into doing a little Indian blessing. Give Dennis a proper send-off."

"I can ask Clifford Many Horses. I'm sure he would like to see the calf before the crowds come."

The woman was squinting up at him past the brim of her cowboy hat. "He can give Spirit the stamp of approval. Ten o'clock in the morning? You'll arrange it?"

"I'll ask him."

11

Nighttime settled over the mission. The Boy Scout meeting at Eagle Hall had ended an hour ago; pickups taking the kids home had stuttered through the cottonwood tunnel onto Seventeen-Mile Road. Father John had locked up Eagle Hall and checked to make sure the front doors of the administration building and the church were locked. In the residence, the bishop carried a cup of coffee upstairs and, for a little while, Father John had heard the faint tap-tap-tap of a keyboard. Then footsteps overhead, followed by silence. The bishop was usually in bed by ten o'clock. Father John poured himself another cup of coffee and carried it into the study across the front hall from the living room. He opened his laptop and watched the icons people the screen. Pipes gurgled somewhere in the walls of the old house.

He searched for sites about white buffalo calves and their significance to Plains Indians. Dozens of sites came up, and he clicked on one that looked promising: the video of the keynote talk at a symposium on Indian spirituality by Professor Harold Jumping Elk of South Dakota State University. Father John recognized the name. Professor Jumping Elk's book on the Indians as the Creator's chosen people was in the stack of books on his bedside table waiting to be read.

The video flickered and settled into the image of a wide-chested man with black hair slicked back into a ponytail and intense black eyes. He wore a black suit with a white shirt buttoned to the collar and no tie, like the chiefs in the bronzed photos from the Old Time. Dropping his gaze, he took his time checking the papers on the podium in front of him. Turning over one page, then the next. The audience was still.

Finally the professor looked up, cleared his throat, and began speaking:

When I think of the sacred white buffalo calf, I think of the beautiful young woman with the yellow-and-red scarf tied around her bald head. She stood at the fence next to the pasture on a farm in Wisconsin. Hundreds of people milled about, and I remember how this beautiful woman waited her turn to get close to the fence. She leaned against the post and stared out at the herd of buffalo. Off to the side was the new white calf, about the size of a lamb, sheltering in the great, protective shadow of her mother. The beautiful lady did not take her eyes away. I saw that she was crying.

Later she told me that she had heard about the birth of the white buffalo calf as she finished chemotherapy. She got into her car and drove from Houston to Wisconsin because, as she said, she believed the sacred calf would be a blessing on her life.

When I looked at the other visitors lined along the fence, staring off into the pasture, I saw that most had tears in their eyes. All kinds of people, not just Indians, although Indian people had come from across the country, Mexico, and South America. Whites, African Americans, Asians — a microcosm of the whole world. In some way, all these people understood that what they saw out in the pasture — a smallish, unassuming animal — was the most sacred creature they would ever see.

I first learned about the sacred white buffalo calf from my grandfather. I remember sitting in a circle inside the tipi that Grandfather kept in his back yard. The government had built frame houses on the Pine Ridge Reservation, but many of the old Lakotas preferred to sleep and eat in their tipis. It was rumored that some of the old ones stabled their horses in the houses while they continued living in their tipis. Anytime Grandfather began a story about the Old Time, the circle inside the tipi became very quiet. We knew the story was about us.

In the very long ago time, Grandfather told us, when the people were alone and hungry, a beautiful woman came from the West. She was dressed in a white deerskin dress decorated in beads and quills. Her moccasins did not touch the earth. She floated toward the village, and the people knew she was a spirit. She was Wakan. She came from the Creator. The woman taught the people many things. To be respectful of creatures, the four-leggeds and the wingeds, who are our relatives, and to be respectful of the living Earth. She told us to be in a holy way. She spoke to the women especially and said their work was as great as that of the warriors who procured food for the people. It was the women's work and the children they bore that kept the people alive. She taught us the sacred ceremonies and gave us the

sacred pipe. The smoke from the pipe is the breath of the Creator.

Before she left, the beautiful woman promised she would return in times of trouble so that we would know the Creator remained with us. She started off in the direction of the setting sun, then stopped. She rolled over and became a black buffalo. She rolled a second time and became a brown buffalo. The third time, she became a red buffalo, and the fourth time she became a white buffalo calf.

After her visit, the plains were filled with buffalo. Enormous herds stretched as far as the eye could see. The ground rolled and shook like thunder under their hooves. The buffalo gave the people everything we needed to live. Food, clothing, shelter, tools. Today archeologists say seventy million buffalo once existed. The ancestors saw the herds and said the people would live forever. When the wars of the plains ended and the people were sent to reservations, the great herds had been reduced to a few straggly animals, one thousand or less. It seemed that the buffalo had been swallowed by the Earth, and that the Indian people would die.

But throughout the generations, White Buffalo Woman kept her promise, and

from time to time, a white buffalo calf was born. Scientists look to genetics and try to determine how many white calves might have ever been born, but the ancestors did not keep track of such numbers. They knew only that the white calf came to remind the people that the Creator was with them.

White Buffalo Woman came to the Lakota, but the message she brought was meant for all people. All the other tribes, and all the non-Indian people. For that reason, the beautiful white woman with a bald head, a yellow-and-red scarf and tears in her eyes, had driven a thousand miles to see the sacred calf and pray for healing. For that reason, thousands of people had come, all of them praying for healing in their lives. They believed that the small white calf was a sign of the Creator among his creatures.

Father John closed the site and glanced through the list of other sites, finally settling on one called Buffalo Today. "Walking Lightly on the Earth" ran across the top of several pages of text. He scanned the paragraphs. Buffalo were at home on the plains, with the lack of moisture and sparse vegetation. Once accustomed to roaming vast

areas, they grazed as they moved without destroying the fragile environment. Confined to smaller areas today, buffalo feed sometimes had to be supplemented with hay. Still, environmentalists pointed out that buffalo lived in greater harmony with their surroundings than cattle. The low-fat, low-cholesterol buffalo meat was considered a healthful delicacy.

Father John closed the site and sipped at the cool, bitter coffee. He swiveled toward the window and stared out at the streetlight dancing in the wind over the wild grass. A small white animal, a sacred sign that would bring thousands of people to the rez. He wondered if Sheila Carey had any idea of what was coming. Chief Banner might mobilize the entire police force, but he wondered if it would be enough.

12

Annie was at her desk when Vicky let herself into the office. Printer humming, smells of fresh coffee wafting through the air, and Roger Hurst, the lawyer she and Adam had hired to handle what Adam called the "little cases," standing at Annie's shoulder, the invisible remnants of a conversation dangling between them. "Good morning." Vicky headed toward the small table that held the coffeepot and stack of mugs.

She adjusted her bag over her shoulder and, gripping her briefcase with one hand, managed to pour a cup of coffee. Out of the corner of her eye, she saw Annie scoot her chair backward and jump to her feet. The secretary's footsteps clacked behind Vicky as she went into her private office. She sat down behind her desk and let the briefcase and bag fall at her feet. Tiredness dragged at her. She had tossed and turned all night, a strange dream running through her head. She was walking across the plains, walking, walking toward some point on the horizon she could never reach.

"You okay?" Vicky realized Annie had been watching her.

"I'm fine. Got off to a late start this morning."

"I thought maybe you'd heard the news." When Vicky didn't say anything, Annie hurried on: "There's a rumor on the moccasin telegraph — nobody's confirmed it — that a white buffalo calf's been born."

Vicky could feel her breath expanding in her throat. She forced herself to exhale. "Where?" she managed. She knew the answer, as if it were written in the air.

"On the rez. Like I said, it's only a rumor, but folks are really excited. Tribal cops are getting ready for a lot of visitors. I mean, thousands. There will be people everywhere. It will be a mess." She stopped. "But if it's true, it will be quite wonderful. You have to wonder, why us? Why would we be blessed?"

"We don't know if it's true." My God, Vicky was thinking. A white buffalo calf. The rarest of creatures, a sacred animal come to help the people in time of need. There was always a time of need, but the white buffalo had never come to the rez. Maybe the needs had accumulated, grown so great that the Creator decided the time was right. She tried to shrug away that line of thought. Rumors were always blowing about. Some turned out to be true, but most died away like the wind. "We'll have to wait and see," she said. Still the image of a white buffalo calf on the rez, a sign that the Creator had not forgotten the people, sent a chill through her.

Annie nodded, but hope and excitement flared like firelight in her black eyes. "You're right. We'll just have to wait. You have an appointment in fifteen minutes. Lucy Murphy. She said she met you yesterday. She called first thing this morning. I was coming through the front door when the phone started ringing."

Vicky took a sip of the black coffee. Lucy Murphy, the girl hovering around Arnie Walksfast in the parking lot outside the court building. White girl, blond hair. She wasn't sure she could pick the girl out of a police lineup. Annie had gone back into the outer office and closed the beveled-glass doors behind her. Through the glass, Vicky could see the distorted image of the secretary settling behind the distorted image of her desk, leaning into a computer that resembled a flying alien ship. She turned on her own computer and checked the day's calendar. Lucy Murphy, 9:00 a.m. Howard Black Cloud, 10:00 a.m. Howard wanting to sue the mechanic shop that had fired him. Nancy Savage, 11:00 a.m. Nancy sure this time she wants to file for a divorce from Fred. Vicky had no idea what Lucy Murphy wanted. The afternoon looked free, but things always popped up, clients called or strolled into the office.

Vicky brought up her e-mail. Thank-you notes from members of the women's club at the tribal college, an invitation to speak about Indian law from the Riverton Lions Club, an invitation to lunch from a woman she didn't know who was thinking about opening a law office in Lander. She closed the e-mail, took another drink of coffee, warm now and almost chewy, and allowed last night's dinner with Adam to work its way to the front of her thoughts, the place it had been demanding all the previous night. Adam, seated across from her, steak and baked potato in front of him, and she with her own steak, both of them talking around the subject, observing the polite preliminaries: the weather, next week's pow-wow.

Finally Adam had apologized for wanting to leave the murder scene. He had been worried about their safety, the two of them standing out in the highway, prime targets if the shooter had happened by, or if the killer had come back. Maybe the same man, who really knew? Not the fed or the tribal cops. A murder on a dark highway, it would probably never be solved.

She remembered hardly listening. His voice blended into the background noise in the restaurant, the clinking of dishes and swooshing of the steel door to the kitchen. She wondered who he was, the Lakota across from her with black hair streaked with silver, the little scar that ran across his cheek, the black eyes and intelligent face, and something about him — the confidence, like that of a warrior in the Old Time — so handsome that the two women at the adjacent table kept glancing his way, trying to catch his eye. So many years they had been lovers, with occasional breaks while he handled natural-resource cases for other tribes, but always he had come back. Always saying he wanted her, when he could have practically any other woman. Always finding a way to let her know that was the case, slyly, not reluctantly. Always hinting to the secret life she knew nothing about.

It was sometime during the night, she guessed, wrestling with the sheets and pillow, half dreaming she was walking across the plains, that it had come to her: Adam Lone Eagle was who he was. The problem with their relationship was hers.

The sound of the ringing phone cut like a knife through her thoughts. She picked up the receiver. Lucy Murphy was here.

A blur, like that of a child in a funhouse mirror, the small, blond-haired girl was seated on the other side of the beveled-glass doors. Vicky opened the doors and smiled at the girl curled like a snail across from Annie's desk. She looked up, an eager, frightened expression in her pale blue eyes. "Come in," Vicky said.

She waited until Lucy Murphy had re-settled herself into one of the visitor's chairs, then she said, "How can I help you?"

"I couldn't sleep all night." The girl had a halting, singsong voice. "I decided you were the one I should talk to. You'd know what to do."

The girl took in a shuddering breath. She kept her hands, slim and pink, clasped together on the thighs of her blue jeans. A silvery ring with a big white stone that looked as if it had come out of a vending machine sparkled in the light from the desk lamp. "I mean, you are Arnie's lawyer."

"Is this about Arnie?"

"You could say so. I'm worried about him.

I mean, I love the guy. I know he's Arapaho and I'm Polish, but so what? We love each other. So I don't want him in any more trouble, but I don't want to get myself into trouble. It's just that, well, there's something he didn't tell anybody. I got to thinking, if the cops find out, and they know that I knew and didn't say anything, it could go bad for both of us."

"If you are asking me to represent you, I must tell you . . ."

"No." The word came as a shout. "I want to do what's best for Arnie, put everything out on the table so there won't be any surprises."

"You had better tell me what you're talking about."

Another shuddering breath. Lucy Murphy stared into the center of the desk, as if what she wanted to say was laid out between a folder and the legal notepad Vicky had started making notes on. "That night at the bar in Riverton, me and Arnie was having a few beers, minding our own business, not paying any attention to the cowboys over at the booths. Music was playing real loud, lights were swirling over the dance floor that isn't any dance floor like I've ever seen, nothing but a little space between the booths and tables. A cowboy and some girl was dancing, and lights were swirling, and I thought, Jesus, this place thinks it's a club in LA when it's nothing but a two-bit cowboy bar. I mean, I been to real clubs."

"What happened?"

"Arnie grabs me by the hand and practically drags me out to the so-called dance floor even though I kept saying I didn't feel like dancing, thank you very much, 'cause the beer was sloshing around inside me and what I really needed was to go to the ladies' room. You don't say no to Arnie. Maybe that's why I love him because, you know, he knows what he wants and he goes after it. It's very — how do you say? — powerful, takes your breath away. Sweeps you along and you're glad to go because, I mean, where else you gonna go? So we started dancing and this cowboy cuts in."

"Did you know him?"

Lucy gave a quick nod. "Rick Tomlin." She hesitated. "He wasn't just any cowboy."

And here it was. Vicky looked up from the name she had just jotted onto the pad. She waited for the girl to go on, but the words seemed to have stacked themselves inside her throat. She was coughing, clasping the hand with the big ring over her mouth, coughing and shuddering. Finally she said, "We used to be together, me and Rick. He was okay. I liked him, except he wasn't like Arnie, powerful and knowing where he was going and taking me along. Soon's I met Arnie . . ."

"Where did you meet?"

"At the same bar. Ironic, huh? I guess that's what set Arnie off. Rick cutting in just like Arnie had cut in before. I mean, when Arnie cut in, I seen my destiny. We started dancing and, let's just say, when I left I didn't go home with Rick."

"What did Arnie do when Rick cut in?"

The girl sucked in a long breath. For a moment, Vicky thought the girl would jump to her feet and run out of the office.

"Look, Lucy," she said. "You were there when the fight started. You had better tell me what really happened." Odd, she thought, that Lucy Murphy's name was nowhere on the prosecutor's witness list.

The pale blue eyes darted about the office and finally settled on a space behind Vicky's shoulder. She still didn't say anything, was just breathing hard, as if she had run up a mountain trail. Finally, in a little voice, a child's voice: "Arnie told Rick to back off, 'cause he didn't want to fight. The cops get called and who goes to jail? The Indian. I seen it happen before. Trouble was, Rick didn't back off. 'Looks to me like you got

140

the wrong gal,' Rick says. 'You got a gal that belongs to me.' "

"Well, I started shouting how I don't belong to nobody except, well, Arnie, and that was my choice. Next thing I know, Rick punches Arnie in the jaw. I mean, he was roaring like a bull. Arnie picked up a chair and hit him over the head. Then he grabbed me and pushed me out the door. He throws the keys at me, and says, 'Get out of here. Don't come back.' I drove to my place. A trailer I been renting south of Riverton. Hour later, one of Arnie's buddies shows up. 'Stay here,' he tells me. 'Don't talk to anybody.' I asked him what happened, but he said it wasn't my business. Just stay out of it. I heard later that the fight moved out to the parking lot and Rick was claiming that Arnie assaulted him. The tribal cops went to Arnie's place, handcuffed him, and dragged him off to jail, wouldn't even let him put on his shoes."

Vicky leaned over the desk. She knew what had happened, a bar fight between two drunken cowboys, white and Indian, the details spelled out in Rick Tomlin's complaint. What was new was that the fight had been over Lucy Murphy, and the girl could have corroborated Arnie's claim of self-defense. Rick had attacked Arnie. "Why didn't you tell the police the truth?"

The girl had gone back to studying the pale hands clasped in her lap. "You don't know Rick," she said. "We was together a really long time, six months at least. We was gonna get married soon as he collected his pay at the ranch. It was gonna be our stake. We were gonna head up to Montana, get out of Indian country. He was gonna work on another ranch close to some town so I could get me a waitress job like I got here at the Diamond Bar and Grill."

"There are tribes in Montana."

"Well, we was going where they weren't."

"You were scared of Rick?"

"Like I say, you don't know him. He's got a big temper. I been staying out of his way ever since the night I took up with Arnie. It was okay long as Arnie was around, but with Arnie in jail I'd be on my own. I had to talk to the cops when they came looking for me over at the grill. I didn't have a choice. I told them I didn't see anything. I told them I ran out the minute I saw Rick coming toward me and Arnie. I never told them about the fight or what it was about. I never told them Rick started it. What if Rick came looking for me? Besides, there was other witnesses. Arnie's Arapaho buddies and all those cowboys with Rick. Let them sort it

out. Trouble is, the cops believed the cowboys."

Vicky sat back, trying to fill in the blank
spaces, the things the girl hadn't said. Rick
Tomlin, cowboy with no love for Indians,
had succeeded in getting Arnie Walksfast
charged with assault in a bar fight. Arnie
had been looking at time in Rawlins. And
the witness whose statement might have
kept Arnie from being charged had kept
quiet. What didn't make sense was the idea
of Rick Tomlin backing off and disappearing when he had every chance of putting
Arnie into prison.

The girl was shaking her head. A piece of
blond hair fell across her eyes and she
yanked it backward, as if she could pull it
out. "All I know is Rick hated Arnie 'cause
I took up with him. He could never let
things go. He held on and held on until he
could get even. I think he came to the bar
looking for Arnie and me. You ask me, Rick
and those other cowboys were planning to
beat up Arnie, put him in the hospital."

"Do you know the other cowboys?" Witnesses on the prosecutor's list, she was
thinking.

"Just cowboys that work on the ranches
around here. None of them looked familiar,
but I wasn't looking real hard. I seen Rick

walking over — the way he walks, real cocky like he's the king of the cowboys, and I started shaking, and Arnie says, 'Don't pay him no mind. Just stay calm.' Then hell broke out and I ran out of there. Next thing I know Arnie's the one in jail charged with assault. That would've made Rick real happy. Something else I know. Rick never would have taken off right before he was gonna get even with Arnie."

13

Arnie Walksfast slumped at the end of a long metal table in the recreation room. Eyes straight ahead as Vicky walked over. The clack of her heels on the vinyl floor reverberated around the blue walls painted with figures of cartoon characters dancing about. Arnie had a defeated look about him, sunken into himself, clasping and unclasping his hands on the table. Vicky slid onto the chair at an angle from him.

"We need to talk."

Slowly, as if it required great effort, Arnie turned his head. His eyes looked glazed, unfocused. Vicky wondered how clearly he saw her. "How you feeling, Arnie?" she said.

"How's rehab?" His voice was a high falsetto, then he switched back. "Nothing matters except what you want. Get this whole thing over, put old Arnie into rehab. Well, what about me? Puking out my insides all night. Can't even keep water down.

Can't sleep. So they shot me with junk. Drugs to get me off drugs." Switching again into the falsetto, he said, "This'll help your nausea. Be a good boy. Take your medicine." He gave a shrug that was like a tremor running across his shoulders. "My head's big as a boulder, might even drop off. Blood pressure shoots up and down, all over the place. I got the shakes. I wish I was dead."

"I'm sorry, Arnie." Vicky laid out a yellow legal pad and a ballpoint.

"That's supposed to make it easier?"

"You've been through rehab before. You know it will get easier." She had never been through rehab, she was thinking. What did she know? Only what she had heard from other clients across the same table in this recreation room, toys and tricycles stacked in the far corner next to a couple of kid-size tables and chairs with yellow daisies painted on the blue surfaces. She had seen enough alcoholism; Ben Holden had drunk enough for both of them. She had never wanted the seesaw life: binges, rehab, binges, rehab. The life that Arnie Walksfast had chosen — or maybe, stumbled into.

Vicky forced herself not to look away from the man. The crooked nose broken too many times, the deep, black caverns under his eyes, the leathery, smoke-hardened face.

"Your girlfriend came to see me. She's worried about you."

"Lucy should mind her own business."

"You didn't level with me, Arnie. You forgot to mention the brawl was over Lucy. She had been Rick's girlfriend, until she dumped him and took up with you. You said Rick threw the first punch. Your buddies backed you up, but it was your word against Rick's and all of his cowboy buddies. Lucy could have helped you."

"What difference does it make?"

"What difference? Rick Tomlin had motive to attack you. You were defending yourself and your girlfriend. He threw the first punch, but when the fight moved outside, he ended up unconscious. How was I supposed to defend you, if you didn't bother to tell me the whole story? What else haven't you told me?"

"What do you mean?"

"The rest of it, Arnie. What happened to Rick Tomlin?"

"He took off."

"Convenient for you. If Rick wasn't around, he couldn't testify against you. You were looking at a felony conviction and time in prison. Seems like a powerful motive to make sure the main witness doesn't testify. Did you have anything to do with his disappearance?"

Arnie planted himself against the back of the chair, lifted his chin, and looked at her down his long, crooked nose.

"What are you, the prosecutor? You're supposed to be my lawyer."

"I need the truth."

"Rick Tomlin is a no-good sonofabitch, beat up Lucy, acted like he owned her."

Vicky shifted forward to the edge of the chair. She was gripping the ballpoint so hard, white knuckles popped on her fist. "What did you do?"

"How do I know what happened to him? The bastard left, that's all I know. Maybe he got fed up with the Broken Buffalo Ranch. Don't hire Raps or Shoshones, did you know that?" He shrugged. "Just as well. No Indian's gonna take what they hand out."

"What are you talking about?"

"Work the hands like dogs. Sunup to sundown. Bunk in a drafty old shack with a couple of thin blankets. Lucky to get a few squares. Aren't there laws against keeping slaves?"

"Nobody has to work for the ranch. Maybe they pay well."

"When they pay. All I know is what I hear them white cowboys complaining about in

148

the bar. Soon's they knock off for the day, they head into town. Can't blame them. Nobody at that ranch gets back pay 'til the owners take some of the bulls and calves to market. Keeps the cowboys hanging on, waiting. They get paid, they take off."

"Lucy said Rick wouldn't have left before the trial. He wanted to see you in prison. The prosecutor could take another look at Rick Tomlin's disappearance and decide that you had something to do with it."

"Bull."

"If you did, I need to know."

"So you can get me more time in rehab? Sent off to Rawlins for ten years? The way I see it, what you don't know won't hurt me."

Vicky didn't take her eyes away. Arnie Walksfast was lying. She had seen enough clients stammer and blink, run tongues over lips, avert their eyes, clasp and unclasp their hands, lie around the truth. She could feel the hard knot of tension in her stomach. "What did you do?"

Arnie shrugged and went back to staring at some point across the room.

Vicky gave him a few minutes, then picked up the legal pad and slipped it into her briefcase. She dropped the ballpoint next to the pad and got to her feet. "You should find another lawyer. I'll notify the court I no longer represent you. I'm sorry."

He looked up at her. "You're sorry?"

"For your mother. It will be hard on her if you end up in prison." Vicky swung about and started for the door.

"Hold on." A note of panic flitted through the man's voice. Behind her came the scrape of a chair.

Vicky turned back. Arnie was leaning across the table, fists clenched, tendons popping in his neck, like a rodeo rider about to drop onto a bucking bronco in the chute. "Okay. Okay." He lifted one fist, as if he were giving the signal for the gate to open. "Let's do this."

Vicky took her time walking back over. Waiting until Arnie Walksfast had sat down, feeling slightly light-headed with the surge of adrenaline. The slightest movement on his part and she would flee the room. She had seen the clenched fists; the black, brooding eyes; the anger flooding the features of Ben Holden. She had learned to escape. She had made a permanent escape.

She took her chair, repositioned the legal pad, and gripped the ballpoint. "What happened?"

"Nothing actually happened. I mean, we didn't beat him up or anything like that."

"We?"

"Some buddies. They don't like white cowboys coming here and taking our jobs."

"You said the Broken Buffalo doesn't hire Indians."

"Yeah. If the white cowboys weren't around, they'd have to, wouldn't they? Lots of Indians don't like those dudes. So we put a little pressure on Rick Tomlin."

"What kind of pressure?"

"He came into Riverton, we told him he wasn't welcome. Guys waited in the parking lot for his old truck to drive up. Told him to turn around and drive outta there if he knew what was good for him. Some guys got into it. Tried to run Tomlin off the road one night. Another time . . ."

"Keep going."

"Maybe somebody took a couple shots at his truck."

"You did that?" My God, was she was looking at the shooter who had been terrorizing the rez?

"I don't know who did it. I don't mind telling you I thought it was a good idea. Get off a few shots to make those white cowboys think twice about staying around. Took some random shots at other pickups so the cops wouldn't put it together that Raps were trying to run off the white cowboys at the Broken Buffalo."

"I have to know if you were part of this."

"I'm telling you, I don't know who did the shooting. Nobody got hurt, but I figure Rick Tomlin got the message that he was — how do you say? — persona non grata. I figure he collected his pay and got outta here, like we wanted."

"What was your role, Arnie?" When he didn't say anything, she said, "I don't want to hear it from the prosecutor."

"How's he gonna know anything?"

"The first one of your so-called buddies that gets arrested for jaywalking or throwing a punch is going to make a deal and serve you up. What was your role?"

"Maybe I told my buddies that Rick Tomlin was a no-good sonofabitch, taking jobs, stirring up trouble. Maybe I said we should drive the guy off the rez."

"So you instigated a terror campaign against the witness in your criminal case."

"He took off, didn't he? There's no more felony charges. I took the plea bargain, and here I am in lousy rehab."

Vicky waited a moment, trying to marshal her thoughts. The case was like a bucking bronco running wild. "If the prosecutor gets wind of your part in the shootings, you will be charged with a serious offense of intimidating a witness. You'll be looking at a long time in prison."

"Well, you're not going to let that happen. You're my lawyer. You're here to see I got my rights."

"Was Lucy involved?" The girl might decide to tell the police what she knew to save herself.

"She was with me once when I was following Rick real close. Gave his bumper a nudge, thinking he'd go off the road."

Vicky had to look away. No wonder Lucy Murphy thinks Arnie had something to do with Rick's disappearance. She thinks the worst, expects the worst, and she is frightened — not only of Rick. Vicky could feel the weight of the silence that engulfed the room. Muffled voices from the hallway filtered through the closed door. "Is that all of it?" she said finally. "You swear you did not harm Rick Tomlin?"

"He got the message, like I said. He took off on his own."

Vicky slipped the legal pad and pen back into her briefcase. The pad was blank. She hadn't written down anything. Everything Arnie Walksfast had said was imprinted in her mind. She stood up. "Stay with the rehab program. Keep your nose clean. Stay out of trouble. I'll report to probation that you've begun treatment."

153

She walked back across the room and let herself into the corridor. Past the closed doors, the sound of a ringing telephone, the staccato notes of voices, and through the reception area and the glass doors that opened automatically into the bright outdoors. The thought drumming in her mind: Arnie Walksfast was lying.

Inside the Ford, the hot breeze blowing across the open windows, the engine humming, Vicky checked her messages. One from Adam; one from Annie. She clicked on Annie's. "Sheila Carey called. Husband's burial today, four p.m. Hope you can make it." Then she clicked on the message from Adam: "Cancel dinner plans. Something's come up. Flew to Denver this morning for meeting. Talk later."

Vicky slid the phone into her bag, backed into the parking lot, and drove into the traffic crawling down North Federal, aware of a feeling of lightness enveloping her, as if she were floating through Riverton.

14

Trout creek road was a meandering two-lane strip of asphalt that split the north part of the reservation from the south. There was more traffic than usual this afternoon. A thin line of cars and pick-ups and SUVs snaked ahead; other vehicles passed in the opposite direction. Vicky flipped the visor against the sun firing the western sky and followed the SUV ahead onto a dirt road. Rolling clouds of dust peppered her windshield. The air tasted hot and gritty.

She was aware of the tension in her back muscles. So many rumors on the moccasin telegraph. Annie had passed along at least a dozen: *A white buffalo calf born on the reservation. Probably on the Broken Buffalo. People coming to see for themselves. Indians from Montana. Pueblo Indians and Navajos, Hopis, Zunis from New Mexico.* The idea of a white buffalo calf being *here* sent chills running through her like electrical shocks.

Vicky could still see Sheila Carey huddled on the sofa, a skin of bravery painted over her features. In shock over her husband's murder. And now strangers would descend on her ranch — they were arriving already — demanding to see the sacred calf that may or may not be there. There hadn't been any official confirmation, but the moccasin telegraph had an uncanny, otherworldly way of being right.

The vehicles ahead had filtered into a rutted two-track. She could see the beds of the pickups bouncing and swaying. Then she was bouncing, gripping the steering wheel hard to keep the tires in the narrow dirt ruts. The traffic slowed, and she had to step on the brake to keep from rear-ending the SUV. A couple of pickups swerved across the borrow ditch and drove over the scraggly pasture grass that bordered the two-track. She stayed with the SUV until she was forced to stop at a gate dropped over the road. A small group of people were milling about, looking off toward the log house and the ranch buildings beyond the gate.

"Get out of here." A cowboy in a black hat stationed like a guard in front of the gate shouted at a lanky, frozen-faced cowboy with a tan, wide-brimmed hat pushed back on his head.

The cowboy stood his ground. "I'm not leaving 'til I see the boss."

The man in the black hat threw a fist toward the dozen or so pickups parked on the sagebrush prairie next to the two-track. "Get your truck and get out of here."

Somewhere out of the dust and the stalled pickups and SUVs, another cowboy materialized and started directing traffic onto the prairie. Vicky followed the SUV through the clumps of sagebrush and mounds of brown earth, past a van with Channel 13 emblazoned in gold paint on the sides. The SUV pulled in on the far side of a silver truck, and she parked on the other side and got out. The cowboy's voice reverberated in the dusty air: "Head on down the road, you know what's good for you."

The lanky cowboy came toward her, tight-lipped, walking fast, propelled by anger, dust climbing the legs of his blue jeans. He yanked open the driver's door on the silver truck. Vicky saw a man and woman get out of the SUV and hurry past him toward the small crowd waiting by the gate.

The cowboy rounded on her. "You know the owners here?"

Vicky glanced about. Nothing in this makeshift parking lot but a row of parked vehicles and a few people on the far side of the pickups waiting to turn in. She was alone with an angry, fist-clenched man. "I've met them," she said. She had met Sheila Carey and a dead man, she was thinking. "I'm here for the funeral."

"Funeral?" The cowboy pushed his cowboy hat forward and regarded her out of pencil-slim eyes.

"Dennis Carey, one of the owners."

"So that's what brought all the people here? A funeral?" The cowboy seemed to relax a little, and Vicky wondered if she should tell him the rest of it — the rumor that a white buffalo calf had been born. She decided against it.

"Reg Hartly." The cowboy extended a calloused hand. A brown car pulled in beside them. Two Indians got out and headed toward the gate. "Just drove up from Colorado. You from around these parts?"

"Vicky Holden." She shook the man's hand, feeling her own tension begin to dissolve. "Attorney in Lander. Are you looking for a ranch job?"

This seemed to stop him a moment. "I'm looking for a buddy." The narrowed eyes fastened on the brown car, as if the buddy might jump out of the backseat. "You ever heard of Josh Barker? Cowboy from the Western Slope? Came up here to work with buffalo and disappeared."

"Disappeared?" Rick Tomlin, another cowboy, had disappeared.

"Folks haven't heard from him in a couple months. Mom's real sick. She's dying, but she's trying to hold on until she sees Josh again."

"Did your buddy work here?" Vicky nodded toward the cowboys at the gate, another pickup turning into the sagebrush lot.

"Not according to them jackasses." He twisted his head in the direction of the cowboys. "Never heard of him. Nobody by that name on the Broken Buffalo. They're lying. Josh sent postcards saying he'd hired on here. Josh was no liar."

"I think those cowboys are new hires." What was it Sheila Carey had said? With her husband dead, it would just be her and Carlos and another hand. If the white buffalo calf was here, she needed more help. "When did your friend work here?"

"Hired on in the spring. Last postcard came around July Fourth. Like I say, his mom wants to die in peace. She wants Josh beside her, and I know my buddy. That's where he'd want to be, if he knew."

"I suggest you come back tomorrow, after the funeral, and speak to the owner, Sheila Carey." Vicky wondered how many vehicles

159

would crowd the road and the parking lot tomorrow if the news was on TV this evening.

"The goons won't let me in."

"I can let her know you're coming."

"You'd do that?" A look of astonishment crossed the man's face. Obviously he hadn't met a friendly welcome in these parts. "You know a campground close by? I brought my gear." He thumped the bed of the silver truck.

"Try Sinks Canyon. And good luck." Vicky started walking toward the gate, stepping out of the way of another car pulling into the lot. Then she turned back. The cowboy was about to lower himself into the truck, one boot on the dirt, the other inside the cab. "There's a bar in Riverton where cowboys hang out," she called. "Somebody there might know about your friend. The O.K. Bar."

"Thanks again." The cowboy saluted off the brim of his hat.

Vicky reached the gate and told the man in the black hat she had been invited to the funeral. "You're going to have to walk up to the house," he said. "Mrs. Carey gave orders no more cars up there." He lifted the gate high enough that, by bending forward, she was able to get to the other side. She picked her way along the edge of the two-track, where the ground was almost level. The front porch was empty; there was an empty feeling about the whole house. She recognized the old Toyota pickup parked near the porch. She started up the steps, then decided to walk around to the back. The burial would be somewhere on the ranch.

As she walked next to the house, she spotted the small crowd gathered in a grassy space fringed with cottonwoods out by the barn. Around the barn were several ranch buildings, paint-peeled and dilapidated looking, and an assortment of ranch vehicles: trucks, flatbed, tractor, forklift. A barbed-wire fence ran along the open expanse of pasture. In the far distance, she could make out the swaying brown humps of the buffalo herd.

Sheila Carey broke from the crowd and started toward her. "Glad you could make it. Where's your friend?"

"I'm afraid Adam was called out of town."

"Too bad. It's a small group." A flash of what might have been physical pain crossed the woman's face. Vicky looked over and counted seven people: Chief Banner and another officer in crisp uniforms, standing ramrod straight with caps laid against their waists; two cowboys and two women she didn't know; and the cowboy who called himself Carlos, stationed between a narrow hole dug into the earth and a small mound of dirt. Walking over from a pathway that paralleled the barbed-wire fence was John O'Malley and, beside him, the elder Clifford Many Horses. She knew in an instant what they had seen in the pasture, and the chill that ran through her was so strong, it stopped her in her footsteps. It was true. The white calf was here, just as all the people at the gate believed. She caught John O'Malley's eye and smiled.

"Now that we're all here," Sheila said, "we can get started." She ushered John O'Malley and the elder to the far side of the gravesite next to Carlos, who was holding a small wooden box. Then she fit herself into the space on the other side of the cowboy and looked out across the distance. The whoosh of the breeze filled the quiet. Clumps of grass in the pasture lay sideways, swept over the earth.

Finally, Sheila looked up. "Dennis would be honored that an Arapaho elder agreed to bless his grave and send his spirit to the ancestors. It's also an honor to have the Catholic priest from the mission, even though Dennis was never — what you would say? — religious. Leave all that stuff for later, he used to say." She gave a little laugh. "Well, later is here. Used to be Catholic, though. Baptized, confirmed. Like he said, awful-tasting medicine that didn't work on him, even though his ma dragged him to church every Sunday until he got so big she couldn't drag him anymore. Anyway, it seemed proper to send him off the way he started. Carlos . . ." She glanced sideways at the black-haired cowboy.

It was all that was necessary. Carlos cradled the box a moment, then, dropping onto one knee, set the box into the small grave. He stood up, hands clasped in a kind of prayer.

Clifford Many Horses took a moment, his eyes on the open grave, before he began fumbling with the ties on the leather satchel. Vicky closed her eyes and waited. So many funerals, so many blessings for the dead she had watched the elders bestow, so many soft Arapaho prayers she had listened to. The breeze seemed to lie down, and quiet settled over the little crowd. She opened her eyes just as the elder held a lighted match to a small bunch of sage tied with a leather thong. He waved the sage back and forth, fanning the smoke into the grave and out toward the little group. *Jevaneatha nethaunainau, Jevaneatha Dawatha henechau-*

chauane nanadehe vedaw nau ichjeva. Vicky felt the words washing over her. A prayer meant to give courage and hope to those left behind: God is with us. God's spirit fills everywhere on earth and above us.

Hethete hevedathuwin nehathe Ichjeva-neatha haeain ichjeva. The good soul will go to God to our home on high.

The sage-filled smoke drifted past, and she took in a deep breath: The sacred smoke, a sign that even death cannot break the bonds of loved ones. She could feel the sense of peace that always came over her at a burial when the elders prayed for the dead and the living.

The elder waved the smoking sage again, then placed it inside a small tobacco can and closed the lid. For a moment smoke escaped about the edges, then disappeared. Bowing his head, he stepped back.

John O'Malley waited several minutes — respectful of the Arapaho Way, she thought — before he moved to the edge of the grave. "Dear Lord Jesus . . ." His voice was low and comforting. She smiled at the thought of all the times she had been comforted by his voice. "Bless the soul of your servant Dennis Carey. Look not on his sins, but accept him into your peace and love. Remember his wife, Sheila, whom he loved and has now left behind, and help her to find comfort in your presence with us. Amen."

"Amen." Vicky heard her own voice, mingled with the voices around her. For a long moment, the word seemed to float above the opened grave. She kept her eyes on John O'Malley, half-expecting him to look over, acknowledge her, but his thoughts were elsewhere, she realized, in the prayers he had just offered, in the concern for Sheila Carey, a widow. He was a priest.

Sheila Carey removed something from the pocket of her blue jeans — a limp purple flower — and dropped it into the grave. She motioned with her eyes to Carlos, who went over to the side of the barn and returned with a shovel. He began shoveling the small mound of dirt on top of the box. When the gravesite was full, he tamped the dirt into a bare, smooth rectangle, then scooped up dried sage and pebbles and scattered them over the grave until it was lost with the earth. Vicky wondered how Sheila Carey would ever find her husband's grave.

The woman was looking out into space. "Let us all pray that my husband's killer will be brought to justice and will go to his own grave." She exhaled a long breath, a kind of acceptance that justice might never be served, then stepped back, as if her thoughts had shifted away from the narrow grave. "You have all heard, I am sure, that our ranch has been uniquely blessed, or so I have been told. We have a very special calf. A few days before Dennis was shot to death, we were out feeding the herd. I was driving the tractor, and Dennis was on the flatbed throwing out bales of hay. He saw her first and shouted at me. 'Look over there.' I stopped the tractor so fast, I nearly threw Dennis to the ground. The calf couldn't have been more than a few hours old, and white as snow. The mother was cleaning her up and, to tell you the truth, even she seemed a bit surprised at the look of her calf. This is not an ordinary calf. White with black eyes and black nose, so we know she's not an albino. Folks from the National Bison Association are sending people to take blood from the dam and the bull to make sure the calf is one hundred percent buffalo and not descended from a rogue Charolais. We only have one bull, so there's no doubt the calf is a genuine genetic mutation, or whatever the scientists call it. We call her Spirit."

She turned halfway around and stared out at the pasture where the buffalo lumbered and swayed through the cottonwoods. There was no sign of the white calf. A few people trailed along the barbed-wire fence after the cowboy in the black hat, looking out into the pasture as they walked.

Sheila turned back. "As you can tell from the cars and pickups that have arrived, the news has gotten out. I was hoping to get Dennis laid to rest before I made the announcement, but people have been showing up all day, demanding to see Spirit. I have hired a few new hands, and I'm going to need more. We've cleared a path along the fence to keep people from wandering all over the ranch looking for Spirit. The path will take them to the place where they can see her in the far pasture. No one will walk out there without an escort. We can only take a few people at a time. Father John and Mr. Many Horses have already gone out. If you like, the rest of you can go with Carlos now. You will have to excuse me. I promised the TV reporter an interview."

Sheila Carey turned around and started past the barn toward the front gate, resolve in her stride. For a moment, nobody moved, then Carlos waved his arm like a baton, and said, "Follow me."

Vicky realized John O'Malley had moved to her side. "I heard you found the body. How are you doing?"

She forced a little shrug, afraid that she might burst into tears. It had been hard to come across the body of a man shot to death in the night, hard to be there with Adam protesting, not understanding. John O'Malley understood. "I'll be fine," she heard herself say.

Clifford Many Horses had wandered over and stopped in front of her. "Our people have been blessed," he said. "You must go to the pasture, Daughter."

She nodded and tried for a smile that would reassure the elder that she grasped the importance of the calf. She let her eyes glance off John O'Malley's, then started after Carlos and the others.

15

Vicky followed the little group along the barbed-wire fence, past the gate with a big chain linking the posts together. Carlos in the lead, looking straight ahead, a spring in his step as if he were leading visitors to see a rare creature at the zoo. Lined up behind him, the ranchers and their wives, Chief Banner and the other BIA officer. Not from these parts, Vicky thought. He looked Navajo. She gave herself a little space behind them. It had been good to see John O'Malley, as if, because he was here, everything was as it should be. She hadn't seen him all summer, but the moccasin telegraph kept her informed: the scholarship he had arranged for Jimmy Summer at Creighton; the Saturday morning coffees with the elders at the senior center; the new day care center he was starting at the mission. The people would miss him when he left. She pushed the thought away. She didn't want to think of John O'Malley leaving.

The late-afternoon sun blazed in a clear sky; the hot, dry breeze rippled the dusty path. Off to the north, the pasture ran into the sky, the earth flat and brown with tufts of grass and sagebrush here and there and cottonwoods clustered near an underground spring or tiny creek. A few buffalo meandered about the cottonwoods, at home on the dry, bare earth, just as they had been at home for centuries. Nobody knew how long. *Buffalo came out of the earth.* She could hear her grandfather's voice as if he were walking beside her, his footsteps in rhythm with hers. She could imagine the excitement, the joy he would have felt to see a white buffalo calf. *We are close relations to the buffalo. They gave themselves that the people might live. The people must always show respect and gratitude. If the buffalo go back into the earth, the people will die.*

It had almost happened. Buffalo had been slaughtered across the plains. She remembered other stories Grandfather told, stories he had heard from his own grandfather: mounds of buffalo bones higher than log cabins, bleaching in the sun. They had been close to extinction, a few herds hanging on, mangy and starving, hides drooping over skeletons weak from running and running from the guns. Her people and the other Indian nations had also been close to extinction. She blinked at Grandfather's words in her head: *Eight hundred Arapahos had straggled onto the rez. We were a pitiful bunch.*

Vicky stayed with the others around a curve. It was then she saw a small herd of buffalo, grazing placidly, content, the wind shearing the fur on their massive heads. A cow looked up, snorted, and went back to grazing. Out on the pasture, moving among another stand of cottonwoods, were at least two dozen head. And beyond them, Vicky could see more buffalo.

Carlos had stopped. He gestured with his fist at the herd in the cottonwoods. Vicky stopped behind the others and searched the herd for a small, white calf. "Watch and wait," he said. "Takes a few minutes before the mother shows herself. She knows when the calf has visitors. Always shows off her calf when Sheila and me come out. There!" His fist jumped up and down.

Vicky saw the huge, brown buffalo cow moving out of the trees. Swaying at her side was a white calf. She looked smooth and unruffled, as velvety as snow. Vicky felt her legs go weak. She set her hand against the post to steady herself, afraid she might fall down. *The calf will be a sign the Creator is with us.* Grandfather's voice still running through her head. She could sense the power in the small animal. Something holy and ineffable. She wiped at the moisture on her cheeks and wondered what John O'Malley had thought — a priest from another way, so different from her own. She wondered if he had sensed the power, understood the meaning. Surely the Creator gave different signs to different peoples.

She should have brought an offering. She glanced beyond the little group to where a small, tan-colored bag was attached to the fence. Clifford Many Horses would have brought the bag, she knew. Inside was tobacco, a worthy and fitting offering. She tried to think what she had in her bag that she could leave as a sign of respect. A sign she had been here. She rummaged in the bag until she found the soft case that held her sunglasses. She took out the glasses. The case was red, with blue-and-yellow designs and ties of black ribbon, the Arapaho colors for the four directions, east, south, west, and north. She reached up and plucked a strand of hair. Then another and another, winding them together until she had a thin, black string, which she rolled into a ball and slipped inside the case. She tied the black ribbon onto the fence. The case shivered in the breeze.

"You seen the crowd at the front gate. We have more groups to bring out." Carlos started walking back, a familiar confidence in the square of his shoulders, as if he assumed the others would fall in behind.

Banner turned around. His eyes were like black pools. The Navajo officer behind him rubbed a fist across his own eyes. They felt the same, Vicky thought. Everyone except for Carlos, walking away. The white ranchers and the women stood still another moment, gazing at the small white calf. Then shrugging at each other, they started after Carlos, as if the calf made some difference but they weren't sure what it might be.

"It's wonderful." Vicky fell in next to Banner.

"Part of me wishes it was born on another reservation. We're going to be double-shifting all the officers until we see how many people come. Might have to call for help from outside." Vicky felt the chief glance sideways at her. "I hear your client got lucky."

"Arnie's in rehab."

"Drunk or sober, he's a troublemaker. There's a rumor he's behind the random shootings. Three so far." God, Vicky was thinking. Did nothing escape the moccasin telegraph? "Things have been quiet since Arnie boy's been waiting for trial. Now he's in rehab, I suspect the shootings will stop."

Vicky didn't say anything. She was aware of the scuff of the ranchers' boots ahead. She could guess what had happened. One of Arnie's friends arrested, probably on a DUI or disturbance or assault, begging to make a trade. Arnie's involvement in the random shootings in exchange for his own skin. "I'm not aware of any additional charges filed against my client."

"Not yet," Banner said. "Let's say I'm giving you a heads-up."

"What about Rick Tomlin. Any word on him?"

"He's gone, Vicky. Nowhere in these parts or we would have heard. Somebody would have given him up."

"Right." Gone, she was thinking.

"Cowboys like him are drifters. Start out in New Mexico or Texas and drift north until they hit the border, then start drifting back. Tomlin's in Montana or Idaho."

"Sheila Carey thinks he could have killed her husband."

"FBI is working the case. They haven't found any trace of Tomlin, which means he's out herding cattle in the middle of nowhere. Nobody knows where he is and nobody can get to him." Banner stopped, and the Navajo officer behind him also stopped as if they were chained together, two officers protecting each other. "You ask me, Mrs. Carey and her husband would've been a whole lot better off hiring from the rez. The warriors have ties. Family, responsibilities, ceremonies, all the things that keep them close to home. Wouldn't have these drifters like the cowboys out front, work for a while 'til they get bored and set off for someplace different."

"We have Arapahos working for us." The two ranchers stopped and turned back, their wives stopping behind them, glancing at one another. A fringe of black hair showed below the cowboy hat of the tall, gangly-looking rancher. The other man was a couple of inches shorter, squat, with long, powerful-looking arms, a big cowboy hat, and a shiny, smooth spot at the base of his skull that made her think he was probably bald. "Nobody understands horses better than Raps," said the squat rancher. "They can ride anything. Take the herd out to pasture, bring them back. I got to agree with you, Chief." He tipped his head toward Banner. "They got ties around here, so you know they're not going to take off just when you need the herd rounded up."

"Free country," the other rancher said. "I guess Dennis could hire any hands he wanted. Maybe he felt more comfortable with white guys. No offense." He threw a glance between Banner and the other officer. "I heard he had enough trouble getting along with his help. Maybe he thought Indians would be even more trouble."

"Where did you hear that?" Banner said.

"Just some things he said at meetings. Ranchers hereabouts get together to chew the fat, talk over common problems, like we did the night he got shot. Dennis was always hiring or firing. Claimed he couldn't get anybody he could depend upon, but he kept trying." He gave a ragged laugh that sounded as if he were clearing his throat.

"You ask me," the short rancher said, "Dennis knew he was going to get killed."

"What makes you think so?" Banner said.

"Last couple meetings, he was a nervous wreck. Couldn't sit still, couldn't stop talking. Real jumpy. Truck backfired outdoors. He jumped a foot."

"Drinking a lot," the other rancher put in. "Four or five shots every meeting. Staggered outside and got in his truck. Jesus. I told him more than once he shouldn't be driving. Give me the keys, I said. Me and Chet'll take you home. But nothing doing. Everything in control, he said. You ask me, he was out of control. Something was on him, tracking him like a big mountain lion, and he knew it. He was just waiting until it took him out."

"You tell the fed this?"

"Lot of good it done." The gangly man leaned sideways and spit a string of saliva onto the dirt. "Just a hunch. We don't have proof. Wasn't like Dennis took us into his confidence." He gave another snort-laugh, and the other rancher laughed with him. "Anyway, we gave our opinion, for what it's worth." He shrugged. "Well, time we was getting back to our spreads. See you around, Officers." The ranchers lifted two fingers and saluted toward Vicky. "Ma'am," one of them said. Then they were off, the men and their wives heading toward the crowd clustered at the gate, past Carlos coming down the path with six or seven visitors in tow.

"You know anything about Dennis being nervous?" Vicky realized Banner was staring at her.

She shook her head and looked in the direction of the patch of ground where the ashes of Dennis Carey had been buried. "I never met the man."

Carlos and the little group passed by, making a half circle around them. A mixture of Indians and whites, somber and reflective, as if they were on their way to church. Banner and the Navajo started toward the gate, and Vicky stayed with them until they had reached the front of the house. Sheila Carey stood on the porch, talking to two men. One held a camera on his shoulder.

"See you later," Vicky said, veering to the right. She made her way across a patch of shade to the porch steps and waited. After a few minutes, the two men stomped down the steps, faces cracked in grins. The cowboy with the black hat walked over. "This way out to the north pasture to see the calf," he said.

Sheila came down the steps, her eyes trailing after the three men. "Well, that's it." She might have been speaking into space. "It'll be all over the news tonight. Spread across the nation, I expect." Her voice rose and fell on notes of anticipation.

"It meant a lot to see the white calf," Vicky said. "Thank you." She waited a beat, then she said, "There's something I wanted to tell you." The woman turned slowly toward Vicky, as if she were turning toward a minor inconvenience. "I spoke with a cowboy from Colorado, Reg Hartly."

"Colorado? What does he want? A job? I'll need more help with the crowds coming."

"He's looking for a friend. Josh Barker. One of the cowboys told him nobody by that name ever worked here, but he said Josh had sent postcards home saying he had been hired on the Broken Buffalo."

Something happened in the woman's face, as if the muscles and sinews were starting to collapse. "One of the cowboys that hated Dennis. Hated him! Took off one day after a big argument. Just got in his truck and drove out of here. Just like Rick Tomlin. Left us high and dry with dams getting ready to calve. I'm sick of questions about those sonofabitches!" She was shouting, and Vicky took a couple of steps back. "Do you understand? Sick and tired of questions."

"I didn't mean to upset you."

"Upset me?" Shock registered in her features, as if she realized she was shouting. She lowered her voice, but angry red marks were moving up her throat and into her cheeks. "Why shouldn't I be upset? Cops knocking on my door looking for Tomlin. Expect me to know where he is. Now this cowboy looking for some other cowboy. The new hires don't know who worked here before, and I plan to keep it that way. Anybody comes around asking questions,

179

they'll get rid of them. God, let the cops find them. Rick. Josh. Whoever. One of them killed my husband." She took off her cowboy hat, ran her hand through her reddish hair, and set the cowboy hat back on. "You tell your cowboy friend, he shows up, I'll have him tossed out on his head."

Sheila swung around, marched up the steps, and let herself into the house. The screen door banged behind her in the wind.

Vicky started for the gate, aware that the people there had been watching, like an audience at a play, surprise and shadows of worry on their faces. She was about to duck under the gate when she saw the wooden post just inside the gate. It had a new, bleached look about it. She hadn't noticed it before. Affixed to the top was a metal container with the word DONATIONS printed in bright red letters.

16

Father John could hear the cheering and shouting from the ballpark. He managed to fit the Toyota pickup between two SUVs at the curb alongside Riverton's city park. A big crowd had gathered for the game between the Riverton Rangers and the St. Francis Eagles, the team he had started ten years ago, his first summer at the mission when he had been looking for something familiar to do, a priest from Boston finding his way on an Indian reservation. Baseball bridged a lot of divides.

He ran across the grass toward the diamond. He was late; the game had probably ended. He hoped the crowd was cheering for the Eagles. Last time they had played against the mighty Rangers, the winningest team in the league, the Eagles had barely managed to hold on to a 4–3 lead. Everybody had thought the win was a fluke. Even some of his own players, he suspected. Back at the mission, they'd had a meeting. A pep talk. Don't underestimate yourselves, he'd told the kids seated cross-legged on the lawn in front of the administration building, brown faces turned up at him, eyes shining like black pools. Don't think you didn't deserve to win, because you did. You worked hard. You're winners. He remembered repeating the phrase numerous times until the black eyes started to smile and blink in agreement.

Now he jogged around the edge of the diamond to the dugout on the third-base side. The kids were jumping up and down, high-fiving one another, hollering and yelling with joy. A couple of kids were rolling on the grass. He could feel the excitement. "What's the score?" he yelled.

"We won, Father," one of the kids shouted. Then the whole team rushed around him, chanting, "We won! We won!" Someone shouted, "Five–zip. Can you believe it?"

"Of course I can believe it." He threw his head back and laughed. Across home plate, in the Ranger's dugout, he could see the slumped shoulders, the lowered heads gathered around Steve Mantle, the coach. He liked Mantle. He was fair to the kids. His son played for the Rangers. He could imagine what Mantle was telling his players. *Hey, everybody has an off day once in a while. You're still the best.* The same thing he would have told the Eagles had they lost.

Marcy Hawk caught his eye and walked over, blue baseball cap with Eagles in big white letters on her head. Marcy had been helping him coach this season, and she was good. Black-haired, round, brown face; in her thirties, short, stout with an arm that could hurl power balls. Her son, Liam, was one of the pitchers; the kid had gotten his talent from his mom, Father John thought. He'd asked Marcy to coach today, since he wasn't sure how long the burial ceremonies at the Broken Buffalo might take. Looked like Marcy had pulled in Dexter Horseman's dad, Dennis, to help with the coaching. The Eagles had been in good hands.

He had driven Clifford Many Horses home and visited for a few minutes, listening to the old man relive the experience of seeing the white buffalo calf. A stunned look about him, going over and over it: the small white calf turning from her mother and stepping out alone, facing the barbed-wire fence as if she were *seeing* them. Tears had welled in the old man's eyes as he talked, just as there had been tears when he'd seen the calf. "Spirit. Spirit." He had said. "A beautiful name."

Father John had waited with the old man until Betty had come with her dad's dinner. Then he had broken a few speed laws to get to Riverton before the game ended. "Congratulations!" He waved to Marcy and Dennis, awash in kids.

"It was electric!" Marcy shouted over the kids. "They could do no wrong." She managed to work her way through the kids until she was next to him. "Liam did just like you've been coaching him. He threw strikes. Never got behind in the count! You know Liam." She rolled her eyes. Her son was a lot like her, Father John was thinking. Always sure of what he was doing. "Likes to throw fastballs. But he did like we practiced and struck out five hitters. Even struck out the kid nobody wants to pitch to, the one that goes yard on other pitchers."

"Way to go." Liam had positioned himself in front of Father John, a smile as big as the prairie on his face. Father John patted the kid's shoulder.

"I was focused, Father." Liam worked the words around the big, open smile. "I wanted to do my job. Nathan was catching, he signaled the pitches like we practiced. If he asked for a fastball down and away, that's what I pitched. They only got four hits off me in six innings. They didn't score a run.

184

No way. When they did hit the ball, the team made all the plays."

Father John wondered if Liam Hawk would ever forget this day. "We were a team, like you always say, Father. We worked together."

"That they did." Dennis walked over. "Dexter here" — he ruffled the black hair of his son — "had four hits and batted in two runners. Randall Hunter got us on the scoreboard early with a solo home run. Then Nathan drove in two runners with a key double." He nodded to the skinny kid bouncing on his feet, tossing his cap into the air.

"Peter Boxley was on second when Randall came up again," Marcy said. "Randall hit a single up the middle and Peter scored on a play at the plate. And Liam" — she patted the top of her son's cap — "totally shut them down. I put Mason in for the final three outs, and he did us proud."

Out of the corner of his eye, Father John could see the Rangers lined up for the postgame handshakes. The kids had been so busy celebrating the unexpected win, they had forgotten that handshakes should come first. "Time to congratulate your opponents," he shouted.

"They didn't win," a high, thin voice

shouted back.

"You know the rules of good sportsman-ship. Congratulate them on a good game." There were a few groans; kids were shuf-fling their feet.

"I don't like what they say to us." Liam glanced up at him out of black, pleading eyes. "Like, 'Dirty Indian.' 'Go back to the rez.' Stuff like that."

"You shake their hands anyway." Father John said loud enough so all the kids could hear. "Doesn't matter what they say. You tell them they played a good game. You show them how to be good sports."

They started to turn around, a slow, reluctant motion, and slot themselves into a single line that started toward the other line. He could hear the voices calling, "Good game. Way to go." The lines moved fast past each other, palms barely touching. It was the ritual that counted. Marcy was grinning beside him. "What a sweet win," she said.

Father John waited until the kids had finished the show of sportsmanship, then fell in beside Marcy and headed for Steve Mantle and a couple of other coaches on the Ranger's team. "I hear it was a great game," he told Mantle.

"For your kids." Mantle was about six foot two, almost as tall as Father John, with sandy-colored hair that stuck out in tufts around the red baseball cap with Rangers on the front. He towered over Marcy, who had plastered an earnest look on her face and begun assuring the other coaches their kids had played very well.

"We look forward to our next game," Mantle said. He shot a meaningful look at the two coaches next to him, probably other fathers on the team. Father John recognized the look. Extra work at practice on whatever the coach thought the kids had messed up.

When they got back to the dugout, the kids had picked up the bats, balls, and catcher's gear and stuffed them into bags that they were lugging across the grass toward the parked cars. Father John thanked Marcy for coaching today and doing such a good job, gathered up a glove and bat he found in the dugout, and started down the outfield foul line.

"Hey, Father!" Mantle came jogging across the field, waving one hand as if he were feeling his way, a brown equipment bag slung over his shoulder. Father John waited for the man to fall in beside him. He was breathing hard, flushed. "Is what I heard about the rez true?"

"What did you hear?" Father John knew what the man would say; the moccasin telegraph usually ran into Riverton.

"White buffalo calf born."

Father John stopped and faced the man. "It will be on tonight's news."

"Born on the Broken Buffalo a week before Dennis Carey got shot? Sure surprised me. I expected a white buffalo calf would get born on an Indian ranch, not on that spread."

"You know the Careys?"

Mantle shrugged and adjusted the wide strap over his shoulder. They started walking again. Out in the street, pickups and cars were pulling away from the curb. A few kids climbed into the waiting cars, excitement still leaking from their waving hands and bobbing heads. "Visited with them once or twice when they came into the office. I run Ranchlands Employment over on Main Street, try to match ranches that need help with cowboys looking for work. Dennis and Sheila came in a year ago last spring after they had the ranch six months or so. Came back last fall. I sent a few cowboys their way. Made some connections."

They had reached the curb, and Father John set the glove and bat in the back of the pickup. He looked at the man, who readjusted his own bag, then started moving his baseball cap back and forth as if he were scratching his scalp. "Don't like speaking ill of the dead, but I never could figure out what they were doing out there. Sat across from me and said how much they needed help. I sent them perfectly good hands that they turned down. Only ones they hired came from out of state."

Father John didn't say anything. He could still see the small, thin girl with black hair and blue eyes and skin as pale as the dawn sky. Nuala O'Brian, a pretty Irish girl with a brogue that had followed her to the U.S. and to some small town in New Mexico he had never heard of. He could still hear the panic in her voice. She was looking for her fiancé and she'd thought, well, because Jaime Madigan was Catholic, he might've come by the mission. He'd hired on to a buffalo ranch on the rez and had gone missing. Had Father John heard of him? He'd told her he was sorry, but he hadn't met Jaime. If he was missing, she should report it to the tribal police.

She had put out her hand, as if to stop that line of thought. Jaime wouldn't want the police looking for him. It's not that he was ever in serious trouble, but, you know, he'd sown a few wild oats before he'd met her. They were going to get married. The owners at the Broken Buffalo said he decided to leave one day. Packed up his bags and drove off. They had no idea where he went.

"Ever hear of a cowboy named Jaime Madigan?"

Mantle tipped his head back and stared at the sky a moment. The sun had set over the Wind River range an hour ago, and the clouds were fading into pinks and reds. There was a pinkish cast in the air. "Sounds familiar, but I can't be sure. Out of state?"

"New Mexico."

"We get a lot of cowboys wandering in, looking for work. I might've placed him on the Broken Buffalo. Stop by tomorrow if you get a chance. I can take a look through the records."

The pale flush of daylight hovered in the sky when Father John drove through the tunnel of cottonwoods and swung around Circle Drive. The mission had a deserted feeling. No parked cars about; a warm breeze tinged with the scent of wood smoke drifted into the cab. The Women's Society had met at five thirty for a carry-in supper at Eagle Hall. The odors of enchiladas, spaghetti, and stew clung to the walls of the old hall after every meeting. He circled past the alley that divided the administration

190

building from the church. Eagle Hall stood behind the church. No cars in the alley.

Walks-On was waiting in the residence on the other side of Circle Drive, tail wagging, eyes shining. The dog had the ears of Superman. He would have heard the old Toyota pickup lumbering through the cottonwoods and coming around the drive. Father John went down on his haunches, rubbed the soft fur behind the dog's ears, and closed his eyes as Walks-On lavished wet kisses on his cheeks. "Good boy," he said. Walks-On had that odd look on his face, as if he were trying to smile.

Television noises, voices talking over one another, floated out of the living room. He stood up and walked into the dimly lit room with curtains pulled and television lights flashing over the carpet and the sofa. Bishop Harry looked settled and comfortable in the recliner next to the sofa.

"You've heard about the white buffalo calf?"

"All over the TV, my boy. Couldn't miss it." The bishop looked up and gave him a smile of gladness and wariness. "You see her?"

Father John perched on the armrest of the sofa, Walks-On dropping at his feet. The bishop muted the television voices and, for a moment, they watched in the silence as the small white calf strolled alongside her mother. At one point she veered off sideways, as if she might scamper away. She looked healthy and energetic. Whatever invisible sign the mother had sent, the calf turned back and started nuzzling beneath the shaggy hair on her mother's stomach until she latched onto the teat. "I saw her this afternoon. She's small and helpless looking, like a lamb. The tribes believe she is a symbol of the Creator with us. Her name is Spirit."

"The Creator has blessed us with many symbols in the world." The bishop kept his eyes on the small white creature sheltering beneath the enormous, powerful-looking buffalo. It struck Father John that the dam would kill anyone — any creature — if she perceived any danger to her calf. "We must open our hearts to see them," the bishop said. "I think the Creator sends signs to get our attention. There were many signs in India." He shook his head. "The Brahman bull. The sacred cow, the sign of all life. The Gaja." He seemed to be staring into a space inside his head, as if he had located a lost memory. "The elephant, the sign of the Creator's heavenly throne. Sometimes we just don't see the signs around us."

"The Arapahos believe the calf is a manifestation of White Buffalo Woman, who . . ."

The bishop held up one hand. "Who brought the sacred rituals and ceremonies to the Lakota, but meant them for all Indian people. I did some research this afternoon."

Father John told him what Clifford had said: the birth of the white calf was like a visitation from the Blessed Mother.

"Then the calf is very holy, indeed. What bothers you?" He shifted sideways toward Father John. His blue eyes were bright and watery.

"The owner of the ranch, Dennis Carey, was shot to death. A young man who worked there last fall has disappeared."

"You sense evil about the place?" The bishop hurried on, not waiting for a response. "Perhaps that is the reason the white buffalo calf was sent there."

17

The camping space was perfect. Bordered by two huge boulders and a stand of ponderosas that muffled sounds from the other campers. Past the ponderosas, Reg could see a slice of Lander in the distance. He had pulled the pickup in close to the campsite, set up his pup tent, and put the rolled sleeping bag inside. Then he had gathered twigs and started a fire in the fire pit. Someone who had been here before had left a stack of logs, and he had rolled the top one into the fire and balanced the small grill he kept with his camping supplies on the sides of the pit. He worked his pocketknife around the top of a can of pork and beans, which he set on the grill. When the brownish liquid started bubbling, he had lifted the can off the grill with a pair of tongs, set it on a flat rock that served as a table. Squatting in front, he had opened the metal triangle that held a knife, fork, and spoon and eaten the hot chunks out of the can.

Reg liked the sound of the wind in the pines, the muffled noises of other campers preparing dinner, the faraway sounds of cars pulling into the campground. He liked the privacy, the lack of ties. He was used to eating and sleeping outdoors, used to the feel of the wilderness. He had been a kid, barely sixteen, when Dad died and he'd dropped out of school and gone cowboying. He had followed his cousin onto a ranch on the Colorado plateau, a great swath of land that bound Colorado and Utah together. You could ride for days without seeing another soul. Cattle. Sheep. Mountain lions. He had seen a wolf once, although no wolves were supposed to range that far south. A thousand creatures scampering about, but no people. From time to time, he'd collect his pay and go back to Grand Junction. No family there anymore. Mom had died years ago; he hardly remembered her. Most of his friends had gone cowboying. They had ties. Parents and sisters and brothers. A few of his friends had even gotten married, although months went by between visits home. Oh, he liked girls, all right. Sometimes he longed for a girl. But most of the time, that fire was put out after a few days in town, a couple of dances, a roll in the hay.

Married life had never appealed to him. Born to be a loner. That was how he thought of himself.

Josh was different, always had been. It had surprised Reg when his buddy told him he was going to hire onto a ranch out on the plateau. *Long way from family,* Reg remembered saying. *You'll get lonely.* Cowboying wasn't for everybody; he had tried to make Josh understand. He could still hear Josh's voice: "Hell, I'll come back to see the folks whenever I like." Then he had gotten fascinated with buffalo and gone to Wyoming to work on a buffalo ranch. He hadn't come back.

Reg finished the pork and beans. He felt warm and drowsy. The sun was out of sight, but the western sky was on fire with tongues of magenta, orange, and purple. The other campers seemed to have settled down, although he could hear a faint medley of voices and a strumming guitar. Shadows moved across the campsite; it was starting to get cool, despite waves of warmth from the campfire. A deep tiredness dogged him. He had driven most of the day to get to Wyoming.

He forced himself to his feet and went

about the routine motions of cleaning up the campsite. Always keep a clean camp! Pounded into him by the first foreman he'd worked under, the summer he turned sixteen. He put the used can in a bag he kept for trash, poured a little water from his water bottle over the utensils and folded them back into the triangle. Then he used the rest of the water to douse the fire, because you could never leave an unattended fire. The first rule of living in the outdoors.

Ten minutes later, Reg was driving the winding roads out of the campground. He turned onto the straightaway that led down into town and stepped on the accelerator. Lander was a small town, Main Street stretching ahead with hanging baskets of flowers that looked dried, past their prime; people strolling sidewalks, licking ice cream cones; and the streetlamps coming on, shooting little circles of light over the pavement. He kept the map open on the seat next to him, even though he had studied it earlier at the campsite, imprinting the network of roads in his mind, and he turned onto Highway 789, past the sign that said Riverton.

Another small town, but quieter, it seemed; only a few people strolling the sidewalks. Lights flickered in the windows of small bungalows, a steady traffic crawled down the streets. He drove north on Federal until he spotted the blinking sign on the corner. Behind the sign was a squat brick building with a flat roof and a light over the door that flared onto the parking lot. Reg parked in the lot between two trucks with the figure of a cowboy riding a bronco on the Wyoming license plates.

Smells of beer, sweat, hot grease, and dust hit him as he stepped into the bar. He had been in a hundred bars across the West, places where tourists never went. He smiled at the idea of himself, the stranger, walking into a local hangout, cowboys leaning against the bar, sipping beers, watching him beneath the brims of their hats. Hoping for excitement. What have we here? Somebody new. And the girls in cowboy boots and tight jeans and shirts opened halfway to their belly buttons, giggling. Tension shot like electricity through the whole place.

He wedged himself into a vacant space at the bar between two cowboys. The bartender, who looked as if he'd stepped out of an old western movie, caught his eye, and Reg motioned to the beer tap. There was an economy of movement, an economy of language among cowboys. Familiar, all of it.

He might have been in Arizona or Idaho or back on the Colorado plateau.

"New to these parts?" Reg realized the big guy on his left, with scabs on his hands, had been eyeing him.

"Passing through."

"Not a lot of work, if that's what you're wanting. Where you from?"

"Drove up from Colorado. You work around here?"

"Looking to get hired on at a spread tomorrow, if I get lucky. Raise buffalo, them crazy ranchers. Now they got themselves a white buffalo calf. You ever hear of that?"

Reg took a long drink of the beer the bartender had set in front of him, swiped at the foam on his lips, and nodded. So that's what was going on out at the Broken Buffalo, folks showing up to see the calf. Somewhere he had heard about white buffalo calves. "Indians believe they're sacred," he said, unsure of the memory he had pulled that from. He turned around and leaned his back against the bar, his eyes accustomed now to the dim light. Hanging around the booths in the back of the bar was another batch of cowboys — Indian cowboys. "You talking about the Broken Buffalo?"

"You heard of it? Jesus. They're looking

for hands in Colorado?"

"I came here to find my buddy. He hired on there last spring."

"Must be a white guy." The cowboy on the other side joined in. He had a big belly that rolled over a silver belt buckle and a grizzled look about him, as if he'd just ridden in from the prairie. "Don't hire Indians out there."

"Why not? It's on the rez."

"Just their way." The first cowboy shrugged. "Owner got shot the other night. From what I hear, he wasn't no Santa Claus. Works his hands pretty hard. Holds off the pay for months until he sells some stock and gets a big contract to supply buffalo meat."

"I heard he lost a contract with a national supermarket chain last spring." The other cowboy jumped in. "Meat underweight. You ask me, he ran a lousy business. Couldn't afford to buy enough hay to supplement the grass, so the buffalo didn't get as big as he was expecting, and he lost his contract. Ranchers I've worked for, they get a loan from the bank to run their business. Pay it back after they make some money."

"Heard he couldn't get a bank to give him a loan." The first cowboy lifted the glass of beer to his lips. The scabs looked like flies on his hand. "I hear they only had a couple hands until yesterday, when they started hiring. Carlos somebody is the foreman. That your buddy, Carlos?"

Reg took another swig of his own beer. "Josh Barker. You heard of him?"

Neither cowboy said anything. They made a sucking noise as they drank. An argument had started up over in the booths, a couple of guys shouting. Then quiet as the Indians shifted about, moving between the booths and tables. A cowboy with a lazy eye in a sun-wrinkled face walked over and leaned in toward Reg. "Josh your friend?"

"That's right. His mother's dying. I came here to find him. Cowboy out at the ranch said nobody by the name of Josh Barker ever worked there."

"I'd say he's a damn liar." The man was big, blond, and hard-jawed. Reg knew the type. Quick to call things as he saw them, ready to back up words with fists. "Josh came in here once in a while. Tall, skinny guy, but nobody messed with him. He could handle himself."

"He say he was working at the Broken Buffalo?"

"That's the place. Liked working with buffalo, he told me. Unpredictable beasts. Have to stay on your toes. Don't turn your

201

back on them."

"When's the last time you saw him?"

"Been a while," the first cowboy said. The others nodded. "Couple months at least."

"He say he was planning on going somewhere else?"

"He sure as hell wanted to get off the Broken Buffalo." Reg wasn't sure if the lazy eye was looking at him or someone else. "Said he was getting out soon as he collected his back pay. Going to Montana."

"Did he say why?"

The cowboy shrugged. "Ready to move on. The Broken Buffalo was a lot of hard work, not much time off."

Reg drained the last of his beer, shifted toward the bar, and motioned the bartender for another. Montana. Another big, empty state with who knew how many buffalo ranches. He felt as if he had picked up a heavy load, and now he wanted to set it down. He grabbed the new glass and drank half of it. The image of Josh's mom dying in her bed, pale and as shrunken as a doll under the covers, kept playing in front of him. He took another drink and tried to blink back the image. "I don't think he'd settle into some new place without letting his folks know. Last time they heard from him, he was working at the Broken Buffalo.

I don't understand why that cowboy out there lied to me."

"Could've been one of the new hires. Maybe he didn't know better. Anybody else besides these guzzlers" — the cowboy tossed his head in the direction of the other cowboys; his lazy eye fastened on a corner of the bar — "your buddy might've talked to?"

"I was hoping you could tell me."

"White priest on the rez."

"Josh wasn't religious." He was thinking that Josh's dad had said something about talking to a priest in the area.

"All the same." The lazy eye seemed to have focused on Reg. "Guy gets in trouble, might go looking for somebody like that. I heard the priest at St. Francis Mission on the rez is a pretty good guy."

"Trouble? You think Josh got into some kind of trouble?"

All three cowboys were shaking their heads, looking at him as if he'd missed the rodeo. The cowboy with the scabby hands finished off his beer and set the glass down hard on the bar. "He hated that ranch with a passion."

"I hear the owner got shot," Reg said. "You saying Josh might've had something to do with it?"

"I'm saying, that rancher pushed around every cowboy ever worked there."

Reg took another sip of beer. "I figure I'll go out there tomorrow and talk to the widow. If she takes me on, I might find out what happened to Josh. Any of you guys know her?"

The cowboy with the big belly took a half step backward. "Seen her at the powwows selling buffalo hamburgers. Pretty good looking, but . . ."

"What?"

The cowboy shrugged. "Something hard about her, like she got kicked around a lot and wants to make sure from now on she's the one doing the kicking."

Reg tried to form an image from the women he'd known. Bar girls, party girls, daughters on the ranches he'd worked. He finished his beer and slid the glass onto the bar. "Good talking to you." He gave a little two-finger salute and headed for the door, past the tables, past a group of Indians. He let himself outdoors and walked through the shafts of light to the parking lot, conscious of the heavy thud of footsteps behind him.

18

They were the Indians from the back booth. He recognized them the minute he turned around. The overhead light flickered off their brown faces. "What's your problem?"

"What're you doing here?" A big Indian with a pockmarked face seemed in charge, the spokesman, the boss. The chief, Reg thought, and he stifled a laugh that he knew was from nerves rumbling deep inside. The chief had thick shoulders and thick brown forearms with the tattoo of an eagle that seemed to be flying up his right arm. This wasn't the first time he'd had to face off a gang of tough guys in a two-bit town nobody ever heard of, dust blowing off the asphalt. It was like he was walking around with a billboard on his back: *Stranger. Beat me up.* The local entertainment for the week.

"Minding my own business."

"My friend here says he heard you talking about the Broken Buffalo." The chief shifted sideways, and Reg feinted toward the opening. The chief moved back. "What business you got there?"

"I'm not looking for trouble."

"You come all the way from Colorado and you're not looking for trouble? You think we don't have enough cowboys for the work here? You think you can nuzzle in?"

"I'm looking for a friend." A blur of brown faces striped by yellow light hovered behind the chief's shoulders. "Josh Barker. Last I heard, he'd hired on at the Broken Buffalo. He took off, and I'm trying to learn where he went."

"That's not how we put it together. You're just another Colorado dirtbag looking to take a job ought to be ours. You heard the Broken Buffalo's hiring, and you think you can take over your buddy's job."

"Soon as I locate Josh, I'll be on my way back to Colorado."

"Your buddy was smart. Lot smarter than you. He took the hint and got out of here. You should do the same. Highway out there" — he nodded toward the stream of headlights passing on Federal — "goes straight to Colorado. Start driving."

"Look," Reg said. "His mother's dying. If something happened to him, she wants to know so she can die in peace." Had he imagined it, or had something softened behind the black eyes watching him? "Just between you and me, I'm not going to any cops. I just want information."

The chief took his time, jaw muscles working as if he were chewing over the words before he spit them out. "Your buddy drove out of here just like he drove in. On his own."

A truck had pulled around them into the parking lot. Doors swung open. A couple of white cowboys jumped out and sauntered over, as if they had sized up the situation. They stopped on either side of the Indians and dipped their heads toward Reg. "Raps giving you trouble?"

"No trouble. I was just going to my truck." This time the space opened between the chief and another Indian, and Reg walked through. He got into the truck, turned the ignition, and drove past the Indians — Raps, the cowboys had called them. He supposed that meant Arapahos from the rez, Indians the Broken Buffalo Ranch refused to hire. The side-view mirror framed the two cowboys yanking open the door to the bar and disappearing inside. The Indians were still in the lot. He turned onto Federal.

He supposed he had crossed some invis-

ible line, missed some sign that said ENTER-
ING THE WIND RIVER RESERVATION, the
truck pulling hard up an incline, the lights
blazing on top of the hill. A gigantic lighted
billboard ahead said WIND RIVER CASINO.
And Josh, he liked to gamble. He could
smell a game no matter where he went. And
he was lucky, the sonofabitch. He won big,
but he never could hold on to it. Win big,
lose big, and Reg supposed that was why he
kept cowboying. That and the fact that Josh
loved everything about cowboying. Living
outdoors, working with horses and cattle
and buffalo. Buffalo, they were the biggest
challenge. Josh never shied from a challenge.

The truck slowed and balked. Jesus, he
thought, don't break down on me now.
Seemed like more traffic than earlier, more
than he expected on a road that connected
a couple of small towns. Trucks and pickups,
SUVs, cars moving in both directions. An
SUV with Oklahoma license plates shot
around him and pulled in only a couple of
car lengths ahead of the oncoming traffic.
He blinked his lights at a pickup with
brights on and kept a decent space behind
the red taillights of the SUV, the cone of his
own headlights flaring over the black asphalt.

The truck was groaning now, like a tractor hauling a heavy load. Last thing he needed was to break down out here on the highway between nowhere and nowhere. It was a long five-hour drive south to Colorado, and if he found out Josh had headed for Montana, he would have to go in the other direction. *I'll find him,* he had told Josh's dad. For a moment, the words — the promise — had wiped the worry from the old man's face. Ahead, lights from the sign wafted like blue-and-yellow smoke in a black sky lit with stars. The traffic had opened up. The SUV was far ahead, taillights twinkling like tiny match flames. A long break in the stream of oncoming vehicles.

The gunshot sounded like the crack of thunder. Sudden and explosive, out of nowhere. The truck took a little jump. He could feel his heart batting his ribs. For an instant, he thought another truck, black, invisible, must have rear-ended him. But he knew a gunshot when he heard it. He had been firing rifles since he was a kid; his own rifle hung in the frame across the back window. He jammed down on the gas pedal, glancing back and forth between the rearview window and the side windows. He even turned partway around and looked back, expecting — what? Black space had opened around him. The shot had come out of the shadows along the road as he had driven by. He hadn't noticed anything. No vehicle parked in the brush. No movement. Nothing but the gunshot.

A bullet had hit the bed of the truck, he was sure, which had lifted off the rear wheels. The truck was steady now, the uneasy steadiness after a shock. He drove over the crest of the hill, lights from the casino sign flashing on the hood and mingling with his headlights, then slowed into the right turn and followed the smoothly paved road that circled down and around a parking lot. Vehicles lined up row after row in the glare of the overhead streetlights. Beyond the lot, the reservation spread into the darkness.

He stopped in front of the casino, jumped out, and ran for the wide glass doors that were already opening for him. Inside was an officer in a blue uniform, the grips of two pistols visible in his gun belt. The casino floor lay beyond, an acre of slot machines, people sitting in front of them, other people milling about. A jangling, whirring noise, like an undercurrent of electricity, cut through the air.

"Some bastard just shot at me."

"In the parking lot?" The guard went on alert, yanking a phone off his belt.

"On the highway, coming up the hill." Reg could feel his heart still pounding. His voice came back to him like that of a runner, as if he had run up the hill.

"You hurt?" The officer looked him over, then leaned sideways into the phone. "Edward, at the casino. Got a cowboy here says he was shot at on the highway." He went back to looking Reg over. "You going to need an ambulance?" He waited until Reg shook his head, then he said, "Nah. He looks okay. Shook up." He nodded again and slipped the phone back into its case. "State patrol is on the way. You want to sit down. I'll get you some water."

Reg said he would wait outside. He went back outside into the warm evening, lights flaring over the sidewalk and a field of stars blazing in the black sky. He found the bullet hole. A clean shot through the side of the bed, not three feet from the cab. If the shooter was a marksman, he hadn't intended to kill him, just scare him. Or — and this made him stop, frozen in place — he had intended to kill him and had missed. For a crazy moment, he thought about taking his rifle out of the lock and driving back to look for the shooter.

He cleared his throat, as if that could clear away the impulse. If the shooter was still around, he would be a dead man before he got out of the truck.

He walked around the truck and examined the exit hole. The bullet had traveled straight across the bed, but, had it hit his metal supply box a foot away, it could have ricocheted into the cab. He could have died tonight. The thought froze him in place again. Trucks and pickups were turning into the lot, trawling the rows for parking places. The shooter could have followed him here. Waiting to follow him back onto the highway, where he would try again.

He could hear sirens in the distance growing louder. He watched a patrol car come around the bend, red and yellow roof lights flashing, sirens wailing. Then the sirens cut off and the car pulled in close to his back bumper. A patrolman got out and walked over, one hand on the handle of his holstered gun. "You the guy shot at?"

"Reg Hartly. I have ID." The patrolman nodded, and Reg pulled his wallet from his back pocket, extracted his driver's license, and handed it to the patrolman, who had unclipped a small Maglite from somewhere on his belt. He shone the light over the license and handed it back.

"What happened?"

Reg pointed to the exit bullet hole. "I was driving south on 789, pulling up the hill, when out of nowhere, there was a rifle shot. Hit the bed on the left and came out here."

The patrolman had stepped over and was examining the other side of the truck. "Nice, clean entrance," he said. He walked around and studied the exit hole. "You see anything?"

"Nada. There was a break in the traffic, and that made me a sitting duck for some crazy nut."

"You got a beef with anybody?"

"I just got here today." Reg took in a couple of breaths before he said, "There were some Arapahos at the O.K. Bar, gave me a hard time in the parking lot a little while ago. Thought I was here looking for a job. Didn't like the idea of an outsider taking local jobs."

"They make any threats?"

"No. I drove off. I don't think anybody followed me. I was on my way to Sinks Canyon, where I got my camping gear."

"Why are you here?"

"Looking for a buddy, Josh Barker. Heard of him?" The patrolman barely blinked. "Hired onto the Broken Buffalo Ranch. Problem is, he disappeared. I'm hoping to find somebody that knows where he might have gone."

The patrolman pulled out a phone and tapped a couple of buttons. "We got another shooting on 789, on the hill north of the casino. I'm going to need help locating the shooter's nest."

"Another shooting?" Reg said.

The patrolman put the phone back into its case. "Five or six in the last year. Random, far as we know, but Riverton cops will go to the bar and talk to the Arapahos there. We may need to talk to you again. Right now I want you to take me to the spot."

Reg gave him the number of his cell, which the patrolman jotted down on a small notepad he'd pulled from his shirt pocket. "I'll follow you." He gestured toward the truck with his head.

Reg got behind the steering wheel and jiggled the ignition to coax the engine into life. He pulled a sharp U-turn and drove past the patrol car onto the wide, curving road and out toward the highway. Headlights from the patrol car shone in his rearview mirror. He glanced at both sides of the road for the spot where it had happened. Everything looked the same, shadowy clumps of scrub brush and sage and wild grass in the darkness. He realized he was halfway down the hill. Here, he thought, where the truck had been straining and groaning.

He pulled over close to the borrow ditch on the east side of the road as the patrol car moved in behind him, red, blue, and yellow roof lights flashing against the darkness. He jumped out and walked over to the patrolman lifting himself out of the car. "It was around here, I think. It's hard to tell for sure."

The patrolman straightened his shoulders and looked off into the dark scrubland. Two other patrol cars had appeared out of nowhere, a line of cars parked alongside the borrow ditch now, other patrolmen walking over. "Shooter hid out there?" One of them said. "Lousy place to hide."

Reg left the patrolmen standing in a circle, heads bent. Organizing a search, he guessed, talking on radios. Roof lights flashing; radio in one of the cars crackling. He had to wait for a break in traffic before he could pull a U-turn. Then he wedged the truck into the southbound lane, the traffic moving slowly past the patrol cars. He could feel the heaviness in his legs, the exhaustion working through him. He thought about crawling inside the pup tent, feeling the comfort of the sleeping bag around him. He couldn't shake the memory that had hit him earlier: Josh liked to gamble.

He turned right at the top of the hill and followed the curve back to the front of the casino. He shouldn't park here, but he didn't think they would shoo away a man who had just been shot at. He got out, slammed the door, and walked past the sliding glass doors.

The officer looked at him. "You doing okay?"

He was okay, he said. He was thinking that his blood had stopped pounding in his ears, and the fear and shock had melted into an anger that burned like a wet fire and would take a while to burn off. "I'm looking for a buddy of mine," he said, "liked to gamble. Any regulars here might have gotten to know him."

"What's his game?"

"Twenty-one."

"Over there." He threw a palm toward the far corner of the casino. "Look for Debbie Moon. She's dealing. Might've heard of your guy."

19

A girl with black hair; cinnamon complexion; and dark, shining eyes, who might have been a model for a tourist commercial on Indian country, dealt the cards to three players at the twenty-one table. Wearing a light blue shirt and dark slacks with a thin silver necklace at the base of her neck: the only woman dealing twenty-one. Reg walked past the rows of slot machines, whites and Indians planted on the stools, pushing buttons, eyes glued to screens that flashed and dinged. The place was packed. He wondered if it was always packed, or if these folks were part of the crowd that had come to see the white calf.

He stood off a couple of feet and watched the game. Stacks of chips in front of the players were shrinking. Finally the blond-haired woman seated between two cowboys picked up her chips, slid off the swivel chair, and headed in the direction of the craps tables. The man on her right, cowboy hat pushed back so that the brim slanted upward, cupped a short stack of chips and followed her.

Reg took the seat the cowboy had vacated, leaving an empty chair between him and a bald-headed man bending his head to study the cards that lay face up. Eight and five. Bristles of gray hair sprouted on the back of his neck. In front of Debbie, a face-down card lay next to a jack of clubs. The man took a breath and brushed the cards in his direction. Debbie dealt him a deuce of clubs. Then she turned over her second card. A ten. She collected the chips in the middle and swept the played cards into the discard pile. The man leaned back, shook his head, and stood up. He stretched his shoulders, as if he might change his mind, then walked off.

"You in?" The dark eyes turned on Reg. He fished a twenty out of his wallet and tossed it onto the table. Debbie set a small stack of chips in front of him and began dealing. Four, then a six. She had dealt her first card facedown. Now she dealt herself a ten. Reg brushed his cards, and she gave him a seven before she turned up her other card. Ace of hearts. She took in the chips, swept away the played cards. It was remarkable, he was thinking, the masklike set of her features. She might have been punching divots in a factory line.

"Are you Debbie?"

"You still in?" He nodded, set a chip in the center, and she dealt out the cards. Not much different from the last hand. He watched Debbie pull the chips toward her and place the cards in the discard pile.

"I'd like to talk to you," he said.

"We aren't allowed to fraternize." The mask didn't crack, but — maybe he imagined it — a flicker of light in the dark eyes.

"I'm looking for a friend who's gone missing. Josh Barker? He liked twenty-one."

"Gone missing?" Her hands stopped moving. "Look, you want to play or not?"

Reg set the remaining two chips into the middle. She dealt the cards. He looked down at the eight of spades and the two of diamonds. She had given herself another jack. With her luck, the facedown card would be an ace.

He brushed his own cards, and she dealt him a jack. Then she flipped over her other card. A two of clubs. It was his turn to collect the chips. "You know Josh?"

"Maybe." She put the played cards into the discard pile. "I deal. I don't talk."

"You take a break?"

"Fifteen minutes." She gave a little nod toward the sliding glass doors. "Out front so I can smoke."

Reg walked back through the casino wondering which other dealers might know Josh. Debbie was his best bet. He had seen the flare of interest in her eyes. The officer, still at the door, followed him outdoors. "You need to park in the lot."

"I'll be out of here in a few more minutes." Reg could see the struggle going on behind the fleshy jowls and the paper-thin lips. *Cowboy shot at tonight. Poor guy could have been dead.*

"Make it fast." The officer shifted his massive body around and went back through the sliding doors.

It seemed longer than fifteen minutes, at least twenty or twenty-five, but here was Debbie walking across the sidewalk. He liked the way she carried herself, like a prize filly who knew she was a prize. She was shaking a cigarette out of a package. Then she fumbled with a lighter. He reached over, took the lighter from her, and watched her bend toward the little flame. She stood up straight and took a deep draw. He handed her lighter back. She slipped it and the cigarettes into the front pocket of her slacks. They made a little rectangular outline against her thigh.

"Where you from?"

"Colorado. We grew up together, Josh and me. I drove up here to find him. His mother's dying."

"Why don't we start by you telling me about Josh. Is that the kind of guy he is? Just takes off and leaves. Goes missing, AWOL, the minute he thinks somebody's getting too close? Gonna make demands?"

Bingo, Reg was thinking. Debbie not only knew Josh, she'd been in a relationship with him. "No," he told her. "Josh is not like that. What happened?"

"That's just it," she said, blue-gray smoke coming out of her nostrils. "Nothing happened. I mean, aside from the fact that I fell for the guy, and I told him so. Poof!" She waved away a cloud of smoke. "He disappeared. I figure he took off 'cause, you know, he didn't want to be with me."

"I doubt that's the case."

"Arapaho girlfriend?"

"You know what I think?" He hesitated, then plunged on. "I think he'd been looking for you for a long time."

Debbie gazed at the cigarette burning down between her fingers, then looked away, fighting for control.

"You meet here?"

She nodded, seemingly grateful to move to solid ground. "He was good at twenty-one. Won most of the time. I worried the pit boss might get suspicious, but it was legit. I need this job. I'm not throwing any games, not even for Josh. Maybe I knew . . ." She stopped and considered, watching smoke trail upward. "He'd be gone, and all I'd have was my job, so I better take care of it."

"Where was he working?"

"Broken Buffalo. Where else? God, did he love buffalo. Didn't love that ranch, though. They worked the hands like slaves. Paid them a little on what was owed them. Always promising to pay the rest soon as they had a sale. They never seemed to have a big enough sale. You ask me, that place was barely hanging on. Josh thought so, too. He got away when he could, and I tried to set my work schedule around times he might get off for a few hours. We usually met at my place. Little house my grandfather left me on the rez. I try to keep it from falling down around me." Tears were running down her cheeks.

"I'm sorry," he said. She nodded a thanks. "When was the last time you saw him?"

"Saturday night, end of June. He told me he was going to quit the ranch, soon's he collected his back pay. He said he'd get hired on someplace else. There's an agency in Riverton that lines up cowboys with jobs. He was going to talk to them. He never said he was leaving. He never told me good-bye."

"I talked to a cowboy out there today. He said Josh never worked there."

Debbie let the cigarette butt drop out of her hands. She ground it with a heel until it was a brown smudge on the pavement. Then she looked at him out of wide, uncomprehending eyes. "That's crazy. Josh worked hard for those bastards." She jerked her head sideways and looked away, as if a thought had struck her unexpectedly. "You don't think . . . ?" she began.

"Josh didn't kill the owner."

"No." She let out a long sigh. "He could never kill anyone. But I wasn't surprised when I heard Dennis Carey got shot on the highway. We have a crazy shooter on the rez."

Reg was quiet. He decided not to tell her that he'd been shot at tonight.

She turned toward him, and said, "I hear Carey got shot up close. Like he knew the killer, even pulled over for him. Wouldn't surprise me if one of those cowboys finally killed him. Wouldn't surprise me at all." She lifted her lovely chin and stared up at Reg. He was thinking that Josh would never have

223

walked away from this girl. "Where do you think he went?"

"He might have gone looking for another job. Montana. Idaho."

"Only place he wanted to go was home. Colorado. He talked about it all the time. He was going back to the family ranch, talk to his dad about raising buffalo. He said I'd like it there." She was crying full out now, dropping her face into her hands, shoulders shaking.

Reg drew her to him. He could feel the softness of her, the love for his buddy deep inside her. "I'm gonna find him," he said.

Adam was usually quiet, Vicky thought. He never liked to talk about his trips — even a short trip to Denver — as if he would have to relive the experience by talking about it, and living it once had been enough.

Tonight he had hardly stopped talking, but not about the trip. He had heard about the white buffalo calf before he came by her office to pick her up for dinner, and it had set him off. He was like a bronco that couldn't stop bucking in the chute. She had finished her spaghetti in the casino restaurant, and he had eaten only half of his. The restaurant was full. She could feel people at the adjacent tables glancing over, as if Adam were an actor delivering a monologue.

"A white buffalo calf on the rez!" He must have said it a dozen times. Pine Ridge, Rosebud, those reservations he could understand. The Creator had sent white buffalo woman to *his* people. Why would the calf, a sacred symbol of the Creator, come to another reservation?

Vicky waited until he took a breath, then she said, "White Buffalo Woman came to all the nations." She had grown up with the stories. All the relatives, seated around Grandfather, listening to stories of the ancestors. No matter how bad the times, or how poor they had been, the Creator never forgot his people. White Buffalo Woman had appeared to the Lakota so that all the nations would know and remember. She had promised to send the multitudes of buffalo. She had promised to return in the hard times.

Adam had talked on about listening to the same stories. Sitting around the fire in his grandfather's tipi out in back of the house the government had built. The old man, Adam said, had preferred to live in a tipi. She had laughed at the memory it stirred. Her grandfather said that his father had been the same. A lot of the old Indians didn't want to give up the old ways when they came to the reservations. *He didn't want to live in a wood box.* She could hear her grandfather's voice; it made her feel like a child again. *He kept the ponies in the house. They liked it there.*

"Tell me about the calf." Adam twirled the spaghetti and took another bite. He chewed slowly, thoughtfully, his eyes on her.

"Larger than a lamb, although it looks very small and . . ." She wanted to say *vulnerable,* but she heard herself say: "Holy. The rest of the herd kept its distance. Even the buffalo must know."

Adam smiled, then took another forkful of spaghetti. "I wouldn't want to be around if the herd thought anybody meant to harm her. Let's go together tomorrow to see her."

"People are already coming." She glanced at the tables around them. "Most of the people here will probably be at the ranch tomorrow. Of course we can go," she added, seeing the shade of disappointment moving across his face. The traveling around the country, the meetings in corporate offices of oil and gas companies, the fancy suits and expensive ties — all of these things had bothered her, she realized, raised questions she couldn't answer. Who was he? Always some part of Adam that seemed blocked off, reserved for the world he moved in, a

226

world that revolved around oil and gas and water and timber on reservations, and had nothing to do with her world of DUIs and wills and adoptions and keeping some scared Arapaho out of jail.

But here was someone different. Here was the Adam Lone Eagle she had been trying to find, the Lakota with memories of the old stories and ceremonies, the descendant of warriors and chiefs, stunned, shocked, excited about the miracle of a white buffalo calf. He hadn't forgotten who he was; she was the one who hadn't understood that.

They lingered over cups of coffee, both reluctant, Vicky realized, to break the quiet sense of having landed somehow on the same ground. She was aware of the crowd waiting at the hostess desk, and so was Adam, because he caught her eye and motioned that they should be going.

Vicky saw the cowboy as she and Adam stepped past the sliding glass doors. Tall and thin in a ropy, muscular way, with a tan cowboy hat, walking around the front of the silver truck she had seen parked out at the Broken Buffalo. She hurried across the sidewalk. "Excuse me?"

The cowboy jerked his head in her direction, then came back around the truck. Vicky was conscious of Adam moving in beside her. "Reg? You're looking for your friend from Colorado. We talked earlier today out at the buffalo ranch. Any luck?"

The cowboy nodded slowly, as if he had finally placed her. "The Indian lawyer lady," he said. "I've found some people who said my buddy Josh worked on the Broken Buffalo. No doubt about it."

"You should report him missing." That made two cowboys missing, she was thinking. One named Josh, the other Rick Tomlin. "Both the BIA police and the FBI."

He was still nodding. "I'm going to the ranch tomorrow and have a talk with the owner lady."

"Listen, Reg. I told Sheila Carey you wanted to talk to her about Josh. She said that if you showed up, she'd have you thrown off the ranch."

"Thrown off the ranch?" He gave a loud guffaw. "Well, now I know I gotta go see what that lady's all about."

"What was that all about?" Adam kept one hand on the steering wheel and stared into the shaft of the headlights ahead on Highway 789. Traffic seemed lighter than when they had driven over to the casino. Still, more vehicles than usual. The TV had been reporting the news of the white buffalo calf since late this afternoon. The news was going viral.

"The cowboy's here looking for his buddy, Josh Barker, who according to some guy at the Broken Buffalo Ranch, never worked there. Another cowboy, Rick Tomlin, the main witness against my client, has also disappeared."

"Cowboys drift on the wind. Maybe whoever said Josh hadn't worked there just didn't know him." He glanced over at her. Pinpricks of light from the dashboard jumped in his eyes. "You should be grateful the witness took off before the trial."

20

Elena looked dressed up for Easter. A flowery blue dress cinched at her waist and a little pink scarf tied over her head. She wore the usual black sturdy-looking shoes with ties that flopped about as she came into the office.

"Everything okay?" Father John stood up. The old woman seldom walked over to the administration building. The residence was her domain. She had on shoes for walking a hard-dirt path on a ranch.

"Dinner's in the slow cooker. Ready whenever you and Bishop Harry want to eat, in case I don't get back."

"There will probably be a huge crowd."

"I don't mind standing in line. It's a small sacrifice." She tilted her head toward the window and the white pickup on Circle Drive, exhaust shooting from the rear pipes. "My grandson, Jeff, is taking me. The sacred calf blessed us." She hesitated, and when he didn't say anything, she went on: "Jeff never showed any interest in the old stories and the old ways. Basketball and video games, that's all he thinks about. Who cares about the ancestors? They're dead." She shook her head, drawing in her lower lip. He could see her blinking back the tears. "He saw the calf on TV last night, and everything changed. Wanted to know the old story of White Buffalo Woman, how she changed into a buffalo and promised she would return when we needed her. Now she is with us again, a holy spirit from the Creator Himself in that little white calf. Well, Jeff kept me up most the night, wanting to know more and more. I told him what I remembered my grandfather telling me. I don't mind saying, I thought my heart was gonna burst with happiness."

Father John smiled. "I'm glad to hear it." He had been on the reservation for ten years now. He had seen a number of young men like Jeff turn away, wanting to be modern, wanting to be like everybody else. But he had watched many of them turn back and stay strong.

"It's okay? My taking time off?"

He nodded, still smiling. It wasn't necessary to say anything. They both knew that Elena pretty much ran things.

Father John waited until the old woman's footsteps receded in the corridor and the heavy front door banged shut before he sat back down at the laptop open on his desk. It had surprised him how quickly the news out of the Casper TV station had burst across the internet. Dozens of newspapers, radio shows, TV news shows had featured the white buffalo calf. Dozens of blogs posted on the significance of the calf. He read through several. All filled with wonder. So much longing, he thought, for something holy in the world.

He shut down the laptop, waiting while it cycled silently through different phases before the screen went dark. A four-year-old laptop, practically an antique, but he was attached to it. Familiar with its ways. He was about to start down the corridor to tell the bishop he was going out for a while when he heard the thrum of an engine coming around Circle Drive. He walked over to the window and watched a silver pickup bump to a stop in front of the administration building. A tall cowboy in a tan hat jumped out of the driver's seat. He had the slump-shouldered, bowlegged look of a rodeo rider. His boots scraped on the concrete steps.

Father John went out into the corridor

and motioned the cowboy inside. "How can I help you?" he said.

"Looking for the priest around here."

"You found him. Father John O'Malley." He could feel the cowboy's gaze taking in his red plaid shirt and blue jeans, his cowboy boots.

"You got a minute?"

Father John ushered the cowboy into his office. "Have a seat," he said, gesturing toward a side chair. It wasn't often cowboys wandered into the mission and wanted to talk, but from time to time they wandered in. Working on a ranch a hundred miles from anything that resembled a town, lonely, something gone wrong in their lives, and they found their way to the kind of place they remembered from when they were kids, a timeless, steady place, like a church or a mission. "Where you from?"

"Colorado Plateau. Name is Reg Hartly." Father John shook the man's hand. He could feel the tension beneath the rough, calloused palm.

"How can I help you?" Father John walked over and sat on the edge of the desk.

"I got a buddy that's gone missing. Came up here and hired on the Broken Buffalo last April. Left in late June. Nobody's heard from him since. Not his girlfriend, not his

233

folks. His Mom's dying, so I came to find him. Josh Barker. I was hoping you might've run into him."

"What makes you think he came to the mission?"

"I heard he got crossways with the owner. Figured if there was some trouble, he might've come looking for advice. His folks are Catholic, and Josh got brought up that way."

Father John stood up, went around the desk, and sat down. The old leather chair creaked under his weight. *I committed murder.* The voice from the confessional had never left his mind. In the middle of the night, driving across the rez, opera blaring, walking down the path to the residence, the voice trailing him: *I committed murder.*

He pulled over a pad and wrote Josh Barker on the top. Below the name, he wrote: Broken Buffalo. April–late June. There were no murders on the rez in June, nothing reported in the news, no bodies *found.* Dennis Carey wasn't shot until last week, long after Josh Barker had left. And yet, Sheila Carey had convinced herself one of the cowboys who had worked on the ranch had killed her husband. If Josh Barker was the man in the confessional, what had he done?

"What kind of trouble do you think your friend was in?"

The cowboy shrugged. "Didn't get on with the owner. From what I hear, nobody did. Cheated on the hired hands, paid late and then only part of what was owed. Always promising to settle up. Look." The cowboy held up one hand. "I know somebody shot the SOB. Wasn't Josh. He had too much going for him. Someday he was gonna take over the family ranch on the Plateau and build it up. He had plans, Josh, and he wasn't stupid. No way would he throw away his life over some cheating rancher. I figure he would've lit out of here, if he was able."

Father John didn't say anything for a moment. He drew a long black line under the name Josh Barker. Then another line. "Josh never came to the mission." Then he added, "As far as I know." He had no idea who the man in the confessional had been.

The cowboy started to get up, then settled back in, the dark shadow of a new thought playing on his face. "Some Indians took a shot at me last night. Trying to scare me off. I hear there's been other pickups shot at around here. Those Indians don't like outsiders like Josh or me taking jobs they think belong to them. I been thinking . . ."

235

He nodded and stared off into space. "I was awake all night trying to put it together. The way I got it figured, those Indians scared off Josh and other cowboys. Either scared them off, or . . ." He let the rest of his thought hang in the air. "The guy they really hated was the one hiring the cowboys. I figure they're the ones that killed Dennis Carey."

"You reported what happened?"

The cowboy nodded.

"I suggest you talk to FBI agent Ted Gianelli. He's investigating Carey's murder."

"I'm thinking I'll have a talk with the widow. I hear she's hiring new hands. I get on the ranch, I figure I might get a line on what happened to Josh." He jumped to his feet and started for the corridor. The straight back, the squared shoulders said it all: One way or another he would find Josh Barker. He had no intention of talking to the FBI.

Father John got up and went to the window. The silver pickup backed onto Circle Drive, gravel spraying behind the rear wheels. Then it shot forward. He could see the silver flashing through the cottonwoods. He was thinking about the beautiful Irish girl who had sat in his office in the same chair Reg Hartly had occupied. Nuala O'Brian, black-haired and blue-eyed, freckles sprinkled over her nose, had driven across the snow-blown plains from New Mexico looking for Jaime Madigan. He'd been raised Catholic, she had said, so it made sense that he might've come to the mission if he'd gotten into trouble. What kind of trouble? He had asked. She had shrugged. She didn't know, but there was always trouble, wasn't there? He'd told her the truth and watched the blue eyes darken in frustration and fear: He had never met Jaime Madigan. He had suggested she file a missing person report with the FBI and the tribal police. She had shaken her head, and he wondered if she had filed any reports. She had seemed so defeated — a little stoop in her shoulders — as if the mission had been her last hope. Jaime Madigan, he remembered, had also worked on the Broken Buffalo.

He walked down the corridor and found the bishop bent toward his own laptop.

"News is spreading." The bishop barely glanced up. "More visitors coming. Whole area will be affected." He was smiling at something on the screen, probably a picture of the white calf.

Father John said he was going out for a while. The bishop nodded, still smiling, eyes glued to the screen.

He found Ranchlands Employment wedged between a coffee shop and an outfitter halfway down Main Street. The office and the stores shared the same flat-roof, white-brick building with the sun blinking in the plate glass windows. Riverton was crowded. A group of people stood in front of the restaurant across the street waiting for lunch. Pickups, SUVs, and cars filled the spaces at the curbs. He had to drive two blocks beyond the office, make a U-turn, and drive back before he saw another pickup pulling out. He parked the Toyota into the vacant space and switched off the CD player. The notes of "Di sprezzo degno se stesso" hung in the breeze for a half second. He headed down the sidewalk past the outfitter, with displays of saddles, bridles, blankets, wading boots, and fishing poles, and let himself through the door with the initials RE imprinted on the front like a brand. A bell jangled into a small waiting room with three plastic chairs against the window and a small table littered with used magazines. A counter bisected the room. There was no one behind the desk on the other side. The odor of coffee clung to the office.

Father John walked over and pressed the bell on the counter. The sharp noise punctuated the cacophony of the door bell, which was still jangling. A minute passed, then another before a side door opened and Steve Mantle emerged, carrying a coffee mug. "Been expecting you," Steve said. "Come on back and have a seat." He motioned with his head toward the far end of the counter. "Just brewed some fresh coffee. Tempted?"

"Never can resist the temptation." Father John went over and lifted a section of counter. Steve had set the mug down on the desk and was gathering up magazines and papers that spilled over the seat of a wooden side chair. He dropped the stack next to the coffee mug and started back across the room. "How do you take it?" he called over one shoulder.

"Milk or cream. Powdered is fine."

Steve disappeared behind the closed door. Father John could hear the quiet shuffling of a focused task. Then the man was back, carrying a mug like an offering. He handed it across the desk and sat down in a swivel chair. Father John perched on the side chair and took a sip of coffee. The hot liquid bit at his throat.

"Been doing a little research this morning," Steve said, rolling closer to the computer screen. "Pretty slow lately. Most ranches have all the help they need. Only one hiring is the Broken Buffalo." He was tapping at the keys, the hunt-and-peck method, fingers moving quickly. "Here we go. Placed a couple of cowboys out on the Broken Buffalo a year ago last spring, six months or so after the Careys bought the place. Jack Imeg and Lou Cassell. I heard they left last fall. Dennis Carey showed up and said he was looking to hire a couple more hands. I had some cowboys looking for work, so I sent them over. Rejected all of them. They were good men, experienced with buffalo. So I called Dennis. 'Don't seem like I understand what you're looking for,' I told him. 'Maybe you'd better tell me what you didn't like about those cowboys.' 'Like them just fine,' he said. That was a lie. He didn't hire a one. Told me he had a small operation. Everybody had to get along real good. So he had to go with his gut feelings on whether the cowboys would fit in."

He tapped a few more keys and stared at the screen a long moment. "I interviewed all those cowboys. They'd fit in anywhere. Professionals, you know what I mean? Grew up on ranches around here, born in a saddle. Worked with horses and cattle since they were knee high to a grasshopper. Live in the outdoors, all kinds of weather. Nothing bothers them. Totally self-sufficient, those guys. A rare breed, getting rarer, you ask me, with more small ranches selling out to so-called agribusiness. Fancy name for corporations. It's like these cowboys are left over from another time. Hell, they can live off the land their whole lives. Hunt, fish, eat wild veggies and fruits. Tan skins and sew up their own clothes and moccasins. Use buffalo sinew for the thread and buffalo bones for awls, just like the Indians used to do. They can even fight off grizzlies. Know a couple of cowboys that did just that, and lived to tell the story, too. Most of them hired out to get enough money to start their own spread. None of them was good enough for Dennis and Sheila Carey."

"Too independent for the Careys? Maybe they thought they wouldn't take orders, or wouldn't stay around."

"Wouldn't stay around? You ask me,

nobody stays around that place. I had a mind to tell Dennis Carey to take his business somewhere else. There's a ranch employment agency in Casper covers the whole area. But my business is not that good." He heaved a long sigh. "Can't afford to drop clients even when they're nuts. So I sent over more prospects, and they hired a couple. Jaime Madigan and Hol Hammond."

"Jaime Madigan?"

"Irish lad. Red hair, freckles as thick as buffalo stew." Steve Mantle leaned forward and squinted at the computer screen. "Came from someplace in Ireland I never heard of. Grew up roping cattle, like he was in the West. Always wanted to come here, and one day he got enough together to fly himself and his girlfriend to New Mexico. Worked a couple years on a ranch on the Pecos until the owner sold out to a corporation. You know him?"

Father John shook his head. He told Mantle that he had met Madigan's fiancée last winter when she had come looking for him. He could still feel the worry, the desolation in the young woman wringing a tissue in her hands. *Jaime would never leave me.* She had finally returned to New Mexico, he supposed.

"Jaime left the ranch in February," Mantle said. He had been missing a month, Father John was thinking, when Nuala O'Brian had come to the mission. "Both of them, Jaime and Hol, collected their pay, packed up their gear, and took off. Told Carey they had a line on work in Idaho. He asked me to send over some prospects. We went through the same dance for a couple weeks. Nobody quite what they were looking for. Nobody that would fit into that ranch of theirs."

Steve tapped another couple of keys and blinked at the screen. "Finally hired on Josh Barker and Rick Tomlin." He looked up. "You ask me, that was a mistake, with all their careful interviewing. Tomlin was a troublemaker. In the bars whenever he got time off, or took the time. Maybe you read about him in the *Gazette*. Got in a fight at a bar in Riverton last June. Accused some Arapaho of assaulting him. Case was supposed to go to trial a couple days ago, but Tomlin never showed up." He was shaking his head. "He was one cowboy that didn't fit the mold. I wouldn't call it professional to accuse somebody of assault, make yourself the star witness, and not show up. Can't recall the Arapaho's name."

"Arnie Walksfast."

"You know him?"

Father John nodded. He was thinking that he'd known Arnie since he was a kid. Came out for the Eagles a couple of seasons. A good fielder, and the best hitter on the team. The next season, he didn't show up. Father John had gone over to the small house with blue paint peeling off the sideboards and a musty odor of old things inside. Arnie's mother had raised him alone. Father John wasn't sure about the boy's father. He had never heard the man mentioned. Arnie was getting hard to handle, he remembered the woman saying, running with the wrong bunch. She had been crying, and trying hard not to cry, sinking deeper and deeper into an overstuffed chair, as if it could have swallowed her. He had told her he'd be glad to talk to Arnie, and she had said she would ask him to stop by the mission. She couldn't *tell* him to go. *Order* him to go. Warriors don't take orders, she'd said. Arnie had never shown up, and Father John had gone back to the house two or three times. Just Arnie's mother, sinking into the chair, desolation clinging to her like smoke.

Arnie had been in and out of trouble ever since. Father John had gotten used to seeing his name in the newspaper, or hearing the news on the moccasin telegraph. It was

Vicky who fought to keep him out of jail. From the rumor he'd heard, Vicky had managed to have the assault charges reduced in a plea deal that sent Arnie off for another round of rehab.

Still, it was strange that the cowboy who'd accused Arnie of assault had failed to show up.

"What happened to Rick Tomlin and the other cowboy?"

"Same as the others. Packed their gear . . ."

Father John put up a hand. A pattern was emerging; always a pattern, if you could detect it. Beneath the obvious lay the logic. "All the cowboys white?"

"Yeah. Dennis never came right out and said he wouldn't hire Indians. The guy was savvy. Didn't want to bring any federal busybodies down on him for discrimination, but I got the message. Didn't trust them, even though I placed lots of Indians that turned out to be steady, hard workers. Nobody can manage horses like Arapahos, I told him. He was sitting in your chair. He just shrugged. He said, 'You know the kind we like.' "

The pattern surfaced like a bunch of dots that formed a picture after you've stared at them long enough. But something else caught Father John's attention. "Two cowboys were from Colorado. What about the others?"

Steve went back to tapping keys and blinking at the screen. "Colorado, New Mexico, Utah."

"Nobody from around here." Another pattern, the picture dark and steady now. "Why do you think the Careys only hired outsiders?"

Steve Mantle shrugged. He pushed back from the computer and stared off into space, as if he might find the answer. "I told you, Carey was nuts. Don't repeat that, please. I don't want word getting out I'm bad-mouthing clients. What am I saying? You're a priest. Used to keeping secrets, huh?"

Father John took a moment. There was still something else, flitting past like a whisper. He tried to listen hard, but the whisper drifted away. Finally he put on his cowboy hat and was about to thank the man and get to his feet when he grasped the rest of the pattern. "Looks like the Careys hired cowboys two at a time. And they both left at the same time. Is that right?"

Steve Mantle sat quietly. "Not exactly."

"Not exactly?"

"Sent four or five applicants to the ranch

in June after the last cowboys left. Dennis hired two, like usual. Carlos Mondregan and Lane Preston. They're still there. Been sending cowboys over the last few days since that white buffalo calf was born. So far Dennis . . ." He paused and drew in a deep breath. "Sheila's had to take over, and she's hired five. Still looking, from what I hear, but the word's out now. Cowboys are going to show up at the ranch on their own. Don't need the help of old Steve Mantle."

Father John didn't say anything for a moment. At least for now, the pattern was broken.

And yet, it had only been broken in the last couple of days. "According to my count," he said, "you placed six cowboys on the ranch in the last year and a half. Dennis hired them in pairs. They quit in pairs. Is that usual?"

"Coincidence." Steve lifted his shoulders, then let them fall. "Cowboys ride the range, bunk together, eat together. They get to talking. One plants an idea in the other's mind. Heard of a good opportunity in Idaho or Montana. Always rumors on the cowboy circuit, so they decide to take off together."

"You see the same thing on other ranches?"

Steve was quiet a moment, staring down

at the keyboard. Finally he looked up. "Broken Buffalo's the only place I ever seen it."

22

The brown pickup parked in front of the administration building didn't look familiar. Father John drove around Circle Drive, his eyes on the pickup. A long dent — a slash — along the driver's side. Splotches of primer paint here and there. Frame sinking on bald tires. The pickup might belong to any number of people on the rez.

He pulled in next to it. As he got out, he saw an Indian emerge from the shadows in the alley between the administration building and the church. Shuffling, bent partway forward, as if an invisible rope were pulling him along. He glanced up past the brim of a brown cowboy hat. "Got a minute, Father?" he called.

"Of course." Father John knew the man. Lewis White Feather, in his fifties with the look of a man thirty years older, placing one boot after the other on the gravel as if the earth might shift beneath him. He had the grooved, weatherworn features and the sallow, yellowish complexion of a man who had divided his time between the outdoors and the bars. Father John could smell the whiskey from ten feet away.

"Been waiting for you." Lewis drew up next to him. He was making an effort — oh, Father John recognized the effort — to appear steady and in control when everything was spinning out of control. "You heard about the calf?"

"I have."

"She's a miracle from the Creator. Don't matter how bad things get, the Creator is still with us. Still cares about what happens to the people. I went out to the ranch this morning. Had to wait a couple hours with a bunch of other Indians for some white cowboy to escort us out to the pasture. 'Escort.' That's what they call it. Hurried us along after we got out there, but I left my gift of tobacco. Tied a medicine bag to the fence. There was lots of gifts going up on the fence. Folks paying respect and leaving signs of thanksgiving. You know what a white buffalo calf means?"

"Hope."

The Indian grinned and nodded. "We got hope. We can do better. Spirit come to let us know we aren't alone. The Creator is with us. We forget that lots of times. I came here to take the pledge."

"Where would you like to take it?" Father John tried for a smile of encouragement. He had given the pledge to many Arapahos. An oath, taken on the Bible, not to drink alcohol for a month or two months or longer, if the man — or the woman; he had pledged many women — thought they could do it. Lewis had taken the pledge two or three times before. He had managed to stay sober afterward. Until the end of the pledge period.

"I went out by the Little Wind River while I was waiting. I can feel the spirits of the ancestors there."

"Hold on a minute." Father John took the steps in front of the administration building two at a time and let himself inside. Bishop Harry's voice floated down the corridor. The phone had probably been ringing since he'd left with people wanting to talk about the calf. Whenever there was what he thought of as a touchstone, a junction between Indian beliefs and Christianity, the phone started ringing. People dropped by. *What do we think about this?* He had asked himself the same question. Even the bishop, he knew, had asked the question. Sometimes there was no knowing, no explaining. Only

accepting that the Creator worked in mysterious ways.

He took his Bible from the shelf behind
his desk, found his stole in the drawer, and
hung it around his neck. Outside, Lewis was
staring down the alley toward the trees that
fringed the river. He fell in beside the man,
trying to keep to Lewis's slow, deliberate
pace. Past Eagle Hall, past the guesthouse,
where Lewis had stayed a couple of years
ago after his wife, Marty, had thrown him
out. Set his moccasins at the front door,
was how Lewis had explained it.

They walked down the path that wound
through the stands of cottonwoods and
scrub brush. The air was cooler, the dirt
softer in the shade. "Ancestors had
troubles." Lewis's voice was quiet, reflective. "Just like now. People need jobs to feed
their kids. Kids need to go to school. The
ancestors, they never lost hope. They come
here to give us a better life."

Father John was quiet, waiting for the man
to go on. He had heard stories about the
ancestors, stories handed down in families,
bits and pieces of information he had never
seen in any history book, about what it was
like when the Arapahos had arrived on the
Wind River Reservation almost a hundred
and fifty years ago. It was the Shoshone

reservation. Chiefs Black Coal and Sharpnose had gone to the Shoshone chief, Washakie, and asked if the people could come under his blanket. Eight hundred Arapahos, survivors of the Indian Wars, sick, hungry, with no place else to go. Washakie had agreed. *We were a pitiful sight,* he remembered one of the grandfathers saying.

"My grandfather's father was here," Lewis said. Father John could hear the gurgling sounds of the river; not much more than a creek, really. The path was widening, as if it would spill into the creek. Lewis stopped at a fallen log and gazed at the water tumbling over boulders, glistening in pockets of sunshine. "People didn't have food. His little daughter was dying. They prayed to the Creator to help them." He shifted slowly around until he faced Father John. "I think the Creator must have sent a white buffalo calf back then as a sign the people needed to hold on to hope. Same as now."

Lewis put up one hand, palm forward in the Plains Indian sign of peace. Father John held out the Bible, and Lewis set his other hand on top. "I pledge to stop drinking for . . ." He gulped, as if he were trying to pull the words out of his throat. "Sixty days. I pledge sixty days. I ask the Creator and Jesus our Lord to help me. I thank the

Creator for sending the calf that showed me what I had to do."

Father John made the sign of the cross over the man. "God bless you." Then he said, "God will bless you, Lewis."

He waited until Lewis White Feather had lifted himself into the brown pickup and settled around the steering wheel. He leaned down toward the open window and told Lewis to stop by the mission any time he wanted to talk. AA meetings on Tuesday nights. Once in a while Lewis came. The pickup cranked into life, spit out black exhaust, and wobbled around Circle Drive into the cottonwood tunnel, grayish exhaust trailing behind. "God help you," Father John said out loud.

Bishop Harry was still on the telephone. Father John marveled at the patience in the old man's voice as he walked down the corridor to the back office. The bishop leaned sideways into the phone clamped to his ear. "Yes. Yes. We must be very grateful. Yes, indeed. The white buffalo calf is sacred." After a moment, the bishop smiled, and said, "It is no trouble. Call anytime." He dropped the phone into the cradle and looked up, light flickering in his eyes.

"The calf has everybody talking and thinking about God." He nodded toward the phone. "How can that be anything but a miracle?"

"Would you like to see the calf?"

The bishop nodded. "Very much."

"We'll take a drive out to the ranch later."

"I'm afraid I have bad news."

Father John had turned around and was about to head to his own office. He turned back. "Another random shooting on the rez last night," the bishop said.

"I've heard. A cowboy from Colorado by the name of Reg Hartly. Fortunately he wasn't hurt."

"A couple of callers mentioned the shooting. People don't know how to take it. The birth of the calf should bring peace and hope. Instead, people are frightened. Took place out on the highway north of the casino. About a mile from the mission."

Father John held the old man's gaze a moment. Reg Hartly hadn't said where the shooting had taken place. Dear Lord, a mile from the mission! He turned slowly and started back down the corridor. The phone rang as he walked into his own office. He took the space between the door and the desk in three steps, but before he could pick up, the ringing stopped. Bishop Harry's voice reverberating in the old building: "Yes,

yes, we have certainly been blessed."

He sat down at his desk and squared the notepad in front of him. He drew a black line halfway down the page below the names of Josh Barker and Jaime Madigan. Then he wrote the date and the words "Interview with Steve Mantle, Ranchlands Employment." Coach for the Riverton Rangers, he was thinking, determined to beat the Eagles and claim the league championship, father of a boy on the team. Good coach, good man.

He starting writing down what Steve had told him. Get it down, get it down before it evaporated like smoke. Six cowboys hired by the Broken Buffalo in a year and a half, outsiders, all of them. White. Hired in pairs, left in pairs. Except for Carlos Mondregan, the man he had met when he and Banner had gone to notify Sheila Carey about her husband, and another hand, Lane Preston. Other cowboys hired in the past few days to handle the crowds. Four or five that Steve knew about.

He flipped to a new page and made a column of names. Two by two down one side of the notepad, in the order in which they had been hired and had left. He wrote the dates next to the names. Jack Imeg, Lou Cassell, a year ago last spring, left last fall.

Jaime Madigan and Hol Hammond, hired last fall and left in February. Rick Tomlin, Josh Barker, hired in April. Left in late June. He drew circles around Jaime Madigan and Josh Barker, who seemed to have disappeared. Then he drew a circle around Rick Tomlin, who'd failed to show up to testify at Arnie Walksfast's trial.

He opened the laptop, gave it the minute or two it required to wake up, and typed Nuala O'Brian in the search engine. A list of sites came up. Singer at McCloskeys pub in Dublin. Physical therapist, Danbury, Connecticut. Second grade teacher in New Orleans. None of them the girl who had sat in his office swallowing back tears. He'd had the feeling it was all the girl could do to keep from running out the door screaming with heartbreak and fear.

Then he saw it. Nuala O'Brian's Day Care, Albuquerque, New Mexico. He waited until the bishop's voice went quiet before he picked up the phone and punched in the number. "O'Brian's Day Care." The voice on the other end was sunny and energetic. He could picture the woman out on a playground pushing kids on a swing. He told her he was calling for Nuala O'Brian.

"I'm afraid she's not here. If this is about registration, I can help you. We are still accepting children for the fall semester."

"Can you tell me how I can reach her?"

The question seemed to stop the woman. She took a couple of seconds before she said, "May I ask what this is about?"

"My name is Father John O'Malley. I'm at St. Francis Mission on the Wind River Reservation. Nuala came to see me last winter about her fiancé."

"Jaime? This is about Jaime? He's been found? He's dead, isn't he?"

"I'm afraid I don't have any news." Father John let the words settle a moment. He hoped the man wasn't dead. "How can I reach Nuala?"

"She's in Ireland. I'll give her the message next time she calls."

Father John thanked her and gave her the mission's number along with his cell number. Then he hung up, drew a line under the notes he'd made, and wrote Nuala O'Brian and the telephone number. He stared at the words a moment before he wrote: Jaime Madigan still missing.

The phone rang again, but when he answered, the bishop was already on the line. He slipped his cell out of his shirt pocket and slid his finger over Vicky's name. "Vicky Holden's office." The secretary's voice was familiar; so many times he had called when he needed to talk to Vicky. Would she have time to see him today?

"I will give her the message," Annie said.

23

He was in a traffic jam. A two-track dirt road across the plains, and a line of pickups, SUVs, and dust-covered cars stretching ahead. Reg pounded on the steering wheel, frustration burning like acid in his throat. The line moved forward a couple of feet. He moved with it, closing in on a white SUV with a New Mexico license plate. God, at this rate, he would be here all day, the sun beating down, the air like fire. The air-conditioning in the truck had conked out last summer, and he hadn't had the cash to get it fixed. The windows were down, but the temperature was ninety-five and rising.

The line inched forward again. Reg tapped on the gas, then the brake. Stop. Go. Stop. Go. He studied the people in the truck behind him. Indians. Man in a black cowboy hat behind the wheel, woman in the passenger seat fanning herself with a magazine. Two black-headed, brown-faced kids in the rear seat popping up between them. Air-conditioning must not be working for them, either. They had come a long way. The license plate was from Oklahoma.

People from across the country coming to see the white buffalo calf. He had never seen a white buffalo, even though he had spent two years working a bison ranch in southern Colorado and had watched the birth of a lot of calves. Fuzzy, wiggling, black. Sometimes he wondered if the white buffalo was nothing but a legend, handed down through generations of Indians to convince themselves they had a special connection to the Creator. He would send the white buffalo in times of need — except He never did, in Reg's experience, and God knew Indians had seen lots of needy times.

Now a white buffalo calf born on the Broken Buffalo. He had to admit he looked forward to seeing it. Which would probably mean waiting in more lines. His fist made a hard, popping sound against the steering wheel. He stared at the SUV and tried to grasp the image at the edges of his mind: The owner of the ranch in Colorado, seated on a log around a campfire one evening after they had been riding the fence, looking for breaks. A small buffalo herd grazing off in the pasture, huge, black hulks against the gray sky. "One of those white calves the Indians talk about gets born here, you know what to do."

Reg had waited. They were sipping beer and had just finished eating stew out of cans. He hadn't thought about doing anything different if a white calf were born. Leave the mother and calf alone. The mother would have gone off a ways from the rest of the herd to have her calf. She would introduce the calf when she was ready. Not until she was ready would she allow the tractor and flatbed to come close enough so that Reg or one of the other hands could fork off a bale of hay.

"Shoot it."

"What?" Reg had spit out a mouthful of beer to keep from choking. Buffalo were expensive animals; it cost money to raise a herd. What sense did it make to destroy a calf?

"Those are my orders."

Now he understood why. Thousands of people converging on the ranch to see the white calf, trampling the pastures, breaking through fences. Lines of traffic clogging the roads, like the road he was on now. What rancher would welcome such a blessing?

See where it had gotten the owners of the Broken Buffalo? Dennis Carey shot to death. The widow left to cope with thousands of visitors. A new thought hit him: what if there was a connection between the birth of the calf and the man's death? Reg shrugged the thought away. The Indians had taken care of Dennis Carey, he was sure of it. And one thing he had learned cowboying was to take care of his own business and nobody else's. The calf and all the visitors and the ranching itself were the widow's problem now. All he wanted was to find out what had happened to Josh.

He realized the line had stalled. The same clump of sagebrush outside his window, the same hawk diving and swirling overhead. He slammed a fist hard against the edge of the wheel, then jerked the wheel sideways, stomped on the gas pedal and pulled around the white SUV. He kept going, past the line of vehicles, bouncing over the ridged, hard-packed earth, tearing through the scrub brush like a race car driver. Keep truck upright, avoid obstacles, keep going.

He could see the gate ahead, the cowboys bent toward the passenger window of a black truck. Finally one of the cowboys waved the driver over to another line of vehicles waiting to get into the pasture that had been turned into a parking lot. The lot was already full, with rows of vehicles stacked around the arroyos and brush. Two other cowboys were running up and down waving trucks and cars toward the far end of the rows. The cowboy who had told him yesterday that Josh Barker had never worked here didn't seem to be anywhere around.

He ignored the tall, horse-faced cowboy running toward him, arms flailing, motioning him back into line, and drove for the gate. He slid to a stop, jumped out, and walked over to the stocky, dark-haired man staring at him from beneath the rim of his cowboy hat. He looked Hispanic. Not many Hispanics in this area, but he'd known a lot of Hispanic cowboys in southern Colorado. Reg could see the handle of the pistol on the cowboy's hip. Smells of dust and sagebrush blew in the air. Men shouted, engines growled. The horse-faced cowboy appeared at his side and grabbed his arm. He pulled away. "I got an appointment," he shouted.

"Let him go." The Hispanic cowboy fixed the other man with a death-ray gaze. Then he turned to Reg. "Who are you?"

"Reg Hartly. Here to see Mrs. Carey. She knows I'm coming." It was true. The Indian lawyer lady had told Mrs. Carey to expect him. What he didn't tell the cowboy was that Mrs. Carey had threatened to have him thrown off the ranch if he showed up. "Okay if I go on up to the house?"

"You here about a job?"

Reg took a moment. The idea had been floating around his mind since last night. Hiring on here, seeing what he could learn about Josh. "Yeah. I hear she's hiring." He threw a glance at the line of pickups, the other cowboys running about. "Need a lot of help to handle this crowd."

"Wait over there." The Hispanic cowboy nodded toward a couple dozen cowboys standing off to the left. They'd been waiting in the sun awhile. He could see the dark bands of sweat on the backs of their shirts. Another group of cowboys was forming. At any moment the Hispanic could announce the quota had been filled, and he would lose whatever chance he might have to get to the ranch house.

"You don't understand. Mrs. Carey's expecting me."

"Good story. Too bad you're the fiftieth guy to use it." The cowboy was implacable, face stone-set. "Over there."

Reg shifted about. He didn't want to push things. The last thing he needed was for the Hispanic to call the house to check on his story. He was about to start toward the first group of cowboys, all watching him, sloped forward, thumbs hooked in the pockets of their blue jeans, desperation in their faces.

"Hold on."

Reg turned back.

"Ranchlands send you?"

"That's right." Reg didn't hesitate. Ranchlands could be anything, but it was a way in.

"Why didn't you say so?"

"I told you Mrs. Carey was expecting me."

"Go on up to the house. Leave your truck here. No vehicles past the gate." He reached over and lifted the gate. Reg darted under.

The log house stood at the end of the dirt road, windows blinking in the sun. He walked fast, eager to leave the noise and confusion behind. A white wooden chair creaked on the porch as he came up the steps. He was about to knock on the door when it swung open so fast that he thought Sheila Carey must have heard his steps. The Hispanic cowboy had probably called up to the house after all.

"Ranchlands?" The woman was small and attractive: reddish hair falling around her shoulders, green eyes appraising him as if he were one of the ranch animals.

"That's right."

She gestured with her head for him to come inside. Still appraising him, he thought, taking her time before she said,

"We'll talk in the study."

He followed her around the oak staircase that dropped into the entry, past pocket doors folded into the walls. The study was large and filled with sunshine that streamed through the windows. A fan hummed in the corner next to the desk, sending gusts of warm air across the room. "Have a seat," she said, jabbing a finger toward a straight-backed metal chair. She dropped into a black-framed chair behind the desk and set a notepad in front of her. "Start with particulars. Name. Where you come from."

"Reg Hartly. Colorado." He watched the complacent expression on her face dissolve into a hard knot of comprehension. A red flush started up her throat.

"I told your Indian lady friend . . ."

"She's not a friend."

"Vicky Holden seemed to be under that impression. Concerned about your missing buddy. I fail to see how the cowboys on this ranch could be any business of hers. Ranchlands sent you?"

Reg clasped his hands between his knees and leaned forward. "Yeah." He was thinking Ranchlands must be some kind of employment agency. "Look, Mrs. Carey, I came here to find Josh Barker. He's gone missing. One of your hands told me Josh never worked here."

"I suppose Steve Mantle gave you some story about your buddy working here. Well, I keep the records on this ranch, not Ranchlands. I don't care what that lying sonofabitch Mantle told you." She swiveled sideways and looked out the front window. He would check out Ranchlands, he was thinking. They might have records on Josh.

Sheila Carey squared herself again at the desk. "You can walk out of here, or I can have my cowboys beat the crap out of you and carry you out. Your choice." She stretched an arm over the desk and picked up the phone.

"Josh isn't the only reason I'm here."

The woman sliced the air with the phone. "Get out."

"I hear you're hiring."

Something seemed to change behind her eyes. She stared at him a long moment. "Why would you want to work here?"

"I'm running short of cash, and you need a lot of hands."

She seemed to consider this a moment. "You got experience with buffalo?"

"Couple years on a buffalo ranch in Colorado. I know how to work around the animals. They're tricky, require a lot of skill. And smarts," he added. "Seems to me you need help controlling crowds right now, but ranch work has to go on. Most those cowboys out there never got close to a buffalo. Wouldn't know what to do if one charged him."

"What would you do?"

"Stay out of the buffalo's way, and it won't be charging."

The shadow of a smile played at the edges of her mouth. "You sound like my husband, Dennis. You heard he was murdered?"

"I'm sorry."

She nodded. Reg half expected her to say she was sorry, too. Instead, she leaned forward and dropped the phone into its cradle.

"We pay when we butcher and sell the meat or when we sell a calf or bull. We've got a contract with an organic health food chain, stores all over the west. I'm telling you this so you'll know we're good for the money."

"How long would I have to wait?"

"Don't worry. You'll have plenty to eat. You'll sleep in the bunkhouse, nice and dry, plenty warm in the winter. I can let you have an advance from time to time when I get the cash. You understand, we're a small operation and — and I've been forced to hire extra hands. Lot of expense with this

269

buffalo calf, but . . ." She hesitated, then seemed to shut down, whatever she had been about to say pushed back. "You got your gear?"

"In my truck." He had packed up the tent and sleeping bag, the small kit of utensils, and cleared the campsite in Sinks Canyon. He hadn't known what he might find at the ranch. Some word on Josh Barker — who had never worked here. At least that was what Sheila Carey and her hired hand wanted him to believe. Never worked on a spread that he'd written home about. Had even sent a photo of the ranch house.

"Take it to the bunkhouse in back, then go find Carlos, my foreman. He's at the gate. He'll give you instructions. We have fences to mend."

"I'd like to see the calf."

"Spirit? You'll see her when you ride the fence."

24

"Now for the news. Another random shooting took place on the reservation last night."

Vicky had been about to turn onto Ethete Road when the news program started. She had spent the last hour meeting with Charlie Red Deer, one of the elders, confined to his bed now, a stick figure beneath the white sheets. Wanting her to draw up his will. Connie Red Deer had bustled about, delivering glasses of water, while Vicky made notes. There wouldn't be much to leave four daughters. A hundred acres of scrub brush, a few ponies, a herd of ten cattle.

She kept her foot on the brake and stared at the radio in the dashboard.

"The shooter fired a rifle at a passing truck on Highway 789 north of the casino. Driver of the truck, identified as Reg Hartly, a Colorado resident, was not injured, although the bullet entered and exited the truck bed. State patrol combed the area east of the highway where the shot came from but were unsuccessful in finding any evidence. This is the fifth random shooting on the rez this year. Anybody with information should contact BIA law enforcement."

Vicky shifted into neutral and switched off the radio. Except for the warm gusts of wind blowing past the open windows, the Ford was quiet. She was grateful for the silence. Reg Hartly. Why hadn't he mentioned the shooting when she'd run into him last night at the casino? Had it happened later? Another white cowboy in the area. Arnie's friends could have assumed he was looking for a job they believed should go to them. But Reg wasn't looking for a job.

Someone honked behind her. She glanced in the rearview mirror at a pickup sliding in close. A cowboy in a black hat glared at her over the steering wheel, then lifted his hand and pointed toward the road. Vicky put the gearshift in drive and turned left, watching the pickup charge to the right, swinging back and forth, tires squealing. She found her cell in her bag and pushed the button for the office.

"Vicky?" Annie's voice was loud, tense. "You heard the news?"

"I just heard. I need you to call the rehab

272

clinic and tell them I have to see Arnie Walksfast."

"I understand." Vicky wondered if Annie did understand. She hadn't told Annie or anyone else what her client had confided in her about the shootings, but that didn't mean Annie hadn't absorbed the truth somehow. Or heard rumors on the rez.

"What have you heard about the shootings?"

"Nothing solid."

"But you've heard something."

"You know how gossip is."

"On the moccasin telegraph?"

"Speculation, that's all. Maybe the warriors decided to run off cowboys from out of state. Might be hoping word will get around this isn't a real friendly place for outsiders. You ask me, the Indians are hoping they'll get hired on the local ranches."

"Have you heard any names?"

"Nobody's snitching, if that's what you mean. Besides, it's just rumor. Could be some nutcase in Riverton shooting at folks. Tell you the truth, people are scared. So far the shooter's targeted white outsiders, but who knows when he might decide to shoot at locals? I mean, can he always tell the difference? Somebody's going to end up like that white rancher. You think they're connected? The shootings and the murder?"

Vicky could hear the sound of dread in Annie's voice. It matched her own feeling. "I don't know," she managed.

"Father John called. He wants to see you sometime today."

Vicky told her to call him back and say she would stop by the mission in a couple of hours. Then she ended the call and drove toward Riverton.

The waiting room was cool; an air-conditioning unit hummed overhead. Vicky had tried to sit in one of the plastic chairs pushed against the wall, but she found herself pacing back and forth. The glass doors at the front radiated the sunshine. Beyond the doors was the long driveway that ran across the front of the clinic, and beyond that, the parking lot. A few cars scattered about. She had parked in the front row. The nurse in green scrubs who had met her in the waiting room said Arnie was still in physical therapy. Did she want to wait?

She would wait, Vicky told her.

Finally the solid metal door across from the front opened, and the same nurse — blond hair pinned into a bun, light, pale skin and light, pale eyes — motioned her forward. "He's resting in his room."

Vicky followed the woman down one corridor, then another, past a row of windows that looked onto a gymnasium, patients walking treadmills and lifting weights. A mixture of Indians and whites, trying to work off alcohol and drugs. The nurse had stopped at an opened door and ushered Vicky inside. "He meets with the psychotherapist in thirty minutes."

Arnie Walksfast was propped up on the bed, half sitting, half lying, irritation pooling in his black eyes. "Mind if I don't get up? Had enough frickin' exercise today."

"We need to talk, Arnie." Vicky closed the door, walked past the metal chair kept for visitors and stood at the side of the bed. "You heard what happened last night?"

"This is rehab. It's not the moon."

"Let me lay it out for you. Sooner or later the cops will track down one of the shooters. When that happens, he'll start shouting names to save his own neck. If you are involved, you will be indicted for conspiracy to commit murder, assault with a deadly weapon, and a whole lot of other charges the prosecutor will think up."

"What do you expect? I'm gonna call somebody and stop the shootings? I'm not the boss. I told you, a bunch of us decided to make it tough on the bastards coming here for our jobs."

"You know who's involved."

"I'm not gonna snitch, if that's what you're getting at."

"You're going to wait until some random cowboy gets killed? A man's already been killed. Every law enforcement agency in the area is working the case, and sooner or later they're going to turn up the shooter. If your buddies had anything to do with it, you could end up in prison for the rest of your life." Vicky took a long moment, her eyes fastened on the man slumped on the bed. The smallest twitch in his cheeks, a tightening of his lips? She wasn't sure if she imagined them.

Finally she said, "I can arrange for you to talk to Ted Gianelli."

"You crazy? I'm not talking to any fed. What kind of lawyer are you? You want to throw me to the wolves?"

"We make a deal. You tell him what you know about the shootings, and in return, he might be willing to cut you some slack."

"No frickin' way!" Arnie bolted upright. Vicky felt the crack of a knee against her hip as he swung both legs over the side of the bed. "What I told you is — what do you call it? — confidential. You can't tell anyone, or I swear I'll find some way to ruin you.

Maybe even . . ."

"What? Shoot at me while I'm driving down the highway? Hope to frighten me enough to leave the area like you and your friends are trying to do with the cowboys? I'm trying to help you, Arnie. You can close down these shootings before it's too late."

"Go to hell!"

Vicky took a long moment. Her tongue felt dry against her teeth, miniature tombstones in her mouth. "I think you had better find another lawyer. I'll inform your probation officer I'm no longer representing you." She swung around and started for the door.

"Wait a minute." She glanced back, holding on to the doorknob. "They'll take me out if I snitch."

"Who?"

"What does it matter? You snitch, you die. Maybe not next week or next month. But nobody forgets. I'll be driving down the road some night and a truck will crowd me, force me into a ditch. I won't see the guy coming for me. Most I can do is get a message to one of my buddies to knock it off."

Vicky didn't say anything. Admitting he had the influence to stop the shootings meant Arnie was involved. Sooner or later Gianelli or the state patrol or some other cop from some other agency would break the case wide open, and Arnie's mother would be in her office, begging Vicky to save her son.

But Arnie Walksfast would be alive. She turned away, flung the door open and retraced her steps down the corridors. The nurse in green scrubs glanced up from the clipboard in her hand. "Everything okay?"

Vicky kept going.

She sat in the Ford, breeze blowing in her hair, aware of her heart thumping against her ribs. Why did she care so much? Another Indian, a warrior, on his way to life in prison, and there was nothing she could do. Nothing *right.* She had been hoping to appeal to his sense of self-preservation, and maybe she had. He knew how to stay alive, and he understood he would be dead if he talked to Gianelli.

She turned the ignition, backed into the lot, and drove onto the street, heaviness weighing on her. There was nothing she could do except forget he had told her about the random shootings. And Dennis Carey's murder had been different; he had pulled over and waited for his killer.

The afternoon heat was unrelenting, a fireball falling out of the sky. She drove

278

through town. People everywhere, wandering the streets, stacking up outside shops and cafés. How many more on the way? When she had checked the internet this morning, she'd been stunned by the number of sites on the white buffalo calf. Bloggers in Venezuela and Geneva talking about the calf. My God, would they all come? The rez could collapse under the weight. And how could Sheila Carey handle the crowds?

She drove south on 789, where she settled behind a pickup taking its time, the cowboy behind the wheel looking about, as if to get his bearings. She wondered where the shooter had hidden in wait for Reg Hartly. She understood the truth now. The shootings were not random. Arnie had admitted his buddies had shot at Rick Tomlin to force him out of the area. And now Reg Hartly, another white cowboy who could be taking a job. Maybe Josh Barker had been a target.

She slowed for a right turn and headed west. Looming over the road against the heat-whitened sky was a blue billboard with large white letters that shone in the sun: ST. FRANCIS MISSION. She made a left, plunged into the long shadows through the cottonwoods, and took a deep breath. The air was cooler here, the heat at bay. Then out of the tunnel and back in the sunshine as she curved around Circle Drive. Annie would have called the mission, but John O'Malley could be anywhere: visiting elders at the senior citizens' center, stopping by to see the shut-ins, making the rounds of parishioners in the hospital. Anywhere. But the old red Toyota pickup that looked as if it had escaped from a junkyard stood in front of the administration building.

She pulled in alongside, found her cell in her bag, and called the office. "I need some information," she told Annie. "See if you can get the names of the people whose vehicles were shot at."

Annie said she would get on it, and Vicky was about to hit the end button when she remembered something else. "See if you can find out where Lucy Murphy is staying."

She let herself out of the Ford and made her way up the familiar concrete steps.

25

"Sempre Libera" drifted through the office like white noise, punctuated from time to time by Bishop Harry's voice down the corridor. Phone calls were still coming in. And, Father John had to admit, the old man had the patter down, encouraging people to go and see the white calf for themselves. So many sacred things in the world, it is good to *see* them.

He finished going over the numbers for this month's budget, checking and rechecking the columns on the laptop in the faint hope the sum might land somewhere outside of the red zone. No matter how hard he tried to keep the expenses within the mission's income — a nebulous amount that depended on the generosity of strangers — there were always unexpected expenses. Sandy Moon's new baby, born last week without an esophagus, flown to a hospital in Denver. Last Sunday he had taken up a special collection so Sandy could stay in a motel close to her baby, but in the end he'd had to take money out of the mission budget. The so-called budget. He laughed out loud, as if St. Francis were a business with defined income and expenses.

He had just closed the program when he heard the scrunch of tires on Circle Drive. The noise stopped. A moment later a door slammed. There was the tap-tap-tap of familiar footsteps on the concrete steps. The wind must have caught the front door, because it cracked shut, sending a tremor through the old floor. He got to his feet as Vicky walked into the office. "Have a seat. What can I get you? Coffee? Coke?"

"Water." She dropped onto a side chair.

"I can do that." Father John went out into the corridor and took the first right into a little hallway that led to the archives and what passed for a kitchen. Nothing more than a closet, really: sink, small refrigerator, one cabinet stuffed with paper cups, a can of coffee, and an assortment of mismatched glasses. He filled two of the glasses with cold water, then added a couple of ice cubes from the freezer tray, which sent the water cascading over the sides and into a puddle on the floor. He found a towel, swiped at the puddle, and carried the glasses back into the office.

"Annie said you wanted to see me?" Vicky took the glass he held out for her. No longer sitting; pacing in front of the window, a small, shadowy figure backlit by the sunlight. He was used to the way she liked to talk and walk at the same time. So many things about her he had become accustomed to.

He sat on the edge of the desk and took a drink of the cold water. Even the thick old walls hadn't kept out the day's heat. "I spoke with Steve Mantle at Ranchlands Employment. Do you know him?"

Vicky shook her head. "But I've heard of the business. They place cowboys on ranches in the area." She sipped at her water, watching him over the rim of the glass. "Did they place anyone on the Broken Buffalo?"

"Six cowboys in the last year and a half. Jack Imeg and Lou Cassell were the first hired. Then, last fall, Jaime Madigan and Hol Hammond. In April, the ranch took on Rick Tomlin and Josh Barker."

"Let me guess," Vicky said. "All from somewhere else."

"That isn't the only pattern. In each case, two cowboys were hired together and left together. Mantle said that was unusual. Cowboys might decide to move on, but not at the same time as the guys they were hired on with."

"Josh Barker? Mantle has records that Barker was hired at the Broken Buffalo?"

"He and Rick Tomlin worked there two months."

Vicky swung around, walked to the door, then came back. She finished the water and set the glass down on a tablet at the corner of his desk. "A cowboy by the name of Reg Hartly has come here to find Barker. I asked Sheila Carey about Barker myself. She flew into a rage, told me to mind my own business." She started pacing again. From the desk, past the window, to the door. Around and around. "Barker's disappeared. No one knows what happened to him. He's not the only one. Rick Tomlin was the main witness against my client, Arnie Walksfast . . ."

Father John nodded. He had heard that Rick Tomlin hadn't shown up for the trial. He told her that Reg Hartly had stopped by the mission hoping he might know something about his buddy.

"The prosecutor tried to find Tomlin, but Dennis Carey insisted he had packed his gear and left."

"That's what the Careys told Mantle about the other cowboys. Decided to move on to Montana or Idaho. Jaime Madigan's

284

fiancée came to the mission last winter. She was also hoping I might have heard where he'd gone. I have a call in to her now. The woman I spoke with thought I was calling with news about Jaime, which means he is still missing."

"Rick Tomlin. Josh Barker. Jaime Madigan. Three out of six cowboys missing from the Broken Buffalo. The others may also be missing, but no one has come looking for them." Vicky stopped pacing and put up one hand to stop the objection he was about to make, as if she had read his mind. "I know there's no proof that anything happened to them. Cowboys move around. Isn't that the cowboy myth? Riding toward the sunset? What about Jaime's fiancée? Did she file a missing person report?"

Father John took a minute before he told her he wasn't sure. "I suggested it, but she seemed reluctant. I think she was half-afraid he might have wanted to get away. Maybe wanted to leave her. What about Tomlin? Does he have any family? Anyone looking for him?"

"An ex-girlfriend." Vicky had started pacing again. "I doubt she would file a missing person report. The same is true for Reg Hartly. He is determined to find Josh himself. He thinks if he can get hired at the ranch, he might find something or someone who knows where Josh went." She came back to the desk and faced him. "Something else, John. Reg Hartly's truck was shot at last night."

Father John was quiet a moment. Then he said, "What about the other cowboys? Were they shot at?"

Vicky looked away, and he realized there was something she wasn't telling him. She was an attorney; he was a priest. They kept secrets. After a moment, she looked back. He could see the worry darkening her eyes. "I've asked Annie to get the names of the other shooting victims," she said. "Maybe you can convince Jaime's fiancée to file a missing person report with the FBI. I'll talk to Reg Hartly and Tomlin's ex-girlfriend." She started into the corridor, then turned back again. "Let's stay in touch."

Vicky stood in the rippling shade of a cottonwood and tried to call the number Lucy Murphy had left with her. The mission was quiet; nothing but the sounds of the wind in the branches. She liked the quiet here, a sign of strength and permanence, John O'Malley part of it. "Hi! Little ol' me here, but not here, if you get my drift." A high-pitched, cheery voice that barely

camouflaged the dark emptiness under-
neath. "I like messages, so leave me one." A
buzzer noise sounded, and Vicky said,
"Lucy, it's Vicky Holden. I would like to
talk to you. If you are home, please pick
up." She waited through the silence. "Call
me soon."

She checked her text messages: one from
Annie: "Talked to Arnie's mother. Says
Lucy lives over in the trailer park off 789.
She doesn't know the number."

Vicky slipped the cell into her bag and
walked over to the Ford. The trailer park
was ten minutes away. Finding a white girl
in the maze of metal trailers anchored to
the ground and occupied by an ever-
changing parade of white and Indian resi-
dents would probably take much longer.

Within minutes she was on the highway,
slowing for a right turn onto a ribbon of
dusty asphalt that wound through the trailer
park. The place looked as if it had been left
behind. No children in the dirt playground,
swings dancing in the wind. She drove
slowly, watching each trailer for a sign
someone was home. Finally, a line of wash
flapping next to a trailer with a little metal
porch attached in front. She pulled in next
to the porch and waited. It was impolite to
knock and force herself upon whoever lived

here. If someone was inside and wanted a visitor, the door would open. She waited a few more minutes, then got out and slammed her own door hard in case no one had heard her drive up. She took her time on the metal steps, then rapped on the door, leaning in close for sounds of movement: the scrape of a chair, a running faucet suddenly turned off.

The door opened slowly. A white woman in her twenties, black roots in her long blond hair and a baby with chubby legs on one hip, blinked into the sunlight as if she were trying to bring the world into focus. She was leaning sideways with the weight of the baby. "No soliciting. Can't you read signs?"

"I'm not selling anything." She hadn't always read signs, she was thinking. She had missed a lot of signs in her life. "I'm looking for someone who lives in the park, and I was hoping you could help. Doesn't look like anyone else is at home." Vicky shot a sideways glance at the trailer next door. "Do you happen to know where I can find Lucy Murphy?"

"Who wants to know?"

"I'm Vicky Holden. I'm the attorney representing Lucy's boyfriend."

"She in some kind of trouble?" The baby

kicked his chubby legs and waved a blue plastic spoon. The girl adjusted him on her hip.

"No." Dating Arnie could be trouble, Vicky was thinking. "She may be able to help me."

"I don't like sending strangers to people. I mean, I don't feel good about it." The baby poked the spoon into her neck. She tried to take it away but gave up the effort when he let out a piercing scream. She switched him to her other hip and leaned in the opposite direction.

"Could you call her?" Lucy hadn't taken her call, but she might take a neighbor's call. "I have her number."

The girl seemed to consider this. "I've got it. Wait here." She shut the door. The baby started screaming again, probably because she had set him down. After a moment, she was in the doorway, the baby slung back onto her hip, gulping big, wet sobs. "She says she knows you. Number thirty-nine. Just keep going around the curve."

Vicky thanked her and headed back to the Ford. She could see the girl and the baby framed in the side-view mirror as she pulled onto the dusty asphalt.

Lucy Murphy stood on the tiny metal stoop

of the trailer with the number thirty-nine plastered next to the door frame. She was barefoot, in cutoff jeans and a wrinkled white T-shirt, hair mussed, eyes sleep-blurred. "I don't have time to talk. I gotta get ready for work."

"I only need a minute." The girl didn't move, anxiety and something else — sadness — pouring off her like perspiration. Finally she kicked the door open and stepped backward inside. Vicky followed. The trailer might have been any trailer in the area. Narrow table and bench of red plastic, worn pink. Tread marks in the throw rug, green vinyl floor popping up at the edges. A sink, stove, and miniature refrigerator configured somehow beneath a window with a long, vertical crack. A curtain across the aisle to the back. Tobacco odors mixed with the musty, closed-up smell.

"This about Arnie?"

"I'm here about Rick Tomlin."

The girl rubbed at her eyes with bunched fists. "He's gone. I made up my mind I'm not worrying about him anymore. He didn't worry about me. Cut out of here without even a 'so long, been nice to know you.'" She shrugged a couple of times, as if she were working out kinks in her shoulders. "I'm with Arnie now. Only . . ."

"What?"

Lucy looked at some point in the middle of the trailer. "We been having problems lately. He don't want to see me. Blames me for getting him into all this trouble. He says if it wasn't for me, Rick wouldn't have come after him at the bar and they wouldn't have gotten into the fight." Her voice started buckling; she was struggling to hold back the tears. "I don't understand. I love him, you know. Yesterday was our anniversary. I went to the rehab center, and the nurse said he wasn't seeing visitors. He wasn't seeing me. Not even on our three-month anniversary."

"How long had you been with Rick?"

"Rick?" She blinked, as if she were trying to pull a new image into mind. "Two months, I guess. It was rocky, I give you that, but . . ." She hesitated, searching for the rest of it. "At least I knew he loved me, even if he lost control sometimes. Not like Arnie. All about me one day and don't want me around the next."

"Listen, Lucy. I need to know if you filed a missing person report on Rick?"

Astonishment crossed her face. "Why would I do that?"

"Because you were close to him. Did he have family somewhere?"

291

"An old man he hadn't seen in fifteen years. Rick pretty much grew up in foster homes."

"So you were the only one who might have filed a report."

"Arnie would've killed me. He wanted Rick gone."

"Enough to make it happen?" Oh my God. She could be hanging her own client. Arnie had sworn he hadn't done anything other than shoot at Rick's truck to force him to leave the area, and, God help her, she had believed him. Or was it that his mother had never stopped believing in him and she had been caught up in a delusion?

"No! No! No!" The girl was shouting. "Arnie's a hothead, but he's not evil! He wouldn't deliberately hurt anybody. I mean, he had to defend himself when Rick punched him in the bar. You think I should've filed some kind of report? With the cops? No way. I don't want Rick coming back. He'll think I snitched on him. He'll tell whatever lies he can tell to make sure Arnie goes to prison."

"There may be other cowboys missing from the Broken Buffalo. If the fed and the police get missing person reports, they will investigate."

"What are you doing? You're Arnie's

lawyer. You're supposed to keep him out of prison, not put him in. I'm not gonna help you hurt Arnie."

"What about helping Rick?"

"What?"

"You loved him once, didn't you?"

"That's a long time ago."

All of three months, Vicky was thinking. "What if he's hurt? What if he was taken someplace and can't get away?" The possibility seemed real and immediate, not just something she had seen in the newspaper or on the internet or on TV. "I could go with you to see Agent Gianelli."

"Forget it. I'm not going. If Rick turns up, he'll beat the crap outta me. And Arnie will dump me."

Vicky didn't say anything, and the girl hurried on: "He hasn't dumped me yet, if that's what you're thinking. He loves me."

"Where are you from, Lucy?"

"Kansas. Nowheresville, Kansas. I ain't ever going back if that's what you're gonna suggest."

Vicky moved toward the door, grabbed the handle, and pushed the door open. It was as light as cardboard. She stepped out onto the stoop, then looked back. "Think about it."

"I'm not going to the police."

"I meant about going home."

26

The sun blazed white over the Wind River range, and an orange, red, and violet panorama streaked the sky. Trout Creek Road, running ahead, was tinged in orange. Father John readjusted the visor against the glare off the hood. The bishop seemed relaxed in the passenger seat, staring over the half-open window at the passing scrublands. The swoosh of the wind melted into the sounds of *La traviata.* Traffic was heavy, with more cars in the oncoming lane than in the intermittent line of vehicles ahead.

Father John checked his watch. Nearly seven. The Broken Buffalo Web site listed viewing hours as eight a.m. to eight p.m. He and Bishop Harry should have enough time to walk out to the pasture. He had called Sheila Carey before they'd left the mission and told her the bishop would like to see the calf. She would leave word at the gate, she said.

"How long will they keep coming?" Out of the corner of his eye, Father John could see the bishop nodding toward the truck with the Utah license plate ahead.

"It could go on several years." Father John tried to ignore a sense of alarm flitting like a ghost at the edge of his mind. Years, season after season, out-of-state cars and trucks crossing the reservation, crowds pouring through the wide-open spaces. How many might stay? Settle on a ranch in the area, start a business in Riverton or Lander? This was a land of few people, not yet taken over. It belonged to itself. And yet . . .

He heard himself saying that the newcomers would be good for the local economy.

"Perhaps." The bishop gave a little laugh. "Change will come. It cannot be stopped."

Father John followed the Utah truck into the turn onto the two-track. Little brown circles of dust splattered the windshield. He slowed down to give the truck more space. Another mile and they were bouncing over the ruts toward the gate ahead. Beyond, the setting sun outlined the roof of the log ranch house. A cowboy had directed the truck into the parking lot. Father John pulled up close to the gate. Carlos walked over and leaned toward the driver's window; the beginnings of a beard bristled on his jaw. "Mrs. Carey said you can drive up to the house. She's gonna escort you to the pasture herself." He waved at another cowboy, who lifted the gate, and Father John drove through.

Sheila Carey was coming down the porch steps when he stopped the pickup. "Carlos called and said you were on the way up," she said as Father John let himself out of the pickup. He started around to the passenger side, but the old man was already out, stretching his shoulders, glancing about the ranch. Small groups of people were waiting by the fence that enclosed the pasture. He introduced Sheila to the bishop, who stopped stretching and shook the woman's hand.

"How are you doing with the crowds?" Father John asked.

"Had to take on more cowboys than I planned." The woman hooked her thumbs into the pocket of her blue jeans. The wind blew strands of reddish hair across her face. "We're managing just fine. I'll walk you out to the calf."

Father John and the bishop fell in on either side of the woman as they started down the path beside the fence, past the groups waiting. Fastened to the fence about every twenty feet were large metal canisters with slits in the tops. On the outside, painted in black, were the words: DONATIONS FOR SPIRIT. Another group, returning from the pasture, huddled around one of the canisters. He watched as people took turns stuffing bills through the slit.

"People want to help take care of the calf," Sheila said, leading the way around the group. "I don't mind saying Spirit costs a lot of money. Oh, I've thought about selling her, but how would I keep her safe? Most ranchers would kill her for the meat. They don't want the trouble. I see what she means to Indians. Whites, too. All kinds of folks know the calf is a sacred sign from the Creator." She stopped and looked up at him. "People here from Chicago this morning."

They were leaving more of the noise and confusion behind the farther they walked, moving closer and closer to nature. A soft, quiet wind rippled clumps of grass and sagebrush and plucked at the barbed-wire fence. Another group was returning, stopping to put bills into the canisters. Sheila waved and nodded in appreciation.

The bishop was doing fine on the hard, smooth-trampled path, one foot planted after the other, eyes on the pasture, as if he might catch an early glimpse of the calf.

Ahead, the fence was solid with gifts: paper flowers, small cloth bags, bunches of tied grass, envelopes, photographs, a couple of knit caps, a baby rattle, packages of cigarettes. All rustling in the wind so that the fence itself seemed to be swaying.

They had walked past the gifts when Sheila said, "We'll stop here. You brought your camera?" She was looking at the bishop. He leaned toward the fence and shook his head. "I only want to see the calf." And not capture its spirit, Father John was thinking. Old people, traditionalists on the rez, would understand.

The buffalo herd had gathered under the cottonwoods, a large, brown circle, placid and content. "They're protecting Spirit," Sheila said. "So many people looking at her. They know she needs quiet. I'm sorry, but we may not see her."

Then the herd seemed to break apart, a few wandering out of the trees and into the pasture, stopping to graze as they went. A large buffalo came toward the fence, nodding and snorting. Scampering behind was the white calf. A chorus of *ah*s went up from the group stationed farther along the fence. Sheila was shaking her head. "She's come to see you."

The bishop stood very still, gazing across

the space between the barbed wire and the white calf. "She is very beautiful," he said after a moment. "Praise God for this blessing."

On the way back, the bishop stuffed a couple of dollars into one of the canisters. Another group had started out to the pasture, and a couple of women stopped to feed a canister. They were almost at the house when Father John spotted Vicky and Adam waiting in the last group. He thanked Sheila Carey, told the bishop he'd be just a moment, and walked over.

Adam barely nodded, but Father John stuck out his hand anyway. "Good to see you." The Lakota's hand was smooth and hard. "Any luck?" He looked at Vicky.

"Lucy Murphy refuses to file a missing person report. What about Jaime's fiancée?"

"I haven't heard anything yet."

"What are you talking about?" Adam moved closer to Vicky, as if to shelter her.

"Cowboys missing from this ranch. Driven off, most likely." Vicky took a couple of breaths. "Reg Hartly's working here."

"How do you know?"

"I saw him riding in the pasture when we parked."

"Maybe you can ask him about filing a report."

"I doubt I'll get to talk to him." Vicky nodded at a point beyond his shoulder, and Father John turned around. Sheila Carey stood on the porch watching them.

A cowboy walked over to escort the group, and Father John headed back to the pickup. The bishop was sitting in the passenger seat, door flung open to the breeze. Father John slid onto his seat, aware of Sheila Carey hurrying down the steps. The friendly hostess, the keeper of the sacred calf, gone, he could see, and in her place, an angry, distrustful woman who gripped the top of the window with both hands and leaned toward him. "You and that lawyer have something to say to me?"

He waited a few seconds to let the tension evaporate before he said, "Some cowboys seem to have disappeared. They had worked here. Rick Tomlin. Jaime Madigan. Josh Barker. Any idea of where they were headed?"

"I don't babysit the hired help. Leave it alone." Sheila spun around, ran up the porch steps and into the house. The door slammed like a clap of thunder.

Quiet lay over the residence. The bishop had gone upstairs an hour ago, and the mission itself seemed to have settled into a deep slumber. Father John filled a mug with the coffee he'd just brewed and went into his study. He made his way around Walks-On snoring on the pillow in the corner and dropped behind his desk. The laptop was open, the screen glowing blue and pink around the icons. He had been searching the internet again for news about the calf at Broken Buffalo Ranch. Dozens of sites — Facebook, YouTube, Web sites, blogs — had materialized. The news had spread everywhere. There was even a blog in Belgium. Trips offered by specialty travel sites to "Experience the sacred buffalo calf in the wilds of Wyoming." Traffic crowding the ranch this evening, visitors yet to come — it was just the beginning. He could feel the hard knot tightening in his stomach.

He glanced through the search history and clicked on the site of a ranch where a white buffalo calf had been born ten years ago. He skimmed the story again: the unexpected birth of a white calf; the visitors coming for years, trampling the pastures, clogging the roads. Then he found the photos he had been looking for: a long fence like the fence at Broken Buffalo, sagging under the weight of gifts. Another photo showed lines of people waiting to see the calf. In yet another, a metallic sea of cars, trucks, and vans stretched toward the horizon. He went back to the first photo, looking for something else among the gifts. There, in the lower-right corner, a metal canister the size of a small trash bin. Scrawled in red paint across the front were the letters DONAT. The rest of the word ran off the edge of the photo.

Father John typed in a new search: monetary donations white buffalo calf. A page of sites came up, and he clicked on the one at the top and read down the black lines of type:

The birth of a white buffalo calf on a farm or ranch has proved to be expensive for the owners. Indians and non-Indians alike believe the rare calf is the embodiment of the sacred. A great number of people can be expected to visit the calf, which can present a challenge to owners. New fences must be constructed, current fences repaired and strengthened, and special areas marked off for parking. Porta potties must be installed. Visitors must be kept on special paths so that they do not ruin pastures and grazing lands. The volume of visitors can outpace the best efforts of the owners. Impatient visitors can be expected to break through fences, park in cornfields, and generally come across the pastures in any way they believe necessary to gaze upon the sacred calf. Most owners will be forced to hire extra hands to control the crowds. Local authorities also see additional expenses in controlling traffic.

Visitors can be expected to bring donations to the calf, considered personal mementos, or even sacrifices. They will also donate money to help defray the costs of maintaining the calf. It is not unusual for donations to exceed a million dollars in a year. Usually the visitors begin to diminish after two or three years, and the donations lessen.

Father John closed the site, sat back, and stared at the icons aligning themselves on the screen. One million dollars the first year. Another million the second year. Fewer donations after that, but still something. He wondered how much Sheila Carey would bank after paying wages for the hired hands, repairing fences, marking out pathways. Most of it, he thought.

He realized the phone was ringing, and he reached around the corner of the monitor and lifted the receiver. "Father John," he said.

"Oh, Father, I'm so glad to reach you. Nuala O'Brian returning your call. It's not too late, I hope. I'm in Mayo." She hurried on: "Ever since I got your message, I've been praying you have good news about Jaime. You do have good news, I hope."

"I'm sorry. I was hoping you had news."

"Me? There's been nothing. I came home to spend Jaime's birthday with his parents. They're getting old. Not in the best of shape. Not knowing what happened to Jaime, well, it's about killed them. The police don't seem to be doing anything to find him. I've called every month, but nothing new has turned up. I have to remind them who I'm calling about."

"Did you file a missing person report?"

"Three. FBI, sheriff, and BIA police. I didn't want to at first because I was" — he could hear her gulping in air — "worried Jaime might have wanted to get lost. Maybe get away from me and our wedding plans. Maybe he wasn't ready to settle down and didn't want to disappoint me. Crazy things were going through my head. If he didn't want me, well, I certainly didn't want to be with someone who didn't want me. But after I talked to you, I realized that the idea of Jaime running away was silly. He's not like that! Jaime runs toward whatever he has to face, and he's faced some hard things in his life. Leaving the farm here and his parents, going off to the States to make money to save the farm. That's the kind of man my Jaime is. So I reported him missing. It hasn't done any good. I keep hearing how cowboys wander around, hire on to ranches, sometimes get paid in cash. You Americans call it *under the table,* so there's no Social Security or tax or bank records. They can disappear. But that is not my Jaime."

She was crying now, and the sobs made a shushing noise on the line. "I don't know what else to do. Can you help me, Father?"

"I don't know," he said. "I can try."

The phone had started beeping another call. He told Nuala good-bye, wondering if she had heard him, as she was crying so hard, and switched to the new call. Before he could say anything, a woman's voice said: "Father! You heard what happened?"

"Who is this?"

"Marcy." She was gulping in air. "Marcy Hawk."

He could picture the short, black-haired woman who had been helping him coach the Eagles this season. Always wearing the blue baseball cap with Eagles across the front. Whistling, clapping her hands overhead, shouting, "Way to go!" after the

Eagles had shut out the Rangers.

"What happened?"

"Coach Mantle's been killed."

"What?"

"In his office a couple hours ago. Burglar broke in and shot him."

27

Red, blue, and yellow lights swirled in the darkness a block ahead. Traffic bunched together on Main Street, crawling past the strip mall where Ranchlands Employment was located. Father John switched to the far right lane and skimmed alongside the curb before swinging into the parking lot. Police cars were scattered about as if they had been dropped out of the night sky. Beyond the cars a half circle of yellow police tape flickered in the breeze. People stood around, heads bobbing, feet shuffling. Several uniformed officers huddled beside the cars, glancing at the notepads in their hands. Plainclothes officers in white shirts and leather vests moved about inside the police tape. Cameras flashed.

Father John drove around the bystanders, pulled in behind the police cars, and jumped out. A plainclothes officer nodded in his direction, lights flashing over the look of annoyance on his face. "Crime scene. You need to go back." He waved toward the street.

"Father O'Malley from the mission." He kept walking toward the police tape. He recognized the detective: George Samuels, Riverton Police Department. He had met him at other all-too-similar crime scenes. The play of lights, the stunned onlookers, the hush of voices. "I knew Steve Mantle and his family. Is his body still here?"

The annoyance in the detective's face melted into recognition. "Sorry, Father. Should've recognized your old pickup. Coroner took the body fifteen minutes ago. We're finishing up with forensics."

"What happened?"

"Burglary, plain and simple. Professional job. Knew what they wanted. Computer's missing. Safe emptied. No sign of Mantle's cell phone. He was shot in the back of the head at his desk, execution style. No way did they want to be identified."

Father John took a moment, fighting the wave of nausea that rolled over him. Execution style. Dear Lord, a few hours ago Steve Mantle had told him about the cowboys he'd sent to work at the Broken Buffalo. Two by two, hired together, left together. But Ranchlands Employment was only part of the man. He blinked at the image of the coach on the other side of the field when the Eagles played the Rangers. Checking the batting lineup, coaching in the runners, clapping his hands overhead when the kid in left field caught a fly. His son, Richard, loading up the bats and balls and gloves, hoisting bags over his shoulder, following his dad off the field.

"How about the family?"

"Wife drove over soon as she heard. Hysterical. One of the policewomen took her home. It's tough, real tough. I don't have to tell you. You seen it before." Too many times, Father John was thinking. Too many senseless endings to too many lives.

The detective threw a glance around the parking lot and drew in a long, slow breath that expanded his chest. "How well did you know him?"

"We coached Little League teams. He was a good coach. Good man. I was here this afternoon."

"What about?"

"I was curious about three cowboys who have gone missing. Steve had placed them on the Broken Buffalo Ranch. They worked for a while, then left. He didn't know where they might have gone."

The detective nodded. "Cowboys don't

always leave forwarding addresses."

"Last March the fiancée of one reported him missing to the fed and the BIA police. You hear about it?"

"Probably came across my desk. I'd have to check. Are you suggesting it might have something to do with the killing?" The detective was shaking his head. "They came for what was valuable. Mantle's wife said he kept cash in the safe, probably a couple thousand. Sometimes he'd loan a cowboy money until he could find him a job. The killer came in here, forced Mantle to open the safe, then took off with the contents and the computer. Hit the jackpot."

Father John waited a moment before he told the detective he was going over to the house to see if there was anything he could do.

Detective Samuels gave a quick nod, then ducked under the police tape and started toward the other plainclothes officers.

It might have been a party. The two-story house lit up, lights flaring over the front yard and bouncing in the trees. Cars jammed the driveway and crowded the curb on both sides of the street. Dozens of people, probably neighbors, blocked the sidewalk. Father John had to drive to the next block before he found a parking space. He walked back, only half-aware of the conversations fading into the breeze as he passed people on the sidewalk. "The mission priest," he heard someone say. A hushed, mournful tone, as if the presence of a priest somehow made the inexplicable real. He hurried up the narrow front sidewalk to the porch, where baskets of flowers hung from the ceiling. The door stood open. Silhouettes of people moved around the brightly lit living room; the faint smell of fresh coffee and the soft noise of voices wafted toward him.

He rapped on the door frame, then stepped inside. A crush of people, like in the grief-stricken homes he was used to visiting on the rez. Neighbors, family, all the relations — and, on the rez, everybody was related, it seemed — gathering together to comfort someone whose world had changed forever. The conversations died back. He could see the expectancy in the eyes turned on him, as if he, the priest, could make sense of this. A pathway seemed to part on its own across the room to the sofa against the far wall. Curled into the corner was Julia Mantle. He had seen her at the games, small and dark-haired, packed with energy, like a cheerleader for the Riverton Rangers. Jumping and shouting at every hit. All she needed, he used to think, were pompoms to wave overhead.

He walked over and sat down on the edge of an ottoman someone pushed toward him. "Julia." He kept his voice soft, the voice of the confessional, of holy things. "I'm so very sorry."

She shifted away from the back of the sofa and made an effort to turn in his direction. Her black hair was shiny and matted where she had been leaning against the cushion. She blinked into the lights that flowed from the ceiling and the assortment of table lamps as if she had just come in from the dark and needed time for her eyes to adjust. She lifted a hand, then let it flutter back to her lap. He wondered what she had taken, what kind of drug to mask the pain that, he knew, would come roaring back, a monster no drug or alcohol could tame. "You heard?"

Father John nodded. "I came to see if I can help you in any way."

"Steve liked you. He said you were a good coach. Your kids play fair."

"He was a good coach."

She buckled under his words, face wrinkling, tears puddling in her eyes. "What will I do? Who will be the father to our children?

Who will look after us and love us? Tell me, Father. What will I do? Oh . . ." She lifted her hand again. It looked as small as a child's, with thin fingers and pink nails. "Don't tell me to pray. Don't tell me God will take care of us. What kind of God lets a good man like Steve be shot like a dog? I don't want your God. I'm alone here. All these people, they'll go away, and it will just be me and the kids, and what are we supposed to do?"

"I don't think your family and friends will go away." He glanced at the little groups hovering about. "They will help you find the way. You will gain strength from them." He had seen it happen: the bereaved carried along on a wave of strength from family and friends. She didn't believe him, though. He could see it in the vacant look in her eyes, as if she were staring into an abyss.

She shook her head and squeezed her eyes shut. Moisture pooled on her cheeks. "He was here with us. He was here." She opened her eyes and gave him a pleading look. "You understand? We were about to eat dinner. It's still in the oven waiting for Steve to come home. How can this be? I mean, his dinner's in the oven."

"I'm sorry."

"He's coming home, I'm sure. He never misses dinner. Dinner with the family is a big thing with Steve because he didn't really have a family. Just him and his mom. She was a waitress, so she used to bring home food from the restaurant. She always worked at dinnertime. He'd find something in the fridge and eat it by himself. Watch TV. Sometimes he wondered where she'd gotten the food. Scraped leftovers off somebody's plate? He never knew, but he was always hungry, so he just ate whatever was there. But what he was really hungry for was a family to eat dinner with. Talk over the day. Steve created the family he always wanted."

Father John didn't say anything. He could almost feel the memories rolling through the small, dark woman across from him, staring off into the past, her legs tucked under her. Finally she brought her eyes back to his. "Steve's not coming home for dinner, is he?"

"No, Julia. He's not." He took a moment before he said, "You said you were about to eat dinner. Why did he go back to the office?"

Now she was staring in the direction of the dining room that opened off the living room. There were people sitting at the table, sipping from coffee mugs. Richard and a little girl sat across from each other. Father John wondered if the kids were in the same seats they always sat in at dinnertime, as if everything were normal. A woman with white hair and an air of authority set a plate of food in front of each child and leaned down to tell them something, her voice lost in the voices around them and the clanking noise from the kitchen.

Julia kept her eyes fixed on the dining room table, as if she were picturing the family having dinner together. *How was your day?* Finally she looked back. "A client called. Steve took good care of his clients. They put the food on the table, he used to say. Family came first, but clients supported the family. He pulled his cell out of his shirt pocket, got up from the table, and went into the kitchen. No media at our table, that was his rule. I knew from the tone of his voice that something had come up and I would have to put dinner back into the oven. 'Sorry,' he said when he came back. He had to go to the office. It would only take thirty minutes. 'We'll wait,' I told him. Oh God." She dipped her face into her hands. "Why did I say that? Why didn't I say, 'You can't go! You can't leave us!' "

"You told the detective about the call?"

"I told him." She peeled her hands away. Little black streaks, like fine lines, ran down her cheeks. "He'll check Steve's cell records. He's got to find out who called! The client that needed to see Steve might have seen the killer hanging around the mall somewhere. He might have seen a car or truck. Detective Samuels has to find the client!"

Father John looked away. It hadn't dawned on Julia Mantle that the client might be the one who'd robbed and killed her husband. Clients were locals, part of their world. She and Steve went to church with clients, ate picnic suppers in the park with clients. Clients didn't rob and kill. *They supported the family.*

"Steve didn't say who the client was?"

She was shaking her head.

"Listen, Julia. If I can ever help you or the kids in any way, please call me. Even if you just need someone to talk to."

She stared at him wide-eyed, as if she had just realized who he was. "Steve always said you were a good man."

Father John took her hand for a moment, then got to his feet. He made his way past the knots of people to the dining room. He saw Richard and the little girl watching him, dark eyes like their mother's, rounded with grief and confusion. He placed a hand on

317

Richard's shoulder. It was thin and knobby, layers of muscles not yet laid down. "This is tough," he said, looking across the table at the kid's sister. Big brown eyes and straggly brown hair. She looked even more fragile than Richard. "You've got friends and family here," he said. "They'll help your mom and you kids."

The little girl pushed a fork through the macaroni on the plate in front of her. The kids might have been twins, except that the girl was smaller. "I seen you at the games." Even her voice was small.

"Remember, you have your mom, and you have each other," he said.

Both kids nodded, as if they understood more than should have been asked of them.

28

Sirens rose and fell somewhere on Main
Street. Vicky sipped at her coffee and
watched Adam stir a spoonful of sugar into
his cup. The sound of sirens was always un-
nerving, with their mournful sense of someone in need of help. The sirens had been
going throughout dinner, starting up, quiet-
ing down, starting up again. Odd how
everyone ignored them — the waiters bustling about the tables, the other diners. The
café, a new restaurant they had decided to
try, was packed. They'd had to wait twenty
minutes for a table, and people still filled
the entry. A few people looked familiar.
They had been in the line to see the white
buffalo calf this afternoon.

Adam took a drink of coffee and set the
mug down. "Traffic accident nearby." He
had been watching her, she realized.

"It must be bad." Vicky could sense people
in the entry watching their table. So many

visitors; every restaurant crowded. She'd heard there wasn't an available room in the motels. The campgrounds were full. Someone in line had mentioned the only available camping place they'd found was up by Dubois, a good hour's drive away. She gulped at her coffee.

"We don't have to hurry," Adam said. "Let's talk a little."

Talk! Vicky closed her eyes a moment. They had been talking for three hours. On the drive to and from the Broken Buffalo, during dinner. Talking and talking about the white buffalo calf. How helpless and vulnerable the calf had looked, Vicky had said. Adam had disagreed. Look at the way the rest of the herd hovered over her, a protective shield, as if even the buffalo knew she was different, a sacred creature they had to protect. On and on they had talked, recalling stories they'd heard as children. Arapaho and Lakota, allies once, in the Old Time. All the tribes tried to befriend the powerful Lakota or stay out of their way. The cultures were similar, the old stories the same.

"The offerings have about filled up the fence," Adam had said. "Seems to me Sheila Carey should be setting another fence in front of it. Something nice about the way folks want to leave a part of themselves for the calf." She had agreed. Yes, it was nice. She had left strands of her hair inside a little case. This afternoon, Adam had left a small bag of tobacco. Small talk, all of it.

Then he had mentioned the metal donation cans. "You ask me, Sheila Carey could make some serious money."

She has serious expenses, Vicky had told him, wondering even now why she had stood up for the woman. There was something about the redheaded Sheila Carey that was off-putting, as if she wasn't what she seemed — or perhaps was more than she seemed. "She's had to hire extra hands, repair and build fences, bring in porta potties."

"I say she's still going to make more money than any buffalo ranch could hope to see in a lifetime."

He could be right, Vicky thought now. What did it matter? The white buffalo calf was a blessing to all the people. The topic they should be talking about, she knew, had risen between them like a boulder fallen out of the sky, too large to push aside, too dense to see around. They had ignored it.

The sirens were louder. A couple of police cars, roof lights flashing, raced past the plate glass windows on the other side of the café.

The waitress swung by and refilled Vicky's cup. "Do you know what's going on?"

The woman straightened up, a hand gripping the handle of the coffeepot, her eyes on Adam. She was small and blond and beautiful in a vapid, obvious way, Vicky thought. "Heard there was a burglary in the strip mall. Some guy got shot." Adam waved a hand over the top of his mug, and she moved toward the next table, swinging the pot like a banner.

"Somebody walked in on a burglar." Adam shrugged, as if walking in on a burglar and getting shot were normal occurrences. Things happened. He leaned toward her. "What do you think?"

"About somebody getting shot?"

"About Denver."

Here it was, then. Vicky sipped at the hot coffee, bitter tasting now, leaving a sharp, unpleasant tingling sensation in her throat. She let the silence stay between them and looked away from the worry in his eyes. They had an uncanny sense about the lies they told each other, she thought. She would not lie. "I haven't had time to think about it."

"Vicky . . ."

Yes. Yes. She gave him a little wave. What sense did it make? No time to think about an important, life-changing decision? "I've been preoccupied with a client. Worried about Arnie Walksfast."

"I thought that case was settled. He's in rehab. You got him a better deal than he deserved, the way I see it. What are you worried about?"

"He could be involved in something bigger than an assault case. I can't talk about it."

"If we were partners, we could talk about it. Maybe you would stop worrying about things you needn't worry about."

Vicky set the coffee mug down and smiled at the handsome, self-assured man across from her. He worried, she knew, but always about important cases. Cases that mattered. Arnie Walksfast and most of the clients who found their way to her office — scared to death, helpless, locked in some tangled legal problem — hardly qualified. Hardly mattered in the glass-enclosed corporate offices of oil and gas companies, where Adam hammered out the best agreements, the tightest contracts to the advantage of tribes across the West. Now he had been offered a partnership in a Denver law firm.

"You should take the offer," she said. "I'm sure the oil and gas companies sit up and take notice when they have to deal with

Trent, Lawrence, and Vickery. It's what you want, a wonderful opportunity. You will be able to do a lot for our people."

"I'm not going without you."

"Don't say that." Vicky clasped her hands in her lap; they felt cold and shaky. "Don't make me the reason you turn down a great opportunity. You would come to hate me, Adam. I don't want that."

Adam pushed his own mug halfway across the table. "I was thinking about something else today when we were at the ranch," he said. "The white buffalo calf is a sacred sign of the Creator's presence. Don't you see, Vicky? She's a blessing for our lives. A personal blessing for each of us. She's a sign we're on the right path, we can go forward together. It is what should be."

The waitress was back with the coffeepot, but Adam waved her away. She stared at him for a long moment before turning toward the next table. The most handsome man in the restaurant, Vicky thought. Here with her, asking her to move to Denver with him. Start a new life together. Telling her the calf was a personal blessing.

Adam held up a hand in the Plains Indian sign of peace. "Let's not talk about it now. I don't want you to make a decision if you haven't thought about it."

"Is there anything else I can bring you?" The waitress was back, all smiles and ingratiating bows toward Adam. Vicky felt as if she were invisible.

"You can bring the check." Adam gave the woman one of his warmest smiles.

"I'd say she likes you."

"Don't, Vicky." Adam sat forward and pulled a thin wallet from the rear pocket of his blue jeans.

"It's a compliment."

"I don't want it."

Vicky dug into her bag on the bench beside her, extracted her wallet and tossed a twenty and a five into the center of the table. "Put that on the bill."

He pushed the money back toward her. "Let me at least take you to dinner." He smiled at her. "Peace?"

"Peace." She took the bills, slid to the end of the bench, pulling her bag with her, and got to her feet. "I'll meet you outside."

It had cooled a little, but it was still warm outside, the wind gusty and dry. Whirls of dust spun across the sidewalk and trailed along the curb. Headlights streamed up and down Main Street, campers and SUVs and cars with out-of-state license plates. People pushed around her and shouldered their way into the restaurant, where others were still milling about the hostess's desk. She wondered how long this pilgrimage would continue. A year? Two years? Until the white calf was no longer a calf?

The sirens had stopped, but there was still commotion in the next block, still people standing about. Adam was probably right. Somebody had walked in on a burglar. The thought sent a chill through her. It could happen to anyone. She dug through her purse for her cell phone. She had turned it off at the ranch — a ringing phone would have been incongruous, a sacrilege, an imposition on the sacred and timeless. She had kept it off during dinner. Now she checked her messages. There were four, all from Annie. She called her secretary's cell.

"Vicky, I've been trying to reach you." Annie's voice was breathless and tense.

"What's happened?"

"Arnie left rehab."

"What? When did he leave?"

"About five o'clock. The rehab nurse called and said he didn't show up for dinner. He seemed fine this afternoon, went to physical therapy and spent an hour with his counselor. They thought he was making progress. They checked his room, and he was gone. She has to report to probation."

"Did he tell anyone where he was going?

Leave any written messages?"

"Nothing. I think they were pretty surprised. Never saw it coming."

Of course not, Vicky was thinking. Arnie Walksfast was a chameleon. He could be whatever you wanted him to be. "Have you talked to his mother?"

"I didn't know if I should call her."

"I'll handle it." If she could find him, Vicky was thinking, she might be able to talk him into returning tonight. The probation officer might look more favorably upon his leaving if he returned within a few hours. "Call me if you hear anything else."

Vicky pressed the end key, aware of Adam standing beside her. "What's up?"

"Arnie left rehab."

"Nothing you can do about it. He's made his own choices." She could feel the pressure of his hand on her arm, steering her along the sidewalk toward the parking lot next to the restaurant. "The waitress told me she heard the guy who got shot was named Steve Mantle. Ran an employment office."

Vicky pulled away and stopped walking. "Ranchlands Employment."

"You know him?"

"He found jobs on ranches for cowboys. He placed at least six cowboys on the

Broken Buffalo."

Adam stood beside her, not saying anything. Waiting, she knew, for some explanation. What did this have to do with her?

"At least three of the cowboys are missing. One of them had pressed the assault charges against Arnie, then didn't show up for the trial. No one knows where he went."

"You think Arnie might be involved in his disappearance?"

"I don't know." Vicky started toward the lot, hurrying, catching a heel in a sidewalk crack, righting herself, aware of Adam's hand on the middle of her back, steadying her. She darted past the parked cars, waited for Adam to open the passenger door on the BMW, and slid inside.

"I'll take you wherever you want to go." Adam slid behind the steering wheel and pulled his door shut. He was looking at her as he turned on the ignition. Lights from the dashboard striped his face.

"Just take me to the office."

"Vicky . . ."

"There are some things I want to check on." The car turned through the lot and burst into the traffic. The lie was like something heavy and unreal between them. She knew that he knew she was lying; she could sense the barely controlled anger in the sound of his breathing. She stopped herself from telling him that he wouldn't understand. They drove in silence.

29

Vicky closed the door and leaned against it. The office glowed in the light from the streetlamps: Annie's desk and chair, the computer, side chairs against the wall. She could hear the click of Adam's footsteps receding on the sidewalk, the sharp ratchet of the engine turning over. Then the fading noise of the BMW moving down the street. Sadness washed over her. Shouldn't there have been shouting and tears, some force of emotion, to mark the end of a relationship? Something more fitting than silence? They had started with so much hope, she and Adam. Such a promising direction, as if on some day in the future she would love him and he would love her and they would go on, but that day had never arrived. They had loved each other as much as they could, she thought. As much as was possible, but it hadn't been enough, all that wanting love. They had needed more.

She flipped on the switch and watched the light from the ceiling shimmer in the beveled-glass doors. She walked over, flung open the doors, and went to her computer. Nothing in her e-mail that needed attention, nothing about Arnie. She clicked on the Web site for the *Gazette.* A bold, black headline ran like a banner across the page: LOCAL BUSINESSMAN MURDERED THIS EVENING. She scanned down the lines of text.

Steve Mantle, owner of Ranchlands Employment, was shot to death this evening in his office on Main Street in Riverton. Police believe Mantle was killed in the course of a burglary. The office had been ransacked, and numerous items were taken. Mantle had run the employment company, which placed ranch workers in the area, since 2002. Active in the community, he was a member of the Presbyterian church and had coached the Riverton Rangers for three years. He is survived by his wife, Julia, and two children, Richard and Mary Ann. Riverton police ask that anyone who may have noticed anything unusual around the office of Ranchlands Employment between 6:00 p.m. and 8:00 p.m. contact them.

Practically broad daylight. Someone in the strip mall must have seen a burglar and killer going into Ranchlands Employment. And yet, people tended to their own business, picking up dry cleaning or pizza, locking up the front door for the day — normal, normal — not expecting anything unusual.

She dragged her cell out of her bag, called the number for the rehab clinic, and asked to speak to the nurse in charge. Several moments passed before a woman's voice, deep and confident, came on the line. "This is Ruth Avery."

"Vicky Holden. I represent Arnie Walksfast."

"Yes. I called your office as soon as we realized Arnie had left the hospital."

"Is there anything you can tell me about why he left? Something he might have said? Any note?"

"I'm afraid not. He seemed to be doing well in treatment. Very accommodating."

A red flag, Vicky was thinking. Arnie had been belligerent and angry when she had seen him. He blamed everybody for his predicament. Everybody except himself. If he had turned accommodating, it meant he had decided to leave. "Have you reported his absence to the probation department?" God. Arnie's probation could be revoked.

He could spend a year in jail.

"I'll have to report him missing tomorrow morning."

"Yes, of course." Which left some time to find Arnie and talk him into returning voluntarily, unless . . . She thanked the nurse and ended the call, a chill moving through her. Arnie had walked away from the hospital around five o'clock, and sometime between six and eight, the man Arnie and his friends blamed for putting outsiders into jobs on local ranches was shot to death. My God, what had Arnie gotten himself involved in? Shooting at cowboys, trying to scare them away? And now, at least three cowboys missing — there could be more — and a businessman murdered?

Vicky started to call Betty Walksfast, then ended the call. If Arnie was at his mother's, a telephone call would send him fleeing somewhere else. She swung away from the desk and hurried back through the office and into the still, warm night filled with stars. In ten minutes she had left Lander behind and was following the sheen of headlights onto the reservation. More traffic than she had ever seen on Rendezvous Road, cars and trucks barreling in both directions, headlights strobing the asphalt. All around, the plains were dark and quiet, limitless. From time to time houses rose at the edge of the headlights. Sometimes the windows were dark, sometimes faint lights glowed behind the curtains.

She followed a truck from Oklahoma and kept going until she saw the lights of Arapahoe on the west. Still more traffic, and she wondered where all the visitors would bed down for the night. Not until she turned into Arapahoe did the traffic fall behind. She tried to remember which of the white, look-alike houses belonged to Betty Walksfast. Which house had Arnie grown up in? Become angry in?

She drew up in front of the house on the corner with a little peaked roof over the stoop. A single light shone in the front window. Parked next to the house was a dark truck with a license plate that hung off a single screw. She waited, half expecting Arnie to fling himself past the door and run to the truck. He would back up and leave before she had the chance to turn the ignition.

No one came to the door. After two or three minutes, Vicky got out, walked up onto the stoop, and knocked. "Betty," she called. "It's Vicky Holden."

The door opened. A small, stooped figure in a pink robe cinched at her waist stood outlined in the rectangle of light. Greasy smells of something fried, like chicken, seeped from inside the house. "I seen you drive up. Wasn't expecting visitors."

"I'm sorry. It's about Arnie. Is he here?"

"Here? He's in rehab. Doing okay, too. I talked to him today." For a moment Vicky thought Betty would close the door, then she seemed to hesitate. "Why'd you come here?"

"He left the clinic this afternoon." The woman hadn't invited her inside, and Vicky wondered whom she had been frying the chicken for. "I have to talk to him. I want to help him."

"He's not here." Now the door was closing, and Vicky wrapped her hand around the edge.

"Listen to me. The clinic won't notify probation until morning. If Arnie returns, everything might be okay. I have to get him back tonight."

The woman was shaking her head. "I'd tell you if he was here. Arnie don't need any more trouble. I told him I'd take him back, but he said he had something to take care of."

So Arnie had come home. Vicky didn't press the point. "Where did he go?"

For a moment, Vicky thought the woman

might fold inward and crumple to the floor. She looked shaky and uncertain, as if the world had started turning about her. "Are you okay?"

Betty blinked into the outdoors, as if she could blink herself back, and leaned against the door frame. "I did my best for that boy. I raised him right here in this house. He went to school over there." She nodded in the direction of the dark expanse of the Arapahoe school yard. "I had help. All my aunties and grandmothers, my nephew was like a big brother. Didn't make any difference. Arnie went on his own way, found his own friends. No good, any of them. See what they brought him? All the relatives threw up their hands and said no more. We're not bailing him out of jail, paying lawyers, vouching for him to some judge. No more promising to look after him. He was on his own. Except for me. I know the goodness in my boy. He's got to throw away all the bad stuff and come back to the Arapaho Way like he was raised."

"Where did he go?"

"I don't know, and that's the truth. He called somebody. Pickup drove up with three or four drunks, and Arnie ran out, jumped into the back. They took off."

"What time did he leave?" The woman

was shaking her head, as if the time couldn't matter. "It's important," Vicky said.

"He didn't stay long. I started making him dinner, but he said he didn't have time."

"An hour ago? Two hours ago?"

"He come here straight from the hospital. One of his no-good friends dropped him off. Then he called somebody else, and next thing I knew, he was gone. Three hours ago, I'd say."

"If he comes back, tell him to call me. I don't care what time it is. Have him call."

Vicky sat in the Ford a couple of minutes, watching the light go out in the window, listening to the sounds of night, the shush of the wind, the crackle of an animal's footsteps. The car was stuffy, the warm breeze blowing through the opened windows like the air out of a vent. Still she felt cold and clammy and a little sick to her stomach. Arnie had left the hospital with every intention of killing Steve Mantle, finishing unfinished business. The man would not be placing any more outsiders on local ranches. Anybody who took his place would get the message.

God, what had she done? Confronted Arnie about shooting at the cowboys, trying to scare them off? Reigniting all the festering resentments, the anger and hopelessness of Arnie and his buddies? Spurred him on to taking care of the man responsible for parceling out the jobs? And all the time she had been hoping that Arnie's crime was hanging around with bad guys — shooters — that the most Arnie could be charged with would be conspiracy. It would have been tough enough, but conspiracy she could have handled. She could have built a defense that he hadn't known what the others were up to. At the least, he hadn't approved, hadn't gone along. But this . . .

This was murder, planned, carried out. If Arnie had left the clinic to murder a man, that meant Arnie was the leader. The others might be conspirators, but Arnie . . . God, leaving court-ordered rehab was the least of Arnie's problems now. She fought the impulse to jump out of the car, run off into the darkness, and throw up.

Finally she turned on the engine. Fingers shaky, slipping off the key. She made herself take a deep breath, then another. She wondered if John O'Malley had heard the news about Steve Mantle. This afternoon — it seemed like a month ago — John had gone to Steve's office, gotten the news about the cowboys Steve had sent to Broken Buffalo Ranch. Two by two, like dancers in a powwow, hiring on, leaving.

She pulled out her cell, found John O'Malley's number, and hit send. It took a moment before the buzzing noise started. The engine hummed around her, the breeze whipped a piece of hair into her eyes. She pushed the hair back and tried to tuck it behind her ear. "Sorry to miss your call." John O'Malley might have been sitting in the passenger seat. "Leave a message and I will call you back." She waited for the beeping noise, then said, "It's Vicky. Please call me."

She drove back through the dusty streets of Arapahoe, left onto Rendezvous Road, right onto Seventeen-Mile Road, trying to push her thoughts into some kind of order that made sense. She could be wrong about Arnie, and she whispered a prayer to the Creator: "Let me be wrong." She had to find him. The instant she saw him, she would know.

She laughed at the thought. She hadn't known anything about Arnie Walksfast. She had thought he had been involved in an assault in a bar. She hadn't seen the turbulence and hatred beneath the surface. The idea of trying to talk him into returning to rehab seemed faintly silly now. A murderer showing good faith by returning to rehab? She would be laughed out of court.

The surface, she thought. Stay on the surface. All she knew was that, at five o'clock, Arnie Walksfast had walked away from rehab. Her job was to talk him into going back. The rest was conjecture, the what-might-have-happened. The Riverton police would have to sort it out.

Traffic had thinned out, but lines of cars and pickups moved along Seventeen-Mile Road. Looming in the headlights was the billboard with the shining white words: ST. FRANCIS MISSION. She slowed for the right turn, ignoring the horn that erupted behind her, and plunged into the tunnel of cotton-woods, which cast long shadows over the road. She pulled onto Circle Drive and drove slowly around the center of the mission. Dim lights shone in the windows of the administration building, the church, and the museum; night lights that were always left on, she knew. The residence was dark, closed up for the night. No sign of John O'Malley's red Toyota pickup. No vehicles anywhere.

He was a priest. He could have been called out. To the hospital, to a house where someone needed to talk to a priest. So many people who needed him more than she did.

She completed the circle and drove back through the cottonwoods. Trying to think, trying to remember. What was the name of the restaurant where Lucy worked? A bar and grill in Riverton, she remembered that much, but there were several in Riverton. She worked nights, late, which probably meant the place served liquor.

She was back on Seventeen-Mile Road, heading to Riverton, when her cell phone rang. It took a moment to find it in her bag. She stopped at the intersection with highway 789. "Call from John O'Malley" appeared on the screen. She slid her fingertip over the answer bar. "Have you heard the news?" she said.

"Are you talking about Steve Mantle?"

"Yes. There's more." Then she told him about Arnie leaving rehab. She could hear herself going on and on about her fear that Arnie and his buddies had killed Mantle until a pickup behind her honked. At the next break in traffic, she turned left onto the highway, still babbling, all the worry and tension of the evening leaking out.

"Where are you now?"

"I'm on my way to talk to Arnie's girl-friend. She works at the" — she had it then, as if the name had dropped into her head — "Diamond Bar and Grill."

"I'll see you there."

30

STEAKS CHOPS BBQ blinked yellow and red on the neon sign close to the curb in front of the redbrick restaurant. Rows of cars and pickups crowded the parking lot next door. Vicky waited for an SUV to back out of a parking space, then pulled into the slot. A trio of people were weaving their way among the parked vehicles, and she followed them toward the front. The big door with glass inserts sighed on pneumatic hinges when one of the men yanked it open. He held it back, a doorman bowing and smiling, as she joined the others pushing into the crowded entry. People everywhere, standing against the walls, hovering around the hostess desk, sitting on small benches. Vicky thanked the man. "Happy to oblige, ma'am," he said, shutting the door behind him. A Texan, she guessed.

She slid past the crowd toward the desk. The hostess was about twenty, tall and white-skinned with black hair piled on top of her head and a harried look that gave her an exhausted, older-woman look. She kept her head down, eyes glued to a seating chart with assorted red checks on the square, black outlines of tables. "Excuse me," Vicky said.

"Sorry, you have to wait your turn." The young woman never lifted her eyes. "We're super busy. I can't help everybody at the same time."

"Is Lucy Murphy on tonight?"

The hostess looked up. Eyebrows raised, shiny red lips revealing a row of tiny, white teeth. "No personal stuff while the waitstaff is serving. Manager will throw a conniption fit. You'll have to call her tomorrow. She's supposed to come in at five, but she was plenty late tonight. You want a table? Half-hour wait."

Vicky waved away the offer. The woman had told her what she wanted. Lucy was here now. Through the low murmur of conversations, the impatient tones, Vicky heard the door behind her sighing again on its hinges. Out of the corner of her eye she glimpsed a tan cowboy hat bobbing above the heads of the people packed into the entry. She tried to make her way toward him, slipping past arms, wedging herself

343

between backs. Excuse me. Excuse me.

"Lucy's here somewhere," she said when she reached John O'Malley. There was a worried sadness about him, the lines at the corners of his eyes deeper, permanent looking. "We can go into the dining room and look for her."

He nodded, and she turned around and threaded her way back through the crowd, aware of John O'Malley behind her and the way people parted for them. The dining room was packed, people seated at tables and in the booths, waitstaff in white shirts and black slacks or skirts, scurrying about with trays of food perched shoulder high on their palms. She spotted Lucy in the far corner, bent over a table, delivering plates of food. The girl stood up straight, lifted the tray off a serving table, and swung toward them. She stood still, as if an electric current had coursed through her. Then she pivoted about and pushed through a swinging door. A flare of noise burst over the dining room: clanging metal, running water, someone shouting. For an instant, Vicky glimpsed the rows of metal tables, white-coated cooks bustling about. Then the door swung shut.

"She's scared. She's going to run." Vicky could see the look of understanding that flashed in John O'Malley's face. He ushered her ahead, back to the entry, through the crowd, and out the door that another man in a ten-gallon hat, probably also from Texas, was holding open. They hurried around the building, half walking, half running.

An alley ran along the back, cars and pickups parked at random, trash barrels overflowing against a wooden fence, a collection of small metal containers lining the back wall. A solid black door in the center of the building burst open. Lucy came running out, clutching a red bag and a stash of black-and-white clothing, fingers working the buttons on a pink blouse. The door made a hollow whacking noise behind her.

Vicky closed the space between them. "Lucy! Don't be frightened." The girl's eyes were lit with fear. "This is Father John from the mission."

"Go away. Leave me alone." Lucy was trembling, backing toward the alley, knocking over a metal container that clanked and rolled along the pavement. "I don't know anything, I swear. Arnie'll kill me."

"He threatened you?"

"Told me to stay out of his business. Go away. I can't talk to you."

"Where can we find him?" John said. "We

won't have to talk to you. We'll talk to him."

"You don't get it." The girl started shaking her head, swallowing tears. "I'll be arrested. I'll be charged with aiding him. That's what he told me. I gotta keep my mouth shut or I'll be in a lot of trouble."

"You picked him up at the clinic?"

"He said it was okay. He said the judge changed his mind, so he could leave. Soon's he got in the car, he told me to keep my mouth shut if I knew what was good for me. That's when I knew he wasn't supposed to leave rehab, and I was his accomplice or something." She looked back at the door. "I'm gonna lose my job, walking off like I just did."

"You can go back," Father John said. "Tell us where Arnie is and go back to work."

This seemed like a new and fantastic revelation. Lucy looked at them with wide, dark eyes. "You won't tell him I told you?"

"We're trying to help him," Vicky said. "I'm hoping he'll let us take him back to rehab before the probation officer knows he left."

Lucy gulped down a couple of breaths, looking between them and the solid, black door. "I need this job, but Arnie can't know I talked to you. He said he had business to clean up."

"Business? Where?" Vicky could feel the knot tightening in her stomach. Clean up by murdering the man responsible for putting outsiders in jobs?

The girl shrugged. "All I know is, Arnie did business with drinking buddies, a bunch of lowlifes."

"Do they hang out at a bar?" John said.

"He said he was going to the rez."

"A drinking house?"

The girl nodded. "Ansel Night Hawk's place. His girlfriend doesn't care. She drinks with 'em."

They drove south on 789, past the warehouses and liquor stores and camper rentals, past the trailer park, and turned onto Seventeen-Mile Road, heading deeper into the reservation. Traffic was lighter, but still steady. An occasional truck passed; lights from oncoming vehicles flashed across the pavement. A field of stars danced in the sky. They had taken John's old pickup, parked in the rear of the parking lot near the back door of the restaurant. The girl had stood there, looking small and helpless as they backed out of the lot. Vicky had wanted to jump out of the pickup, run to Lucy, and tell her again to go home. She could feel the exhaustion moving through her like a cold draft.

"Ansel and Arnie used to play for the Eagles," John O'Malley said, and Vicky realized he was lost in his own memories. "Good kids, both of them."

Vicky told him then about her fear that Arnie and his drinking buddies could be responsible for the cowboys missing from the Broken Buffalo.

"You think they might have killed them?"

She was quiet a moment, sorting her thoughts into compartments: Anything Arnie had told her was privileged. But she had her own theories. Theories based on nothing except her own growing uneasiness and diminishing trust in her client.

"I spoke with Jaime Madigan's fiancée," John said. "She reported him missing last fall, and she has been in touch with Gianelli and the BIA police every few weeks. There's no sign of Jaime."

"So they've stopped looking."

"Unless something turns up, they don't have anything to go on."

"How can cowboys disappear and nobody cares?"

"Nuala cares. Josh Barker's friend has come here looking for him. The prosecutor must have tried to find Rick Tomlin so he could testify against your client."

"They've run into blank walls. Reg Hartly thinks he might stumble onto something at the ranch, but as soon as he hits the blank wall, he'll leave."

"You believe the cowboys are dead?" Father John turned north onto Blue Sky Highway, leaving most of the traffic behind. An occasional pickup rose in the oncoming lane. The houses set back from the road were dark.

"I can't shake the feeling, John. I hate it; I don't want to believe it. What business did Arnie have that was so important he had to leave rehab?" Vicky leaned her head back against the seat and stared at the headlights floating into the darkness. "He's my client, but who is he? A guy who beat up a cowboy in a bar? A murderer? How can I help him if I don't know?"

John O'Malley didn't say anything. He understood, and it was enough.

She could see the glow of lights off the road ahead, the dark shadows of parked vehicles. She thought she heard the faint trace of hip-hop on the breeze, but she wasn't sure. There were no other houses around, no other traffic, just the glow of a drinking house where kids and young people went to drink. Sometimes for days, until someone dragged the kids away.

The pickup was slowing down. Tires scraped the pavement, the engine rattled. They veered right, crossed the borrow ditch, and slid onto the hard dirt washboard of a yard. The headlights flicked over a group of men standing around and lounging on the stoop, shadowy and dark, hunched over beer cans, music thumping in the nighttime silence. The door to the house was open. John pulled in next to a dark sedan with a silvery-primed passenger door. He started to tell Vicky to wait, then changed his mind. She would do what she wanted. He got out, leaving the engine running, the headlights on. Three of the beer drinkers started toward the pickup.

Vicky threw open her door and jumped out. She hurried around the hood and stopped next to John O'Malley, a phalanx of two, she thought, against big, strutting drunkards. "We're here to see Arnie Walksfast," John said.

"Don't know any Arnie Walksfast," one of the men said. He was in his twenties, shirtless, with long black hair pulled back from his face and trailing over his naked shoulders. He wore blue jeans that rode low on his hips and flip-flops that made a swishing noise on the dirt. "Anybody know an Indian named Arnie Walksfast?" he called over a brown shoulder. "Nope. Nobody. So turn around and drive that old wreck out of here."

"Hey, maybe they want a drink first?" Another Indian had staggered off the stoop and planted his boots a couple of feet apart, shifting his weight from one to the other. "Get them a drink! What kind of Raps are we? Forgetting our manners."

"I'm Arnie's lawyer." Vicky could hear the tenseness in her voice. "Tell him I'm here. I can help him."

"Help him?" A fourth man had walked over, and now they stood together, smirking, headlights strobing over their faces. "He don't need no help. We don't need no lawyers around here."

"Is he inside?"

"What?" The Indian blinked and looked around, as if he'd given away the game. "I never said he was here."

"You heard that?" the first Indian said. "Nobody said he was here, so get out before . . . we have to do some damage. Break a couple legs. Never like beating up ladies, but ladies don't come calling where they're not wanted."

Another Indian appeared in the doorway. He had big shoulders and a big head that rolled on his thick neck. "Knock it off, you bums," he shouted. "This here's Father John." He picked his way across the stoop, gripping the shoulder of an Indian sitting on the concrete edge. "Show some respect. Hey, Father," he said, tottering forward, in and out of the headlights. He let out a loud belch.

"How are you doing, Ansel?"

"Doing just great. Having a little fun, that's all. You want to see Arnie? You're not going to bring the police here, are you?"

"We're not going to bring the police."

31

"I'll get Arnie." Ansel swung around, stomped up the wood steps, and disappeared into the dark house. The other Indians moved about in the headlights, forward, receding, like a stream lapping the banks of a river. Gusts of warm wind disturbed the dusty ground. A fetid odor of hopelessness tinged the air.

"He'll take off," Vicky said. Father John could hear the tension in her voice.

"Maybe not."

They leaned against the pickup and waited. The Indians were waiting, too, it seemed, slouching around the front of the house now, folding onto the stoop. Hip-hop pulsed into the quiet. Five minutes must have passed. Father John was beginning to think Vicky was right, that Arnie had bolted out the back and was running across the prairie. Running to what? He had no other choice. He would come out.

There he was, framed in the rectangle of darkness, peering out past his buddies, blinking into the headlights, a shaky, lost look about him. He stumbled across the stoop, braced himself on somebody's shoulders, and picked his way down the steps. Across the yard, hugging the edge of the headlights, weaving forward, the alcoholic walk. In an instant, an unwanted memory, Father John saw himself. Planting one foot after the other, not trusting the earth. It was always shifting.

"Why'd you come here?" Arnie looked around, as if someone else might materialize out of the darkness, the police perhaps.

Vicky took a step toward him. "You have to go back to rehab."

"Tomorrow." Arnie switched his shoulders about, as if he could drive himself back to the house. He started falling sideways, and Father John reached out and grabbed his arm, steadying him.

"Tomorrow's too late," Vicky said. "If you return tonight, your probation officer might take that into consideration. There are no guarantees. He could still revoke probation and send you to jail. Your only chance is to return tonight. By nine o'clock tomorrow morning he will know you walked away. Within an hour, maybe less, the BIA police will be here. You will be in jail by noon."

Arnie squinted into the darkness and lurched backward. Surprise started over his face, as if he had just registered the fact Vicky had come with someone else. "Where you been keeping yourself, Father?"

"Same place."

"Baseball field?"

"That, too. What made you leave the clinic?"

The Indian shifted his gaze between them and mopped at the perspiration that gleamed on his forehead. "I had business. I needed to clear up a couple things."

"You'd better tell me," Vicky said. "I can't help you if I don't know what's going on."

He bent toward Vicky. "You're the one got me worked up." There was a husky belligerence in his voice, and Father John moved closer to Vicky. "Rancher got murdered. Who the cops going to blame if my buddies were out shooting at cowboys? Cops are going to think they did it." He tossed his head back toward the Indians. "Having a little fun, I mean, trying to scare the outsiders away. Besides, we was so drunk, couldn't hit a barn." He hesitated. "Did some good, though. Those cowboys got out of here. Murder, that's something else." He clasped his fist against his mouth. "I'm going to be sick." He stumbled sideways through the full blast of the headlights and crouched in a spasm of dry heaves.

Father John went over, put a hand on the man's shoulder, and handed him a wad of tissue that he'd pulled from his jeans pocket. "Take your time." He remembered the queasy, dizzy miserableness.

Arnie tried to get up. It took a while, Father John bracing one elbow and Vicky bracing the other. Finally he was on his feet. "Like you said" — he was looking at Vicky again, eyes rheumy and tired — "I'd be a conspirator. No matter I'm in rehab spilling out my guts to some therapist, working the machines sick as a dog. I'm still a conspirator 'cause these are my buddies. We do business together. We shot at some cowboys, but we stopped. We figured we might get real unlucky and kill somebody. If my buddies had anything to do with that rancher getting shot, I figured I'd be looking at conspiracy to commit murder."

Vicky glanced at Father John, and in that instant, in the headlights flaring in her eyes, he saw a new idea take hold of her. She was quiet a moment. Finally she said, "Somebody shot at a white cowboy two nights ago."

"It wasn't us." Arnie was shaking, hands

moving at his sides, and Father John expected the dry heaves to begin again. Instead, the man seemed to grab hold of some invisible support. "Wasn't us that shot the owner of the Broken Buffalo, either. Hell, we didn't know he got shot until we heard the news on the telegraph."

"But you worried your buddies might have been responsible," Father John said. "You came here to find out. You believe your buddies are telling you the truth?"

"Yeah. I told you, we stopped trying to run off the cowboys. Wasn't a good idea."

Father John exchanged a glance with Vicky. He could read the conclusion in her mind; it was the same as his. *Somebody* thought it was a good idea. He fixed his gaze again on the Indian: "Did you hear that Steve Mantle at Ranchlands Employment was murdered this evening?"

Arnie blinked, a puzzled look on his face, as if he were trying to fit this new information into the rest of it. He shifted from one foot to the other. "The guy that finds jobs for outsiders? Murdered?"

"Sometime between six and seven o'clock."

"You think . . . ?" He was sputtering, tossing his head about. "You think I had something to do with it? My buddies? Jesus!

357

That's what the cops think? That's why you come here?"

"I told you why we're here."

"Jesus! You tell the cops we took a shot at some cowboys, they'll blame us for everything. You'll bring all the freaking cops down on us."

"I'm your lawyer, Arnie. What you tell me is confidential."

The Indian was staring at Father John. "Don't worry," Father John said.

"It's not like this is confession. Nothing keeping you from . . ."

Vicky put her hand on Arnie's arm. "You heard what Father John said. What about the others?" She nodded toward the Indians still slouching around the stoop. What do they know about the murder?"

Arnie turned around. "Mantle, that white man that gets jobs for outsiders, got shot tonight. He's dead. Any of you guys heard anything?"

The Indians started moving about, getting to their feet, starting toward them. "Dead?" Ansel said.

"Yes," Father John said.

"First we heard." There was an anxiety in the way they looked around at one another. "We been here all day." Drinking, Father John thought.

He walked over and opened the passenger door. "Get in, Arnie," he said.

Arnie pulled back and, for a moment, Father John thought he might refuse, take his chances, run off before the police arrived tomorrow. Then Arnie threw a glance over one shoulder. "I need my backpack."

"Ansel can get it." Father John nodded at the Indian who seemed to be the spokesman for the others.

"Hold on, I'll find it," Ansel said. "We don't need the cops showing up here." He spun around, crossed the yard, and leapt onto the stoop. In a couple of minutes, he was back, carrying a small, lumpy-looking pack that, Father John thought, probably contained everything Arnie Walksfast owned in the world.

Vicky was already in the passenger seat, the door open; Arnie was nowhere in sight. Father John felt a stab of annoyance. He'd been tricked. Arnie had gotten him to look away and had taken off.

"He wants to ride in the bed," Vicky said, then she pulled the door shut.

Father John went around and handed the pack to the Indian, already curled up in the corner beneath the rear window. He shunted the pack under his head and closed his eyes.

"I think Arnie's telling the truth." The faint dashboard light washed over Vicky. Against the black window, her profile looked small and dark. "Maybe I want to believe him. I know he can't be trusted; I learned that in the past. The thing is, he was scared enough to walk away to make sure his buddies weren't involved in the shootings. What does that tell you?"

"He thought it was possible."

"Exactly." Out of the corner of his eye, he watched Vicky lean back against the seat, as if something had been settled.

"He believes them."

"Which could help his defense, I guess. He's not a conspirator."

"What's the motive for killing Carey or Mantle?"

Vicky was quiet a moment. "Revenge, anger, and the sense of falling behind while everyone else goes forward."

Father John slowed down to let the truck behind him pass. It had been riding on his tail since they had turned onto Blue Sky Highway. Something familiar about the truck, but there had been a lot of traffic on the rez — trucks, pickups, SUVs. Now the

360

traffic seemed to have melted into the vast, empty darkness.

The truck dropped back, and Father John pressed down on the accelerator. A gust of wind knocked at the pickup, pushing them toward the borrow ditch. He tightened his grip on the steering wheel. The truck was gaining again, bright lights flashing and bouncing behind them. This time he kept the pickup steady. There was no oncoming traffic. He slowed down to let the truck pass.

"What's going on?" Vicky shifted about, stretching to see out the rear window. "Why doesn't he go by?"

Father John sped up a little. The pickup was shaking around them, the engine growling. No more than a few feet between the truck and the pickup, and Arnie Walksfast in the bed. If the truck rear-ended them, Arnie would be hurt.

Then the truck — huge and black, silver chrome gleaming on the doors, a cowboy hat dipping behind the wheel — pulled around. The engine roared, and gears ratcheted down. The truck veered to the right, forcing Father John to stomp on the brake. The old pickup swung back and forth across the highway before settling into the lane. The right-turn light on the truck had started blinking; the emergency lights came on. The truck was riding the edge of the highway, close to the rim of the ditch, slowing down. Father John pressed down on the brake.

"He wants us to pull over." Father John steered the pickup sideways as the truck pulled ahead and stopped. The driver — short and powerful looking, cowboy hat pulled low — jumped down and started walking back, a measured gait, as if everything were normal. Except for the way one hand was hidden in the pocket of a bulky jacket.

Father John pushed the gear into reverse and turned halfway around. One arm across the top of the seat, eyes on the road behind. He stepped down hard on the accelerator and the pickup shot backward, rocking and skidding over the pavement. He glanced out the front at the dark figure standing in the middle of the road, arms extended, holding something in both hands.

"Get down," he yelled. He was pushing the pickup as hard as it would go. For a terrified moment he thought it might stop altogether, collapse in a heap, but it kept going. He was aware of Vicky crouching below the dashboard, and he yelled again, this time at Arnie bouncing around in the back. "Get down. Get down."

The shot, when it came, sounded like a clap of thunder, sudden and sharp, leaving a dead silence in its wake. He realized he had braced himself for the impact. Nothing. Still he kept trying to put as much distance between the shooter and the pickup. Finally he slowed down and made a sharp U-turn, managing to bring the pickup around so that they were heading back the way they had come. The truck dissolved into the darkness in the rearview mirror.

He stopped at the intersection with Ethete Road, got out, and ran to the back. "You okay?"

Arnie was wide-eyed and blanched looking, mouth quivering. "He tried to kill us! I heard the bullet whiz past."

"You okay?" Father John said again. He could hear his heart pounding.

The Indian nodded, and Father John got back into the pickup. Vicky was sitting up straight, staring ahead. "My God, John. That was how Dennis Carey was shot. That was his killer. Why us? Why us?"

He followed Ethete Road until he came to Seventeen-Mile Road and turned east, scanning the rearview mirror for the large, black truck. After several miles, he saw the billboard of St. Francis Mission blinking in the trace of headlights.

He kept going, looking around, watching everything now because you never knew; you never knew when someone might try to run you down and kill you. At the highway, he turned north. Through the outskirts of Riverton, the dark shadows of buildings and sagebrush passing outside, and into town, under dim circles cast by the streetlights. Why us? Why us? resounding in his head. Another turn, and the clinic lay ahead, bathed in outside lights, a few cars parked in the lot. He pulled up near the front door.

It took a moment to get Arnie out of the back. Difficult, all of it, throwing one leg over the top of the bed, searching for the wheel well on which to balance himself. Father John hung on to his arm until the Indian had dropped to the ground on both feet. They walked him inside, Vicky holding one arm, Father John the other. The nurse was tight-lipped but professional, nodding him into the corridor like a truant schoolboy returning to class.

Out in the pickup, Vicky beside him, Father John took a moment. The bullet had whizzed across the hood, tearing through the windshield. A couple of inches lower and it could have killed her. It could have hit him. Or Arnie. Any of them, stopped in the darkness by a crazy man. He realized why the black truck had seemed familiar. "There was a big black truck among the trucks parked next to the barn at the ranch," he said.

"We've been asking too many questions," Vicky said. "Cowboys missing from the Broken Buffalo. Someone there must think we found the answers. You talked to Steve Mantle this afternoon. He was killed this evening. We were next." Father John watched her digging something out of her bag. "Reg Hartly has been asking a lot of questions." She pressed a button on her cell phone and stared at the hard, bright light of the screen. "He's in danger, John. Hello?" She had the phone at her ear now. "This is Vicky Holden. I'm with Father O'Malley. Someone tried to run us off Blue Sky Highway and shot at us. No. We're okay. The truck came from the Broken Buffalo Ranch. There's a cowboy at the ranch who is in danger. You've got to get officers out there."

"What's this all about?" Father John could hear the voice through the cell.

"The cowboy's in danger." Vicky was shouting. "Get cars out there now."

Father John had already turned the pickup around. They could get there before the BIA, he was thinking.

32

Reg Hartly cracked open the door to the bunkhouse and slipped outside. He shut the door against the chorus of stuttering, snoring noises. The barn and storage shed on either side of the bunkhouse looked deserted. Thirty yards ahead, the house rose out of the earth like a dark, hulking creature. No lights shone in the house; the windows blinked in the starlight. The big truck usually parked alongside the barn was gone. In the dirt yard behind the house stretched the long dining table, surrounded by white plastic chairs and covered in a green plastic cloth that flapped and rippled in the breeze. All the cowboys were asleep in the bunkhouse except for whoever had drawn all-night duty patrolling the gate and the path leading to the house. Another cowboy, he guessed, was patrolling the fence perimeter. Strange that anyone could even think about breaking into a pasture with wild animals that weighed two tons, yet he had spent most of the day repairing places where the barbed wire had been cut. No signs that anyone had actually gotten into the pasture.

Dinner had been late, nine o'clock, after the last visitors had driven away. They would return tomorrow. People couldn't get enough of the white calf. There was something magical, otherworldly, about the creature. It cast its own spell. He wondered what Josh would have made of it. A white calf born on the ranch where he had worked! Incredible! Even now, wherever he was, Josh was sure to have heard about the calf. He wouldn't be surprised if Josh were to drive up and talk the boss lady into hiring him back.

Wherever he was. Reg had spent the afternoon talking to the other cowboys. Had they heard of Josh Barker? He had run into stone walls. They were new hires, almost as new as Reg himself. They expected to work while there was work. When the number of visitors dwindled and Sheila Carey no longer needed extra help, they would move on.

He had done his share of moving on, but he had never cut all contacts. He had never disappeared! And neither had Josh. A few weeks might go by, a month or two at the most, while Josh was driving around looking for a new job, but then he would send his folks a postcard. *Hired on a ranch outside Billings. Sheridan. Cody. Cheyenne. Boise.* A thousand ranches across the West, big spaces separating them. It took time to find a new job.

But no further postcards had come after he had hired on the Broken Buffalo. His dad's letters had gone unanswered. As if Josh Barker had drifted out onto the plains and would never be heard from again, like in the old cowboys-and-Indians movies.

Reg had crawled into his bunk tonight and lain wide awake, staring at the dark outline of ceiling logs, listening to the snorts and grunting around him. He couldn't sleep. Tossing, turning, running stories through his head, trying to find an explanation. Thoughts circling about, always coming back to the Broken Buffalo. The answer was here. He had felt the truth the moment he'd set foot on the ranch. Something not quite right about the place — not straight on. Somebody here knew where Josh had gone, but it struck him that whoever it was might not realize it.

He had focused on the foreman, Carlos. He and the cowboy Lane Preston had been at the ranch the longest, three months now, but Lane had proved another stone wall. Reg made opportunities to talk with Carlos, riding over to where the cowboy was working, offering him a cigarette. Taking a break, smoking together. Carlos wasn't much for words. He had never heard of Josh Barker, he'd said, until Reg came around asking about him. Boss lady says nobody by that name ever hired here, so lay off. She's got her hands full. Then Carlos had let something slip: He had heard that Dennis Carey had the temper of a grizzly. You didn't want to cross him.

What if Josh had crossed him? Made him angry for some reason? Reg let the story play out: They had gotten into an argument, and Josh was never one to back down if he thought he was right. The argument turned physical. Josh threw a few punches. He knew he had to clear out, so he grabbed his gear, threw it into the back of his pickup, and drove off.

It made sense, except that nobody had heard from Josh.

Reg walked over to the barbed-wire fence. The pasture lit by stars, the buffalo swaying like shadows on a lake. Some were lying down, great brown hulks that broke the flat expanse of the ground. He couldn't make out Spirit. Probably huddled in the trees with her mother.

He supposed he should make another stab at sleep. The bell would ring at five. Forty-five minutes to wash up and eat breakfast at the long table. The morning air cool, the sun glowing in the eastern sky, faint and drained of warmth. The work would begin. Hardly a moment to breathe, unless he took a moment and offered a cigarette to some other cowboy. Probing, asking what he had heard, what he had forgotten.

He turned back to the bunkhouse, but it was the storage shed that grabbed his attention. The rough plank building half the size of the barn, an important part of the ranch. He had never seen anyone go inside. He knew the bunkhouse, and he had been inside the barn, the horse stalls, the smell of manure and dried hay, the sounds of horses stepping about, the swishing of their tails. Like a hundred barns and bunkhouses across the west. But storage sheds told different stories.

He picked his way across the gravel and clumps of brush to dampen the sound of his footsteps. A rusty-looking lock hung off the metal bar on the door. He pulled the ring of keys out of his jeans pocket and thumbed through until he came to the small, metal flashlight. He couldn't remember when he had last used the flashlight. He held his breath and pushed the button on the end. Dead. He pumped the button a few times until, finally, a small light burst on. By maneuvering the lock sideways he was able to shine the light directly on it. A key lock. He was in luck. He clicked through the keys again until he found a metal fingernail file, which he inserted into the keyhole. He jiggled the file up and down, back and forth, then jiggled again. Finally, he heard the faintest clicking noise. He snapped the lock loose.

Reg slipped the lock out of the bar and shoved at the door. It squealed like an animal caught in a trap. He waited, glancing about, expecting a cowboy — Carlos — to roar out of the bunkhouse. After a moment, he shoved again until there was enough space to slide inside. He pushed the door shut behind him. The beam from the tiny flashlight lit up the darkness. Tack, blankets, saddles stored everywhere, hanging off hooks on the walls, sitting on shelves. Barrels and metal troughs with water marks on the inside, shovels and tools and wood toolboxes. He flipped open the top of one of the boxes and shone the light around the screwdrivers, hammers, saws.

Then he stepped farther into the shed and

shone the light across the tack, harnesses, and bridles. On one of the shelves were a number of saddles, piled together so that it was hard to tell how many there were. He played the light over them. Worn looking and yet — useful. Spare saddles, waiting in case one of the hands needed a different ride. The heavy leather, browns and tans, gleamed in the light. He ran his fingers along the leather edges, hard and soft at the same time. And here was something under the flap on a tan saddle wedged between two chocolate brown saddles. A mark etched into the leather in black, like a brand. Inside a circle, the initials *JB*.

He kept the light on the mark. The saddle Josh had won in a rodeo in Sedona when he was seventeen. Getting started on the circuit and already one of the best bronco riders. Josh loved that saddle. It meant something. It meant everything. A sign, a reminder of who he was and what he was good at. Josh Barker would never have left his saddle.

From outside came the scraping sound of footsteps on the gravel. Reg shut off the flashlight and held his breath. The footsteps came closer, then stopped. He could feel the presence of someone on the other side of the door, hear the rapid breathing. He had to get ahold of himself, not let his imagination get the better of him. One of the cowboys on duty was probably checking that all the buildings were locked for the night. He stayed frozen in place, willing the footsteps to move on.

But they didn't move on. A sharp clinking sound cut through the quiet. He could almost *see* the cowboy pulling at the lock, feel the cool metal against the man's palm. Feel the shock that the lock was open. There was a loud sigh, an expulsion of breath, or was he imagining it? Another clinking noise, but this was definitive as the lock was shoved back into place. The footsteps crunched the gravel again, moving on.

He couldn't believe it. He was locked inside the shed. He could be here for days before someone came looking for a tool or saddle. He thought about banging against the door, shouting, bringing the cowboy back. But what would he say? That he couldn't sleep, so he had picked the lock and gone snooping in the storage shed? That he had found Josh's saddle?

He had no intention of explaining to any cowboy. This was a matter for Sheila Carey.

He turned on the flashlight and followed the beam to the tool chest. The lid creaked when he pushed it back. He waited a moment, half expecting the cowboy to return.

Nothing, apart from the wind sighing through the cracks in the old building. He ran the light over the hammers and screwdrivers and handsaws until he glimpsed the long, black metal handle of a crowbar. He laid the other tools on the dirt, lifted out the crowbar, and went back to the door. He set the flashlight upright on the ground so that the light flared over the small, square metal plate on the frame, screws tightened and rusted in place. He poked at the edge of the plate until he managed to insert the tip between the metal and the wood frame. He pulled hard, but the crowbar slipped and bounced upward, swiping at his ear. He went back to trying to work the metal plate loose. Welded into the wood, he thought, it had been attached so long.

Finally the plate popped off. He felt a sense of release as the identical plate outside let go. That plate, he knew, held the U-shaped metal hasp that was secured by the lock. He rammed his shoulder against the edge of the door. It groaned, then settled back into place, and he rammed it again. Pain cascaded down his arm, and for a moment he thought he had dislocated his shoulder. He rubbed at it and rammed again. The door creaked open. A sliver of starlight burst into the shed.

Reg pushed the door open about a foot until he could see the area around the barn and bunkhouse. No one about. He slipped outside, closed the door behind him, and went about trying to screw the metal plate back into place. Finally the shed looked as if it were still locked.

He glanced around again, not trusting that no one was there — Carlos, Lane, one of the other cowboys could appear at any moment. The night was quiet, the stars burning overhead. From out in the pasture, as if from a far distance, came the gentle shuffling sounds of the buffalo. Josh had been here. Stood on this ground, rode in the pasture, checked the fences, stood on the flatbed and forked hay to the buffalo. He had been a cowboy here; his saddle was in the shed. But where was his truck? He hadn't seen any abandoned trucks on the ranch.

He crossed the hard, uneven space between the outbuildings and the back of the house. The plastic tablecloth rustled in the stirred currents of air. He walked down the side of the house, something tightening inside him, hard and focused. He understood now, as if he had absorbed the truth in the shed, running a finger over the carved initials. *JB.* But he wanted to hear the truth from Sheila Carey herself. She would tell him what happened on this ranch. She would tell him, or he would kill her. Just as somebody on this ranch had killed Josh.

He mounted the porch steps, not caring about the loud thud of his boots, wanting to awaken the woman, to frighten her. He banged on the door with his fist, again and again. The reverberation came back to him like the sounds of a horse stomping the ground. The wooden door shook under his fist.

Sheila Carey wasn't home. He should have known. The black truck was gone, and he hadn't seen her since this afternoon. He had gone to talk to her earlier this evening about ordering another delivery of hay, but she had waved him away. Not now, she'd said. Something else on her mind, something more important. *Do your job. Let me worry about running the ranch.*

From behind came the roar of an engine, the thump of tires on hard earth. Reg swung around. Headlights beamed in the darkness as a man in a cowboy hat pushed up the gate. Then the vehicle came bouncing along the ruts. A smaller vehicle than the truck; he could see that. It swayed from side to side, going too fast for the road. He went

down the steps and walked toward the headlights.

The pickup stopped across from him. The
doors flew open. A tall man in a cowboy hat
unwound from behind the steering wheel,
and a smaller figure — a woman — jumped
out of the passenger side. They came across
the road, side by side, like policemen, he
thought, bringing bad news. Sheila Carey.
Something had already happened to her!

"Reg!" It was the woman's voice, and in
the dim light from the mixture of headlights
and starlight, he recognized the Indian
lawyer. "Are you okay?"

The man with her — only a few feet away
now — was the priest he had talked to at
the mission. "What are you doing here?"

"You could be in danger," Father John
said. "Get in the pickup, and let's get out of
here. Somebody tried to shoot us tonight,
and somebody killed Steve Mantle at his office. We think others have been killed."

"Josh." Reg heard the flat and incontro-
vertible acceptance in his voice. "I found
his saddle in the shed. Josh would never
have left his saddle."

"Please," the lawyer lady said. There was a
breathless intensity in the way she spoke, as
if she were running from the shooter. "The
cops are on the way. They'll investigate

what's going on here. You need to come with us now." She swung around and stared out at the narrow road. "Here they are."

"It's not the cops," Reg said. He knew by the way the truck drove straight ahead, as if Sheila Carey knew by heart the best route through the washboard ruts.

33

Father John urged Vicky toward the pickup.
"Come on!" he called over one shoulder to
Reg.

"I'm not going."

He looked back at the cowboy outlined in
the dim light, a shadow plastered against
the dark earth. The truck skidded to a stop
behind the pickup and blocked the road.
He stepped between Vicky and the woman
in the cowboy hat, who swung both feet out
of the cab and dropped to the ground with
the agility of a rodeo rider jumping off a
bronco.

"What's this?" Sheila Carey threw a glance
at Father John and Vicky, then glared at
Reg. "You got up a welcoming party?"

"Time for answers." Reg's voce was low
and steady and filled with menace.

"Take it easy," Father John said, not taking his eyes from the woman. The cowboy
hat, the short figure in the bulky jacket, the

way her shoulders propelled her forward. Not long ago she had tried to run them into the ditch. She had intended to kill them. Before that, she had shot Steve Mantle.

Vicky had moved up alongside him. In the way she kept her eyes fixed on the woman, he knew that she knew the truth.

"Get off my ranch, all of you. Go back to wherever you came from." Sheila Carey did a half turn and brushed past the cowboy. "I could shoot you for trespassing."

"Is that what you did to Josh? Shot him?"

The woman halted, as if she had been pulled up by a rope. She took her time turning back. "You're crazy."

"I found Josh's saddle," Reg said. "Who killed him? Your husband? Is that what he did? Shot the hands instead of paying them?"

"Get out of here." Sheila Carey folded herself into a crouch, shoulders pulled together, head thrust forward, like a buffalo ready to charge.

"What about the other missing cowboys?" Vicky said. "Did you shoot them? Where did you bury them? Out behind the barn where you buried your husband's ashes?"

Sheila took a long moment, her gaze fixed on the darkness that spread over the pasture behind them, a mixture of thoughts moving

380

through her face, as if she were weighing which one to settle on. The dim silvery starlight glowed in the night; the edges of the pickup's headlights played over the ground. "You don't know anything," she said finally, her voice laced with panic. The light flashed in her eyes — something wild in her eyes. "Dennis did what he had to do. You don't understand. This is all we had, this ranch. We sank everything into this ranch, all our hopes and dreams. All those cowboys wanted was money. Money. Money. Money. They were all the same. Threatened to take us to court. Take the ranch away."

"My God," Father John said under his breath. He could hear the breathless voice — the agony — of the man in the confessional. *I committed murder . . . I had no choice.* Dennis Carey. He had come to the mission twice, a man with something on his mind, stumbling around the words, unable to bring them forth. He had come a third time, and in the dim solitude of the confessional, he had blurted out the words. How many times had he committed murder by then? What was it that had finally driven him to the confessional?

"So it was your husband who shot the cowboys," he said. "It weighed on his conscience."

"Please!" Sheila Carey threw out both hands. "Spare me your psychobabble. Dennis couldn't shut up. Kept feeling the need to talk about it, saying he needed forgiveness. Jesus, he was going to blow up everything we worked for. Destroy the ranch, his own dreams, like they were nothing."

"The guilt was tearing him apart," Father John said. "He came to the mission wanting to talk about it. You were afraid he'd go to the police, confess everything."

"Shut up! Shut up!"

"You shot your husband," Vicky said. A controlled voice, calm, Father John thought, but he knew it was like a heavy blanket she pulled over her to cover the shock and fear. "You tried to kill us tonight. You killed Steve Mantle and stole his computer. Why? To destroy the employment records? A lot of folks around here knew the cowboys who worked on the ranch."

"I keep my own records. I could deny any cowboys worked here. Without Mantle's records, what would the police have? Cowboys bragging about their jobs? Bar gossip."

"What about us, Sheila? You tried to kill us tonight. We were asking too many questions, getting too close to the answers, isn't that right?"

Reg twisted his shoulders about, as if he were trying to break out of a nightmare. "What about me? Coming around here, asking questions. You put me next on your list?"

A look of uncontrolled panic glinted in the woman's eyes. Father John wasn't sure where the gun that materialized in her hand had come from. What pocket had she pulled it out of? Which folds in the bulky jacket? He realized she'd probably had her hand on the gun when she descended from the truck.

Vicky gasped.

"Look, Sheila," Father John said, trying to ignore the gun — the silvery metal with the dark shadows and the enormous black hole — as if they were in his office, talking, exploring options, reaching for an understanding. "The BIA police will be here any minute." He hoped that was true. "They will excavate the depressions in the field where you buried your husband's ashes. It's over now. You don't want to kill anyone else."

She was holding the gun in both hands, knees bent in the shooter's stance, the wildness still in her eyes. "I'll tell you what we are going to do. We are going to walk to the barn. I keep a shovel outside in case I need it. We will get the shovel and walk over to the . . ." She hesitated and, for a moment,

Father John thought she might crumble, fall to the ground. "Cemetery," she said. "That's what Dennis called it. The cemetery. This ranch was all we had. No one was going to take it from us. Soon as we hired on the first cowboys, we knew they were going to make trouble if they didn't get their pay. And how were we supposed to pay them? Nothing but work on this place, and very little money trickling in. You know what happened? Some fool Indians took a shot at the cowboys." She tossed her head and gave a sharp crack of laughter. "We figured they'd up and leave. What idiot wouldn't take off after getting shot at? But they didn't leave. Threatened to report us to the police if we didn't pay up. That's when we figured out how to make them disappear so they couldn't cause us any trouble, and people would think they'd been scared off."

The woman seemed to be bearing down, gripping the gun harder. "Dennis was smart," she said. "He figured everything out. Hire white guys so the Indians will keep shooting. Don't hire anybody from around here. We didn't want girlfriends snooping around after they disappeared. It worked perfectly." Her eyes were dark marbles, unblinking, unmoving, staring at an image inside her head. "You understand, don't

384

you? We had to save the ranch. Dennis wanted that more than anything. He just couldn't take it — he couldn't take what we had to do."

She seemed to come back from wherever she had drifted. "Walk!" she said. "Don't think you are smarter than this gun. I can shoot you here and drag your bodies to the cemetery."

"Drop the gun, Mrs. C." Carlos strolled into the stream of headlights. He was gripping a rifle. "Drop it, I said!" His voice sounded ragged and harsh.

Sheila Carey looked stunned and confused, as if she had lost her way down a familiar path. She didn't move.

"Do what he says." Reg was glaring at her.

Slowly, reluctantly, she lowered her arm and let the gun slide out of her hand.

"Kick it over here," Carlos said, but she was already toeing the gun in his direction. "Kick it!"

She pulled one leg back and kicked at the gun. It slid forward several feet.

"Get it!" Carlos threw a sideways glance at Reg, who stooped over and picked it up. Both cowboys holding a gun now, and it struck Father John that either might be capable of shooting the woman. "So that's what you had planned for me and Lane and

Reg and the rest of the hands? Work our butts off, promise to pay up soon's you sell a bull or butcher a cow. October a good month for sales. But we'd be out in the cemetery with a bullet in our heads. How did you plan to carry that out? Dennis not here to do the dirty work. In the middle of the night? Next morning we'd hear another cowboy had packed up and left?"

A tremor had started through Sheila Carey, legs shaking first, then hips, shoulders, head rolling about. "Don't be fools. We can forget about this." The words were broken, like the words on a cracked CD. "There's money, lots of it. Visitors are going to keep coming. Oh, they love Spirit. They'll never stop coming to the ranch. Close to a hundred thousand dollars left for Spirit so far. A few more months, we'll hit a million. You'll get your cut."

Carlos snorted. "Like the cowboys got their pay?"

"I swear," she said. "We didn't have the money then. Now the money is coming in, just like we always dreamed, Dennis and me."

"You killed my buddy." Reg steadied the gun in both hands and aimed at the woman's chest. "I should kill you."

"I told you . . ." She was still shaking.

"Dennis and me did what we had to do. I wasn't the one that took out the cowboys."

"Your no-good, weak sonofabitch husband! You put him up to it." The gun lurched upward, then settled back down.

"Don't shoot," Father John said. "You're not like them, Reg. You don't want to become what they are. All we have to do is wait for the police to get here."

Reg didn't move, and Father John wondered if the man had heard anything he said. Sheila Carey crouched a few feet away, shaking, wide-eyed, shifting her gaze between the two guns, hands fletching as if she were grasping for air.

Carlos nodded. "Cops are close. I can feel the tremor in the ground. Couple minutes we'll hear sirens, see lights flashing out on the plains."

"You're lying," Sheila said.

"You better hope I'm telling the truth. If the cops don't get here soon, Reg here might take justice in his own hands."

He could feel the earth rumbling himself, Father John thought, or was he imagining it? Willing the BIA to show up before anyone else on this ranch died? "Let me have the gun, Reg. You aren't a murderer." He took a step forward, but the cowboy jerked the gun in his direction and motioned him back.

"Josh's mom is dying. She's been hanging on 'til Josh comes home. I have to go back and tell her Josh isn't ever coming home. I don't want to see her face when I tell her. I don't want to watch her die."

"They're here." Vicky had made a half turn and was looking out toward the road. Father John glanced around. Lights glowed on the horizon beneath the brilliance of the stars. Another half second and he heard the faintest wail of sirens.

He turned back. "The police will handle this, Reg. Let go of the gun." God. The man's finger was on the trigger. A nervous twitch, and Sheila Carey would be dead.

"All we gotta do is keep her here," Carlos said. "No sense in you getting yourself into trouble. She will get what's coming to her."

"It won't bring Josh back to life. Same for the other cowboys out in the cemetery. What right did these sons of bitches have to take their lives?"

The sirens were closer now, three police cars grinding down the narrow two-track, headlights jumping on the braided earth.

"No!" Sheila Carey let out a scream, like a wild, terrified animal. She threw herself around and started running toward the pasture.

Out of the corner of his eye, Father John saw the gun rise in Reg's hand. He spun sideways and chopped at the cowboy's arm, driving it downward. The sharp crack split the air like thunder as the bullet smashed into the ground, ricocheting about, crazy, invincible. Little clouds of dust exploded around them. There was an acrid smell of dust. Father John gripped Reg's wrist with both hands. "Let it go!" he shouted. "Let it go."

The noise of the sirens reverberated through the night; headlights bathed the ground. Father John was aware of the large, dark shadow moving in close, the cowboy hat bobbing forward. "You heard the father," Carlos said. "Let go of the gun."

He felt the release then, muscles giving way as Carlos slipped the gun out of Reg's hand. For a moment, he thought Reg might collapse, then he seemed to gather his energy. He let out a loud howl. "She's getting away!"

Father John looked up. The small, dark figure zigzagged along the barbed-wire fence, darting in and out of the shadows, running wild. Then she stopped. She was at the gate, lifting the wire loop off the posts, yanking at the gate, which scraped over the ground. "No!" he shouted, running toward her now, half-conscious of Vicky running beside him and the sound of the cowboys' boots pounding after them.

"No!" Carlos shouted. "Don't go in there."

But Sheila Carey was already in the pasture. A dark shadow running toward the herd. The buffalo had started to stir, nosing forward, heads tossing. Moving toward the woman, who was still running and screaming, arms flailing against the blaze of silver stars. The sound of her voice drifted over the grunting, thudding noise of the buffalo as they circled around her.

"My God, she's crazy." Carlos had slammed the gate shut. "She's got the herd all riled up. They're coming for her." He turned to Reg. "I'll get the tractor. We have to get her out of there." He took off running in the direction of the barn.

Father John gripped the bars of the gate and stared out at the pasture. Buffalo bumping together, great brown masses of flesh and bone knocking against one another, separating and bumping together again, like a shadowy monster growing and spreading over the pasture. A small figure — a stick figure — stumbled in the middle of the herd that rolled around her. Then Sheila Carey was flying, lifted against the sky, arms flailing, legs distorted, twisted. She dropped into the herd and disappeared beneath the buffalo trampling and crushing the earth.

The roar of the tractor broke the stillness. "Open the gate." Carlos gripped the steering wheel. The huge machine shook around him.

"Too late," Reg called back. "Better let them settle down before we go out there. She's under the hooves now. She got what she deserved." He turned away from the gate, as if he had seen enough. "It's not like they wanted to crush her." His voice low now, as if he were talking to himself. "They're just protecting their place."

Doors slammed behind them, cracking the air. Father John looked around. Shadows moved toward them, in and out of the swirling lights, and stopped in a half circle in front of them. "Come down off that tractor," an officer shouted. "Drop your weapons."

Carlos kicked the two guns out of the tractor and jumped down after them.

"All of you, hands in the air!"

Father John put his hands up and watched Reg and Vicky do the same. "I'm Father O'Malley," he said. "This is Vicky Holden, and these two cowboys work on this ranch.

Sheila Carey, the owner, has just been killed
out in the buffalo herd."

34

The morning was already hot, the sun a white blaze overhead and the heat just starting to build. Father John left the pickup in the parking lot and headed for the gate. The cowboy nodded him past. Everything on the Broken Buffalo Ranch seemed quiet, subdued, almost peaceful. Visitors stood inside the gate, waiting their turn to go out and see the calf. He could see the cowboys leading other groups along the fence toward the viewing spot, as if nothing had changed.

He walked down the road, past the house, which had a forlorn look about it, chairs rocking and squeaking on the porch, inhabited by ghosts. Past the barn, the green tractor crouching behind it, the flatbed next to the stacks of hay. The cemetery was shielded by a six-foot-high wall of black plastic that snapped in the wind. Behind the plastic, he knew, were six excavated graves. He had been here when the bodies were uncovered.

Blessing each body, praying for the souls of the cowboys, aware of the quiet helplessness with which the officers and the coroner had worked.

Was it only one week ago that Sheila Carey had killed herself? It seemed like yesterday. They had taken the tractor and flatbed out into the pasture, Carlos at the wheel, a police officer in the passenger seat; he and Reg and two medics had balanced themselves upright on the flatbed. Reg had used the forklift to drop bales of hay onto the flatbed, and while Carlos maneuvered the metal machines close to the crumpled body of Sheila Carey, he and Reg had broken up the bales and thrown out the loads on the other side of the flatbed. The buffalo had wandered away from the body, and he and the officer and the medics had jumped down. One of the medics shone a flashlight onto the body of Sheila Carey. She was mauled and bruised, face blackened, clothes soaked in blood. She might have been struck by a semi on the highway.

The medics had rolled a canvas stretcher under the body and lifted it onto the flatbed. He had blessed the body as Carlos turned the tractor and flatbed in a wide half circle, inching through the herd, finally breaking out and heading back to the gate.

Dear Lord, take care of her soul, look into her heart and into whatever had turned her into a murderer, and forgive her sins. The woman was in God's hands now. He alone was her judge.

Vicky had flung open the gate and closed it behind them. No one spoke as the medics had lifted the woman's body into the ambulance, which started down the road with sirens off. The red taillights jittered into the darkness.

Apart from the scrape of boots on the hard ground, a ghostly silence had descended over the ranch. Cowboys had emerged from the bunkhouse and shuffled behind the police officers, shock and disbelief imprinted on their shadowy faces. Father John wasn't sure how much they had heard or what they might have put together. They looked confused, lost, as if they had found themselves in a nightmare. The night had spiraled forward then, with Chief Banner asking questions and jotting notes in a notebook the size of his palm. They had made their way in the flare of flashlights to the cemetery, a peaceful place, something sacred about it, and the officers had stretched yellow tape around the ground.

Now Father John walked around the end of the black plastic wall. Three men in blue jeans and cowboy hats were moving around the six excavated graves — long, narrow holes. They kept their eyes locked on the ground. One dropped onto his knee, produced a tiny brush, and swept something into a plastic bag. Huddled together with two other men on the far side of the graves was Gianelli. He looked over, as if he had detected a disturbance in the atmosphere, a new presence. Lifting a hand in acknowledgment, he started along the wall.

"I stopped by your office," Father John said. "You weren't in, so I took a chance I'd find you here."

"Forensics is checking to make sure we didn't miss anything before we fill in the holes." The fed threw a sideways glance at the men examining the ground. "What's on your mind?"

"I reached Nuala O'Brian, Jaime Madigan's fiancée. She plans to take his ashes to Ireland. She said it was where he would want to be. She can ID his body." Not much left of the bodies, he was thinking. Dirt-clogged faces, sunken eye sockets. Carcasses barely recognizable as human.

Gianelli nodded. "Folks in the coroner's office have been working around the clock to ID the bodies. We found Steve Mantle's computer in the Riverton dump, where

Sheila Carey had tossed it. The IT guys retrieved records for the cowboys Mantle placed here, including photos. So far we have positive IDs on Jack Imeg, Lou Cassell, Rick Tomlin, and Josh Barker. Reg Hartly identified Barker's remains. He arranged to take him back to his folks in Colorado. They'll bury him on the family ranch. If the fiancée identifies Madigan, that leaves only one unidentified. Name of Hol Hammond. Lonely looking guy in the photo, long face, half-closed eyes. Looks about fifty, although the record says he's thirty-two. Could be any cowboy drifting across the West." He looked away for a moment. Murder never gets easier, Father John was thinking. It shouldn't get easier.

"I'll let Nuala know she can claim her fiancé's body." Father John started to walk off, then turned back. "What will become of the ranch?"

"The woman died intestate." The fed gave a half shrug. "We're still looking for relatives. Also trying to find relatives of her husband's. So far we're drawing a blank. Seems like Dennis and Sheila Carey were alone in the world, with no family, no connections. Most of the cowboys are staying on. Carlos will continue as foreman until we get things sorted out. Visitors keep coming." He shook his head. "The murders haven't stopped them."

Father John said he would call when Nuala arrived, then he pulled his cowboy hat down against the sun and headed back toward the parking lot. He had reached the house when he spotted Vicky standing at the gate, staring out into the pasture. He walked over and took up a place beside her. He didn't say anything. A group of visitors came along the fence, made a half circle around them and kept going.

"If you look carefully," Vicky said after a long moment, "you can see Spirit out by the trees. Not as clear a view as from farther along the fence." She nodded in the direction the visitors were walking. "But it seems more private and intimate without a lot of other people gawking at her. Just Spirit and me. And now, you."

Father John looked out at the clump of cottonwoods, branches swaying, shadows dancing on the ground. The sun burned through the back of his shirt. He squinted against the bright sunlight and watched the trees for the faintest movement. He saw the mother first, head thrust forward, power moving in her body. And there she was, huddling close to her mother, a white blotch in the shadows. Sure on her feet now, graceful and confident, tossing her head.

"She won't be white for long," Vicky said. "She will start changing colors in a year or two. Black. Brown. Red. But she will remain sacred, and eventually she could become white again. I remember Grandfather telling the story of what happens with a sacred white calf."

Vicky turned toward him and lifted her face. "I came out here hoping to find answers. Why here? Why this ranch with killers? The calf could have been born anywhere."

"Did you?"

"What?"

"Find answers."

Vicky was quiet. He was aware of her beside him, the soft weight of her against his arm, the in and out of her breathing. Finally she said, "I've been going over and over Grandfather's stories of the white buffalo calf. How she comes in peace, and yet . . ." She drew in a long breath. "Sheila Carey died a brutal death. Oh, I know." Vicky put up a hand. "She wanted to die. She knew she would be crushed."

Father John set his arms over the top of a metal bar and clasped his hands on the other side. His hands were freckled and sunburned. He could almost hear Reg

Hartley's voice. Standing in this same place, looking out over the pasture, the night silvery, the sky filled with stars. *They're just protecting their place.*

"What else did your grandfather say?"

"The calf is always a blessing, no matter where she might be born. What is important is that she was born and she is here. A symbol that the Creator is always with us."

"Then you did find answers."

Vicky turned toward him. The sun shone on her face; light glowed in her black eyes. "I remembered something Grandfather had said. The white buffalo divides time. What happened in the past is over now, and we have to let it go. She gives us the confidence to go into the future. She comes to help us start over. Start again."

Tears had welled in her eyes, and she swatted at them with the tips of her fingers. "It's not easy, starting over, because you don't know where you're going or what you will find."

"It takes trust."

She was shaking her head. "The Jesuits sent you here, and now they could send you somewhere else. Nicaragua, Ghana, back to Boston. Would you have the trust to go? Just step off into a future you know nothing about and can't imagine?"

The thought caught him up in itself like a tornado, and he knew he had been ignoring it, keeping it at the edges of his mind. He would leave here. That was the only certainty about the future. Coming here had been like setting out across the empty vastness of the plains, not knowing which direction he should take or how he would *be*. Somehow he had found the strength — the grace, he thought — to trust. Strange, when he thought about it now, how this place and the people had filled his mind and his days. He never wanted to think about leaving.

"What's going on?" Father John said. Vicky started walking along the fence toward the parking lot, and he fell in beside her. Another group of visitors passed, voices subdued, faces serious.

"Adam is moving to Denver. He's joining a firm that specializes in natural resources law. A great opportunity for him. He's the best at what he does."

"Are you going?" A mixture of feelings ran through him. He would miss her if she left. Miss seeing her at powwows and celebrations. Miss working with her. And yet, it would be easier.

"I'm not a natural resources lawyer. Oh, I've tried, and Adam's right that representing tribes and making sure we aren't exploited for our oil and gas, timber and water is the most important thing we could do for the future. But I keep thinking of people like Arnie Walksfast and his friends. They have rights. They're important, too." She stopped and looked up at him. "Arnie has settled down. The probation officer cut him some slack and didn't revoke his probation. I think he might make it this time."

She was filled with hope, he thought. This time, the clients who found their way to her door, scared and hungover and coming down from a high, this time they were going to make it. He hoped with her.

"What about you?" Vicky asked. They had reached her Ford, and Father John held the door while she lowered herself behind the wheel. A burst of heat blew out of the inside, like the blast of a furnace. She started the engine and rolled down all the windows. The breeze whipping through the car ruffled her hair.

"I'd like to stay here," he said.

"I know what you would like, but . . ."

"I'm here now." The time would come when he would have to leave, he was thinking. It was inevitable. He pushed the thought away and closed the door. Then he set his hand on the window frame as if he might stop time and hold everything in place. He could feel the tremor running through the vehicle as it started to back up. He stepped out of the way and watched Vicky make a U-turn and start out of the parking lot.

She was almost to the dirt road when she stuck her hand out her window and waved and called: "I'll be seeing you."

ABOUT THE AUTHOR

Margaret Coel is the *New York Times* bestselling, award-winning author of the acclaimed novels featuring Father John O'Malley and Vicky Holden, as well as the Catherine McLeod Mysteries and several works of nonfiction. Originally a historian by trade, she is considered an expert on the Arapaho Indians. A native of Colorado, she resides in Boulder. Visit her online at marga retcoel.com, facebook.com/margaretcoel, and twitter.com/mcoel_books.